The Devil's
in the
Details

The Devil's
in the
Details

KIMBERLY RAYE

Text copyright © 2013 Kimberly Raye Groff

Published by Montlake Romance

PO Box 400818
Las Vegas, NV 89140

ISBN-13: 9781477807552
ISBN-10: 1477807551
Library of Congress Control Number: 2013933899

For all of my loyal fans who have been

waiting patiently for a new series,

you guys are the best.

Enjoy!

1

Is there a daughter out there who hasn't suspected her mother of being possessed by the Devil at one time or another? Seriously. The impossible expectations. The nagging. The guilt. The dancing—at my cousin's graduation party to Madonna's "Like a Virgin." The. Worst. Moment. Of. My. Life.

Talk about pure evil.

The thing is, in my case, I didn't just suspect. I *knew*.

That's right.

Lillith Damon to the National Association of Interior Decorators and her snooty River Oaks neighbors, good ole Mom to yours truly, Satan to the rest of the world. She'd just walked into the lobby of Houston's Crowne Plaza Hotel, about to drop a bomb in the middle of my biggest matrimonial extravaganza to date.

I know, I know. Satan? A *woman*?

But just think about it. Women have the market cornered when it comes to trickery, manipulation, and power. They just wield it a little more tactfully than men. Who seduced Adam into eating that apple? Eve. Who caused a full-fledged Trojan War? Helen. Who snagged *the* hottest guy in the world and sucked him into Daddydom? Believe you me, I was still holding a grudge against Angelina for that one. Throughout history women have been wielding their feminine wiles to manipulate men and get their way (plus the occasional piece of jewelry).

The mastermind behind it all?

My very own mother.

For millennia, Mom has been the head honcho Down Under along with her three sisters—Levita, aka Leviathan; Lucy, aka Lucifer; and Bella, aka Belial. Together, they represent the four crown princesses of Hell. Google, of course, would argue this, because every reputable website refers to them as *male* entities. The frightening, formidable, ferocious crown *princes* of Hell (shudder).

Manipulation, remember? Men are typically viewed as more intimidating than women, so my mom and aunties perpetuate the myth, making it that much easier to keep a low profile in the real world. No reputable demon hunter would ever suspect a middle-aged interior decorator with a weakness for mocha lattes and cucumber facials of being the horned god herself.

But back to the matter at hand.

"I want the whole shebang," Lillith demanded, not even slowing to let her assistant catch up (or say hello) before launching in. "From rehearsal dinner to reception." Mom was tall with tastefully styled midlength brown hair. A tailored black skirt and jacket hugged her curves, and a pair of sleek, black Manolo pumps completed the ensemble. Not that she was a slave to designer footwear. That vice fell to Aunt Lucy. Mom just liked to look good, and if that meant swiping a pair of my auntie's prized pumps, so be it.

Sure, she could buy her own (evil was definitely profitable these days), but pissing off her sis was so much more fun.

"Oh, and I'll need to have an official bridesmaids' luncheon too." She waved a perfectly manicured hand. "Maybe even a breakfast the day of." When I arched an eyebrow, she added, "I downloaded *Weddings From A–Z*. I want everything done by the book so there's no doubt that I have finally taken a prince."

While Mom is the oldest sibling, and therefore numero uno in the Big H, she still has to share control with my aunties. And if there's one thing Mom hates (besides my best friend, Blythe, polyester blends, and anything early American), it's sharing.

"When Samael and I unite, our powers will merge," she went on. "My sisters won't be able to challenge me again. No more family meetings. No more democracy." Her ice-queen facade cracked for a split second and she actually smiled. "Hell will finally be a dictatorship, as your grandfather always meant it to be."

I sighed. Here we go again.

Gramps had been an archangel once upon a time. Then he'd had it out with the Big Guy Upstairs and bam, he'd been out on his ass. He'd gone into business for himself after that. But finding good help, particularly when you're the Devil, is hard. All the liars and cheaters out there seemed to gravitate toward Gramps. He'd finally decided to stop trying to recruit a trustworthy right hand and sire his own. A son who wouldn't try to overthrow him. Or milk him for all he was worth. Or change the channel when the Dallas Cowboys were in the play-offs.

A great plan, right? Except that Gramps hadn't had a son. He'd had a daughter. And then another daughter. And then another. And then *another*.

Sheesh, you'd think the Einstein of all evil could orchestrate the birth of one measly male. But only the Big Man Up High controls life and death, and my mom and her sisters are proof that he has a certifiable sense of humor.

The jokes hadn't stopped there, either. My ma had tried to make Gramps proud and squeeze out a boy. Instead, she'd ended up with me and my three older sisters. My aunts? Same story. I have thirty-six cousins. All female. Which explains why I'd started making up excuses to miss as many birthdays and family get-togethers as possible.

Gramps had been tempted to try for kid number five, but four nagging women proved more than he could handle. So he'd cut his losses and taken up golf, a hobby that had quickly turned to a passion. Just last year he'd hit the PGA tour to make a name for himself.

He'd left specific instructions that his daughters continue to share duties and rule Hell together, but Gramps still had the final say. Unless, of course, one of them joined with one of his demon chiefs in an official union. What can I say? Gramps is a total chauvinist. Anyhow, complete control would then fall to his trusted son-in-law (attaboy) and whichever daughter took the plunge first.

"I should have done this day one," my mother declared. "Putting up with one egotistical male, even one as bossy and obnoxious as Samael, is much better than three know-it-all females."

"Samael? Isn't he the chief demon of war?" While every demon had a specialty—sex, war, slavery, IRS audits—only first-tier demons served as chiefs. They answered only to the ancients, like Gramps. Gramps and his ancient buddies had all been archangels at one time, but he'd been the only one with big enough cojones to revolt. He'd jumped ship first and taken charge Down Under, with the other ancients as his henchmen. Since Gramps was king bee, his daughters were considered royalty and destined to rule. Meanwhile, the offspring of the other ancients had assumed chief demon positions.

"Samael is the chief of war *and* strife," she said almost proudly. Except my mother didn't do *proud*, which was my first clue that she didn't find Samael half as bossy and obnoxious as she wanted everyone to think. "So?" Her ice-blue gaze met mine. "What do you think? Can you pull it off?"

"Pull off what?" I was still in shock from her showing up at the hotel where I was neck-deep in a wedding that was about to commence in exactly twenty-two minutes.

Provided the bride didn't change her mind about her hairstyle again. The stylist had canceled at the last minute and I'd jumped in to avert disaster. I'd already braided and pinned until my fingers were ready to bleed.

I glanced around at the busy lobby. Guests were still filing into the chapel area and the bride would be coming downstairs any minute. It was almost go time.

"The union, of course," Mother announced. "That's why I'm here. To secure your services."

I blinked. And here I'd thought she'd come to break the news because (a) she was my mom and this was the biggest thing she'd done, next to that hurricane that had leveled Galveston way back when, and (b) she didn't want to risk hurting my feelings if I heard the news secondhand from one of my sisters.

Then again, she was Satan. Rule out the touchy-feely mommy/daughter crap. She was a mother in the sense that she'd given birth to me and seen that I was well taken care of while growing up (think remote Italian villa and a nanny named Sophia), but that was it. I didn't pour out my hopes and dreams to her, and I certainly didn't expect the occasional "Awesome" when I did something superspectacular. Unless said something involved war, famine, or pestilence.

Pestilence wasn't my specialty. The cousins had that one cornered, specifically my cousin Hester. She could wipe out an entire city with the plague or bring a soccer team to its knees with some serious jock itch. As for me, I was better with the one-on-one. My evil birthright? An overabundance of raw sexuality and the ability to seduce any man who caught my fancy.

Yep, you guessed it. My name is Jezebel. Jezebel Damon. But my friends call me Jess. I'm a succubus. I'm also over one thousand years old—that's twenty-four in demon years. What can I say? Time flies when you're having fun.

Preying on men is my pièce de résistance.

Or rather, it was. Then two years ago I met Mark, a bartender/part-time infomercial host. We'd been having hot, wild sex on the bar where he worked nights—until his fiancée walked in.

Uh-oh.

I'd expected her to call off the wedding. Throw a few punches. Burn his clothes. At the very least, post a few derogatory comments on his Facebook page before rushing out to have rebound sex with the first guy she could find. But lo and behold, she'd done none of the above.

Rather, she'd actually *forgiven* him.

I wouldn't have believed it if I hadn't seen it for myself. He'd begged. She'd cried. They'd hugged. The next thing I knew, they'd left me shocked and bare-assed on the bar while they headed home together. A few days later, they'd said *I do* in front of two hundred of their closest friends and family.

I'd been so stunned at Mark's rejection that I'd crashed the wedding and watched the entire thing from the back row. I'd also bawled like a baby (do *not* tell my mother).

You know how people talk about defining moments? Well, that was mine. A long time coming, but better late than never.

For the first time in my existence I'd realized that hot monkey sex wasn't the be-all and end-all between a man and a woman. Oh, sure, I'd suspected it after watching *The Notebook* a record nineteen times (yep, I'm a closet romantic too). But sitting at the ceremony, holding a bottle of bubbles and listening to "Always on My Mind" (the Willie Nelson version), I'd *known*.

There was so much more to a relationship than what I'd been able to experience. Like spending time together and cuddling on the couch and watching TV and putting up with his snoring and pretending to like her five cats.

We're talking understanding.

Acceptance.

Love.

That was my first wedding, and I'd been hooked ever since. Who wouldn't fall head over heels for a towering fondant-covered masterpiece with white chocolate flowers, marzipan lace, and ganache filling?

I'd realized then that I was missing out on what really mattered. And so I'd renounced my wicked ways and given up meaningless flings to plan happily-ever-afters and secretly hope for one of my own.

My mother was convinced I'd taken up my current profession in order to spoil as many Big Days as possible and hook up with hunky groomsmen. She'd even sent me a fruit basket, along with a list of evil to-dos, when I'd first opened up shop.

Shred the wedding dress.

Kill the doves.

Poison the champagne fountain.

Invite the ex-girlfriend.

Sleep with the groom.

Sleep with the dad.

Sleep with the bride.

Hey, we're talking Satan, as in zero boundaries.

For now she was impressed by my stroke of employment genius. But the moment she got wind that I was being featured in next month's issue of *Texas Brides* magazine, all hell would break loose. Literally. She would cut my career short and banish me back Down Under. My chances of finding my own One and Only would go from *maybe* to *ne-vah*.

Which explained why I was about to freak fifty ways till Sunday.

I tamped down my anxiety and tried to get a grip. As startling as her presence was, she hadn't skewered me with her pitchfork yet, which meant she didn't know (thank you, thank you, *thank you*) about the magazine. I still had a whole twenty-seven days to figure out a way to explain that my career wasn't just an ingenious way to make trouble—I was actually the real deal.

That, or I could move to Iceland.

FYI—demons hate cold weather and Mother would never follow me that far north.

I cleared my throat and forced the nerves out of my voice. "You want to have an actual wedding?"

"Of course. I haven't nailed down any specifics, but I was thinking we'd do it next month." The outer edges of her pupils blazed a brilliant red. "Make no mistake. I'll have none of that mundane wedding hurrah. Forget the bubbles. And the butterflies. And don't even suggest a unity candle. The only fire will be the flames shooting out of my eyes should any of my sisters dare interfere. This wedding needs to be intimidating. Dark. Sinister. Frightening." The red faded into her usual ice blue. "If you have any questions"—she snapped her fingers and motioned to the fortysomething woman who stood a few feet away with an iPad in her hands—"Cheryl is the go-to person."

Cheryl Simcox was a human who'd sacrificed it all for the life of her cockerdoodle. Cheryl (single, introverted, and addicted to *Animal Planet*) utterly adored her dog, Pebbles, so much so that when Pebbles nearly died of congestive heart failure, she'd done the unthinkable to save her: she'd conjured up my ma and struck a deal. Since Cheryl was skilled in every software known to mankind *and* could type one hundred and twenty words per minute, my mother had been more interested in her office skills than her eternal soul. They'd worked out a slightly untraditional arrangement—Pebbles's health and a semidecent 401(k) in exchange for a lifetime of personal assistance. Throw in two weeks paid vacation and a monthly supply of doggie biscuits, and Cheryl had gladly accepted Mom's employment offer. She'd been my mother's right hand for over four years now. Meanwhile, Pebbles had regained her health and given birth to six puppies. All female.

What'd I tell ya?

"I've jotted down a few must-haves to help you get started with the plans," Mom said as Cheryl pulled a thick notebook from the large brown satchel hooked over her shoulder.

"Plus sixty-eight pages of don't-even-think-about-its," Cheryl added. "Your mother highlighted those in yellow."

Did I mention my mom is a control freak on top of being the epitome of evil?

"I know this sort of stuff doesn't come cheap." Mom snapped her fingers and Cheryl pulled a check from the satchel. "This should be a more than adequate down payment. The rest will follow as soon as all of the plans are in place."

I stared down at the six-figure amount and tried not to salivate.

"Why not elope?" Yikes. What was I saying? While I was a definite up-and-comer on the wedding circuit, I hadn't actually *arrived*. Translation? I needed the money in the worst way if I wanted to quit running things out of my duplex and lease my own storefront. That, and I sort of had an appreciation for designer handbags. Currently I was lusting over the new Marc Jacobs hobo. This check was more than enough to turn that bad boy from a screen saver into the real thing.

Take the money and run, my conscience screamed.

My mouth, however, had a direct line to my deepest, darkest fears, so I blurted, "A wedding is so time-consuming. And costly. And you have to get the whole family involved." Which meant me and my sisters and my aunties and...*ugh*. I needed a Xanax just thinking about it. "Why bother with the formalities of a lavish affair? Wouldn't it be better to get it over with?" Quick and painless. That was my vote.

"I need proof of the union. If I say Samael and I have officially joined forces, your aunts will think I'm lying." Cheryl nodded while my mother shrugged. "Besides, I've tried it already and it didn't work." She shook her head. "I don't want anyone to doubt my new authority." She motioned again to Cheryl, who promptly produced a BlackBerry and handed it over.

"I seriously doubt anyone would be that bold—" I started, but Mom waved off my opinion as she focused on her touch screen.

"Landon Parks *must* officiate at the ceremony." She gave me a don't-screw-this-up look. "His contact information is in my notes. He's the chief demon of slavery and oppression, which means he's the only one qualified to launch me into an eternity chained to Samael."

My ma was such a romantic.

"He also occupies the body of a local judge, so the marriage will be legitimate both Down Under and in this realm."

"Landon Parks," I murmured. "Got it."

"Oh, and throw in a bachelorette party and a few male strippers. Your grandfather's ridiculous rules stipulate that I have to be faithful, otherwise it negates the union." She eyed the screen and blew out an exasperated breath before handing the device back over to Cheryl. "If I'm going to commit myself for the rest of eternity, I want to have as much fun while I still can. Speaking of which, I have a massage scheduled in half an hour." She cast a knowing glance at the tuxedo-clad groom standing outside the ballroom double doors, nervously checking his watch. She gave me a wink and a suggestive smile. "You'd better get to work."

Ick.

Not that he wasn't attractive. He was, but I was *so* over the spoiling-men phase of my existence. Plus, said groom was hopelessly in love with his bride. Her name was Mary Ann and she was a pediatric nurse and one of the nicest humans *ever*. She'd been a real trouper despite a hellacious mix-up with the invitations. She'd even given a beautiful quote to the magazine on my behalf.

I could never do such an awful thing to Mary Ann, and I should just confess as much to my mother. She would know the truth about me—that I'd turned my back on my birthright and gone legit—when the magazine came out anyway. No sense putting off the inevitable. My career was over and I was headed straight back to Hell.

"I'm on it," I said instead.

What? We're talking *Hell*.

2

"The groom's uncle Jeffrey can't sit next to his ex-wife," I told Burke Carmichael a half hour after my mother had waltzed out of the hotel and left me to digest her request.

I was standing in the main ballroom where the reception would be held, staring in horror at the place cards set side by side on the pale-pink, linen-draped table. "They hate each other." I plucked Uncle Jeffrey's card and handed it to my assistant.

Burke and his identical twin brother, Andrew—the dynamic wedding duo—were two of the hottest guys I'd ever seen. Twenty-nine. Blond hair. Light-brown peepers. Broad shoulders. Six-pack abs. They were also heterosexually challenged, which made them the perfect assistants because their concentration centered solely on creating matrimonial bliss rather than on how to charm me out of my skinny jeans.

Female sexual demons ooze—you guessed it—sex appeal. With one glance we inspire the most lascivious thoughts in humans of the opposite sex. The average guy doesn't stand a chance.

Unless said guy is attracted to men.

As if to prove the point, my gaze collided with Burke's and an image popped into my head—Brad Pitt from *Legends of the Fall*, complete with long hair, tanned skin, and oodles of emotional torment.

As a sexual demon, I don't just wow humans with my sex appeal, I can also read their deepest, most erotic thoughts. Bottom line, I can see the object of any human's hottest fantasy.

Burke had always been a Brad man. While the details might change—Brad à la *Ocean's Eleven* or Brad à la *Thelma & Louise* (my own personal fave)—he was always faithful to the überhot actor. A helpful tidbit if I'd still been in the spoiling-and-seducing phase of my existence.

At the moment, it just reminded me of my own self-imposed deprivation. Two years on the celibacy wagon. I hadn't even had a date.

Your own fault, a voice whispered. I'd promised myself I'd take the bull by the horns and sign up for an online dating service or something, but I was just so busy on the weekends, what with everyone else's weddings. That, and I was doing my damnedest to curb temptation. No dates. No one-night stands.

No disappointment.

I ignored the last thought and paged my way through the notes on my iPad. "We'll sit Uncle Jeffrey next to the bride's relatives on the other side of the room."

If only the seating at my mother's wedding would be this manageable.

Fat chance.

Evil entities weren't exactly known for their camaraderie. The last time Beelzebub had been within one hundred feet of Ashtoreth, they'd beheaded each other. Sure, the heads had regrown and they'd been back at it during the very next get-together, but still. We're talking a massive dry-cleaning bill, and I was sure to puke all over my shoes at the first sign of blood.

Hey, I'm a lover, not a fighter.

I clicked my headset and called for Burke, who'd just headed to the kitchen to check on the menu for the hors d'oeuvres and cocktails that would keep the guests celebrating until the reception dinner began in an hour. Judging by the round of applause coming from the ceremony space, the doors would open any moment and a pack of hungry guests would head upstairs to the mezzanine level for cocktail time.

"Is everything ready?" I asked.

"The signature drinks are flowing and the platters are being loaded."

"Good, because all hell is about to break loose."

And how.

Forget seating. The food choices at Mom's big event would be even more of a nightmare. While every demon could appreciate a decked-out wedding cake (we all had an insatiable sweet tooth), each had a different palate when it came to main courses. I *so* didn't want to be the one to ask a caterer to substitute braised eyeballs for the salmon croquettes. Talk about killing my chances at being voted Houston's hottest wedding planner of the year.

At the same time, if I refused to handle the arrangements, my mother would surely get pissed. I'd be forced Down Under, into eons of service as Hades's chief harlot.

I *had* to do it.

And maybe, just *maybe*, if I pulled it off, my mom would be so busy calling the shots Down Under that she might miss the magazine article and the all-important fact that I'd turned my back on my birthright.

Hey, it could happen.

I held tight to the teeny tiny thread of hope and was about to pop some Life Savers into my mouth to pacify my sweet tooth when the cell phone in my pocket started vibrating.

I wasn't going to answer it. That's what I told myself, particularly when I saw the black raven icon on the caller ID and realized it was my cousin Portia.

Portia was the youngest of Aunt Bella's brood, meaning her demonic specialty was being spoiled-ass rotten. She was Hell's version of a mean girl, i.e., she loved Gucci, gossip, and getting her way.

I didn't want to talk to her right now. But if I didn't pick up, she was sure to fabricate a scandalous reason as to why I'd avoided her call.

"I'm really busy right now," I said when I answered the phone. "Can I call you later?"

"No can do. I'm about to have some collagen injected into my lips and I won't be able to move them for a few hours."

"I'll text," I offered, but she wasn't listening.

"I heard from Trisha, who heard from Sally, who heard from Lara, who heard from Beth, who heard from Aunt Levita that your mom said she paid you a visit today. Word is there are going to be wedding bells in the near future."

Welcome to *My Big Fat Demon Wedding*.

"Not wedding bells. Maybe a heavy metal guitar riff or a gloomy organ," I said, remembering my mom's minimal list of must-haves. "Mom's leaning toward dark and sinister for her theme."

"I knew it! Auntie *is* tying the knot. Mother thought it was a trick, but then Auntie Levita said Auntie Lillith said you were planning the wedding for her. A *real* wedding. Imagine that. So when is it? When's the big day?"

"There won't be one if I don't get moving with the plans."

"But—"

"Talk later." I hit the kill button before she could fire off another question. I'd already confirmed my mom's announcement. I wasn't going to leak any details. If Ma wanted my aunts to know when, where, and what time, she would tell them herself or send them invites. This was her big news to spread, not mine.

I *so* didn't want to be caught in the middle of an all-out demonic war.

I was sliding the phone into my pocket when it vibrated again. Talk about pigheaded. Portia just didn't give up.

I was about to hit *Ignore* when I saw a giant margarita glass dancing on my display: it was my best bud, Blythe.

Blythagamamia Stephenolopolis, aka Blythe Stevens. Forget causing droughts and stirring earthquakes. Blythe was a lower-level demon responsible for tempting humans on a more day-to-day basis. Her cover? A hot-to-trot party animal who made being bad look really, *really* good. She'd been a Hooters girl for the past few years until she'd saved enough tips to open her own limo service. Now she cruised the Bayou City all night in a hot-pink stretch Hummer full of partygoers eager to drink and dance and sin the night away.

The thing was, Blythe had long since tired of the endless nightlife. Like me, she wanted more out of her existence. Unlike me, she could actually achieve her dream without finding herself doomed to Hell. There were just too many of the lower-tier demons to keep track of when the higher-ups (Mommie Dearest among them) were focused solely on the push-pull of power at the corporate level.

Blythe was now in her fourth year as an undergrad at the University of Houston, specializing in early education. She wanted to be a kindergarten teacher. While I totally supported her dream (I'd quizzed her for her last exam), I couldn't help thinking she was about to trade one hell for another.

We're talking a room full of screaming five-year-olds.

"What up?" she asked when I pressed the talk button.

"I'm about to start the reception."

"I didn't mean *what up* at this exact moment. I meant *what up* as in *what big catastrophe is about to consume your entire existence?*"

"I guess good news travels fast."

"This is more like tabloid news, like when that woman in Kansas gave birth to the three-headed baby."

"Except this is true."

"Which explains why you sound so emo right now."

"I'm not depressed. I'm scared." There. I'd said it. The desperation that I'd been fighting crept back into my voice. "She showed up here, Blythe. Right *here*. What if she'd caught me all misty-eyed, watching the bride walk down the aisle? She would have yanked me back to Hell faster than you can pop the cork on a champagne bottle."

"But she didn't see you, which means your secret is still safe."

"For now. But with me as her wedding planner, we'll be together nonstop. Plus she wants all this dark and creepy stuff, and I don't know if I can pull it off."

"Sure you can. You're a demon. You majored in dark and creepy."

"Yes, but this is a *wedding*."

"Satan's wedding. Just keep that in mind, do a creepy spectacular job, and you'll be fine. She'll say *I do* and then she'll be so focused on her new power trip that she'll forget all about you. The article will come out, your business will quadruple, and everyone will live creepily ever after."

"And what if she doesn't forget about me? I have a bad feeling about this. A really bad feeling." I spent the next thirty seconds angsting to Blythe until my phone beeped again with an urgent text message. I said good-bye and stared at the display. My cousin Monique.

Monique was Aunt Levita's oldest and the Martha Stewart of the Damon clan. She planned and primped and pulled off most of the family get-togethers, which explained why I ignored the CALL ME! blazing on my screen.

The big plus of being a wedding planner—besides the endless supply of wedding cake—was that I spent my weekends working, hence I had an excuse to miss most family functions.

Namely my cousin Hester's baby shower scheduled for next Saturday.

"*Hip-hip-hooray!*"

The cheer came from the ceremony room full of guests rather than yours truly, and I knew it was time to get back to work. I slid my phone into my pocket a second before the double doors swung wide and the guests spilled out to head upstairs.

The second-floor cocktail area filled up in the blink of an eye, and just like that I found myself neck-deep in wedding chaos. A few of the kitchen helpers had called in sick, so I dived in and started reloading hors d'oeuvre trays.

Okay, maybe I didn't need to worry about my mother after all. At the rate things were going, I'd be dead from exhaustion before the night ended. Who cared about tomorrow?

"What's wrong with you?" Andrew, the other half of the dynamic dude duo, asked when he tracked me down in the back kitchen a half hour later, a concerned look on his face.

For the record, Andrew hated all things Brad, except the actor's last ensemble at the Oscars. His fantasy man? Sean Connery à la James Bond.

"You look totally freaked," he told me.

Damned would be more like it. "Sue and Eli got the flu," I said as I finished reloading a platter of Swedish meatballs and handed it off to one of the servers. "I'm swamped."

"I'm not talking about that. Too much work makes you wired and cranky, not depressed. You look like someone just canceled *Cupcake Wars*."

I shrugged. "New client."

"And the problem is?" He seemed to think. "Holy crap. She's a bridezilla. That's it, isn't it?" When I didn't answer, he added, "Please tell me she isn't another Delaney Farris."

Delaney was our current bridezilla and the reason I'd popped two Valium last week despite my strict Just Say No policy.

"She's not a bridezilla."

"Thank God."

"She's a momzilla." My gaze collided with his. "My mother is the one getting married."

While Andrew wasn't privy to the whole Satan thing, he knew that my mother and I didn't have the closest relationship. He also knew that she was controlling and unsupportive and impossible to please. And that she drove me nuts whenever we spent more than five minutes together.

"I helped my mom plan her last wedding," he offered, "and that turned out just fine. Of course, it was number four in less than eight years and we already had the routine down, but still. I made it. Even if I did want to slit my wrists by the time the reception rolled around." When I blinked against the sudden burning in my eyes, he rushed on, "But that's to be expected. That's what moms do. They drive us crazy. And insult any and every boyfriend we bring home. And try to make us wear peach when, clearly, peach is *so* over."

"She made you wear peach?"

He nodded. "With a lime-green cummerbund."

And I thought my mom was the Devil.

Andrew left to check on the entrées, and the next fifteen minutes passed in a frantic blur of mini quiches and spicy chicken wings. I was just handing off yet another overloaded tray when Burke's frantic voice echoed over the headset.

"Nine-one-one!" he shrieked. "We've got a disaster in the reception ballroom."

"Missing place card?"

"Missing body part."

Panic bolted through me and my first thought was *Ma!* She'd been known to rip apart a man or two in her day. A phone call from one of my aunties had probably sent her into a mad rage before she'd left the building and she'd yanked the arm off some poor, unsuspecting guest. I strained my ears for the tormented wail of a victim and heard only a synthesizer rendition of "Like a Virgin."

Close enough.

"Which body part?" I'd seen a severed leg get reattached on an episode of *Grey's Anatomy* last season. Have I mentioned I'm sort of a TV junkie?

"The head."

Slightly more complicated, but still doable, according to Discovery Channel's *Amazing ER Wonders*.

At least that's what I was telling myself. Better than facing the cold, hard truth: my career was sinking faster than the *Titanic*.

"And if we don't hurry up, we're going to be missing a tail too," Burke added.

Oh, no. Not the tail too—wait a second. "The victim has a tail?"

"Not anymore. It's melting right in front of me. I told the banquet manager not to put any of the hot foods near the ice sculpture and what did he do? He used the thing as the friggin' centerpiece for the carving station. There are heat lamps *everywhere*."

A wave of relief swept through me. "You're talking about the ice sculpture." Followed by a rush of *holy shit*. "You're talking about the *ice sculpture*! *My* ice sculpture!"

As in the full-size replica of an African mountain lion commissioned in honor of the bride and groom, who were going on safari for their honeymoon.

I'd gone through Hell—no pun intended—to find an ice carver skilled enough to do the job. Forget the Yellow Pages. I'd convinced an old buddy of mine, Agarth, master swordsman and demon of dismemberment, to use his skills for good by promising to put in a supportive word for him with Blythe. Agarth had lusted after Blythe for centuries now. Of course, she couldn't stand him, since his idea of an affectionate token had been a human head on a stick last Valentine's Day. But hey, at least he'd gotten her *something*. I, on the other hand, had spent the entire evening watching *American Idol* and stuffing my face with a box of Godiva that I'd bought for myself.

To Agarth's credit, he'd outdone himself on the lion. He'd delivered the finished product that morning and I'd known instantly that my bride and groom were going to love it.

Crap!

I reached the ballroom in time to see Andrew, Burke, and a handful of waiters frantically moving the silver serving dishes away from the now headless lion. Water drip-dropped from the nub that had once been the tail. The body looked emaciated compared to the fierce beast of earlier.

"Maybe we can tell everyone it's an abstract sculpture," Burke offered as he reached for a serving pan full of roasted chicken breasts. "We can say each person is supposed to have their own interpretation of what type of animal it is."

I grasped at that kernel of hope for a nanosecond before Andrew's shriek jerked me back to reality. "Are you insane? No one would buy that. This is a disaster." He snatched up a platter of ham and thrust it into a passing waiter's arms.

"It was a surprise anyway," I reminded myself.

The surprise. I always tried to do something special for each of my brides. Sort of a thank-you for entrusting me with their special day. For the Altman wedding, I'd had a restored Dodge Charger (their first-date car) show up to take them to the airport. For the Lancaster wedding, I'd brought in a saxophone player (the groom had proposed at a jazz club) to play their first dance.

Did I mention that I'm a hopeless romantic?

I forced the tears aside. "Let's get it out of here before cocktail hour is over and everyone moves this way." My mind raced. "Maybe we can do some sort of fruit arrangement instead." They *were* health nuts with a weakness for fresh-squeezed juice.

Okay, so I'm an eternal optimist too.

I hefted what was left of the head into my arms and made a bee-line for the kitchen. I'd just dumped the melting ice into the massive sink and was heading back out into the foyer when I saw him.

Tall. Dark. Devilishly handsome.

He had short dark hair and vibrant green eyes. A black T-shirt hugged his broad chest, and a pair of faded jeans clung to his sinewy thighs as he walked toward me. A rip in the thigh played peekaboo with every step, giving me a glimpse of tanned, hair-dusted skin. Scuffed black boots completed the look and made me think rough, tough biker instead of wedding guest.

Actually, the look made me think *naked* rough, tough biker, and my mind did a quick striptease of the shirt and jeans until I saw nothing but tanned muscle and a very impressive body part.

Confession time. Sometimes when I see a really hot guy, my thoughts take a nosedive south. We're talking years of being a dirty girl. It only stood to reason that I couldn't change ten centuries of bad habits in a measly two years.

No matter how hard I tried.

I drew a deep breath and tried to calm my pounding heart. Yes, I had a heart, and all the other parts that went with it. While I was an immortal demon, in order to exist in this realm I had to occupy a body—we all did. Mine was pretty spectacular, too, with flaming red hair, lots of curves, and a nice ass.

Not that I was going to offer up said ass just because a man had mad sex appeal. I was committed. Determined.

The stranger stared into my eyes and a wave of heat swept through me, stalling in all the wrong spots.

"You're all wet," he said.

And how.

I focused on plucking the damp blouse away from my skin. "Knock-down, drag-out with an ice sculpture, I'm afraid."

"Who won?"

"The king of the jungle."

His grin was instant and startling, a brilliant slash of white that softened his dangerous features for a heart-stopping moment. My body tingled and my nipples tightened.

Bad nipples.

"Bride or groom?" I blurted, eager to drown out the thunder of my own heart. If I could just stay on track and stick to business, I could get through this without molesting him right here in the hallway. Hopefully.

"Excuse me?"

"Are you here for the bride or groom?" I repeated.

"Neither." The grin faded into a serious expression and his eyes gleamed. "I'm here for you."

3

Oh, boy.

Excitement rippled up my spine, followed by a shiver of self-doubt. I had to be hearing things. No way had this hunky guy just said—

"You," he repeated, sending a wave of *yeah, baby* from my head to my freshly manicured toes. His eyebrows pulled together in a frown. "You're the one in charge, right?"

"In charge?" Okay, so I sounded about as intelligent as one of the Life Savers stuffed in my pocket. But you try being coherent with six feet plus of sexy male standing a scant six inches away.

"Of this event." He glanced around. "This wedding."

"Um, yes. That would be me. I'm it. I'm the planner."

"Then you know all of the guests." It was more of a statement than a question.

"By name, yes. But I'm afraid I couldn't pick out all the faces. Don't get me wrong, I'm no slouch at what I do, but no one's that good."

His grin was slow and oh-so-sensuous, and I knew he was thinking about more than my organizational skills. "Oh, I bet you are that good." The words dripped with unmistakable innuendo.

Disappointment ricocheted through me. *Y chromosome, remember? He's obviously picking up your do-me vibe.*

While I was thoroughly attracted and wouldn't mind him sharing that attraction, I didn't want him lusting after me simply because I had the unholy supernatural sex appeal thing working for me. I wanted it to be because of the real, honest-to-goodness *me*.

Lame, I know. But there it was.

I stiffened. "How can I help you?"

The seductive gleam in his gaze faded into a hard, purposeful glint. "The woman who was here about an hour ago—brown hair, midforties, expensive black suit—was she one of your guests?"

It took a second for the description to register, but when it did, apprehension wiggled up my spine and silenced the screaming hormones. I was *so* getting a bad feeling about this. "No," I murmured.

"No, you don't know her or no, she wasn't a guest?"

"Both."

He arched an eyebrow. "If you don't know her, then why were you talking to her?"

"She, um, was asking about a different wedding." No lie there. "She'd heard about my services and wanted to set up an appointment." I gave myself a great big mental high-five for sticking to the truth, at least in a roundabout way.

I know, I know. Ruthless demons shouldn't feel guilty for lying. But I'd turned over a new leaf and vowed to find love. It was never going to happen if I didn't lose all of the bad behavior. Now if I could only stop DVRing *Jersey Shore*, I'd be set.

"Why are you so interested in her?" I asked.

"Personal business." He eyed me for a long moment as if trying to decide something. His nostrils flared slightly, confirming what I already suspected. Namely, that he wasn't my biker fantasy come to life.

He was a demon slayer, and he was looking for a demon.

Thankfully I smelled more like a Krispy Kreme than sulfur. While the potent odor was a dead giveaway, most of my wicked brethren had long since discovered deodorant. It was just too easy to mask scents these days. Lotions, perfumes, candles, a dozen glazed right before work—they all did the trick.

An unfortunate drawback for members of the Legion.

Unlike other paranormal groups who hunted supernatural entities (vampires, werewolves, shifters, etc.), the Legion was an organization committed to tracking down and destroying demonic spirits. And I do mean *destroying*.

See, when a demon "dies" on Earth, his spirit heads back to Hell to wait for another chance at possession in this realm. That, or he stays Down Under indefinitely. There are a few, most of them ancients, who prefer fire and brimstone. But the majority want to be here. That means looking both ways before crossing the street and driving the speed limit. Except for my ma and aunties, of course. They were large and in charge. That meant no line and no waiting. If they bit the dust, they could be back in an instant. Different body. Same evil personality.

But when a demon—my ma and aunties included—dies at the hands of a Legion member, there's no coming back. Rather, said demon simply ceases to exist. Gone. *Forever.* After a somewhat messy explosion, that is.

Legion members were the ultimate threat to my kind.

They were also highly trained and very organized, complete with membership cards, an official procedure booklet, and a 401(k) plan, or so my cousin Helvetica had told me at her last birthday party.

Number one in the procedure booklet? How to sniff out a demon. There were a few other giveaways, as well—we tended to make the electricity go nuts if we were a little angry, and animals were highly attuned to us (which explained why I'd opted for a Chia Pet instead of the real thing). But for the most part, smell was the primo tool for weeding out the bad guys. Otherwise, demon detection was pure instinct.

Some people trusted their guts and were good at it, others not so good.

My hunch said this guy was one of the best.

I returned his stare and, as expected, I didn't get so much as a glimpse of his fantasy woman. No Angelina Jolie wearing a red bustier or Sarah Palin sporting an American flag bikini. Legion members lusted after the kill more than sex, so catching a glimpse of anything other than cold, hard intent was virtually impossible. I read nothing in those few moments before he broke the contact and shifted his attention to the wireless headset hooked around my neck. He seemed to come to some silent conclusion.

"My name is Cutter Owens." He pulled a black business card from his pocket with nothing on it except a phone number in big red font and the familiar Legion insignia—a bloodred *L*—and handed it to me. "If she contacts you again to set up an appointment, I'd appreciate it if you would give me a call."

He was a demon slayer, all right.

The demon slayer.

A shiver descended my spine, although this time it wasn't lust driven. Most slayers were your average humans who took up the profession and joined the Legion to make amends. To accumulate enough brownie points to get them bumped up in the Hereafter.

Cutter Owens had no such motivation. He'd been a thief and a gambler and, some said, a murderer before he'd joined up. He was going straight to Hell and he didn't give a rat's ass about redemption. For him it was all about eliminating as many demons as he could before he went down.

Talk about a reputation. We'd all heard the gossip. Stories larger than life. He was a hundred feet tall. He had two heads. He breathed fire. He shit lightning. He had six penises (okay, that came from one of my succubus buds and was probably more wishful thinking than anything else). Bottom line, he was a bona fide badass.

And he was after the biggest kill of his career—the Devil herself. Aka Mommie Dearest.

"Call me," he murmured, and then, before I could find my voice, he winked one gleaming green eye, turned on his heel, and walked away.

Shock and dismay faded into the thunder of my heartbeat as I stared at his backside, his jeans shifting across the tightest, most perfect ass I'd ever seen.

I swallowed.

Hard.

Hello? Your very existence is about to go to Hell in that new Prada knockoff you just ordered. Now would be a good time to forget Mr. Buns of Steel, pack it up, and head for Alaska.

I nixed the image of naked skin and tanned muscle laid out on a bearskin rug next to a fire. I didn't have time to lust after a man I could *never* have, particularly when I'd sworn off lust in the first place. And I was certain Cutter Owens—demon slayer extraordinaire—would sooner chop off my head than jump my bones if he knew my true identity.

"...getting ready to cut the cake, but they can't do it without the photographer," came Burke's voice over the headset. "She went MIA about ten minutes ago to change her film. No one's seen her since. Help!"

I drew a deep breath, ignored the unease that told me something was about to happen—something *really* bad—and headed for the reception area. I could sort through my own problems later. Right now I was smack-dab in the middle of a happily-ever-after— someone else's, but still—and I wasn't going to let anything screw up my bride's day.

That, and it was cake time.

4

I pulled into my driveway long after midnight, my feet aching and my stomach churning from the three pieces of cake (vanilla with strawberry filling, buttercream icing, and sugar rose petals) I'd wolfed down at the wedding.

I know, I know. I should have stopped at one. But hey, we're talking *months* of walking the straight and celibate. No kissing. No touching. No chocolate body paint. It was a wonder I hadn't scarfed down all four tiers by myself. Thankfully I had the superfast metabolism of a demon, otherwise I'd be calling Jenny Craig.

I killed the engine and stared through the windshield at the modest brick duplex I'd been living in for the past two years. It was a split-level number divided into an upstairs apartment and a downstairs apartment. When I'd first moved in, I'd had the upper level while Mrs. Evelyn White, a seventysomething retired flight attendant, had occupied the first floor. She'd eventually moved on to that great big 747 in the sky, and I don't mean that figuratively. She'd joined a group of senior-citizen air candy stripers and was now zipping from New York to Paris every few days. She'd ditched the duplex to share an apartment near the airport with two of her fellow stripers. Meanwhile, I'd managed to scrape together enough money to pick up her part of the lease. I'd bought a used desk, a sofa, and a few chairs, and just like that my business, Happily Ever After Events, had been born.

It wasn't my dream setup (I *really* wanted an upscale storefront in the downtown Galleria area complete with lots of glass and chrome and thick, plush carpeting), but at least I didn't have to face early-morning traffic. My commute consisted of walking downstairs and dodging the paperboy who'd yet to perfect his aim.

I grabbed my purse and a leather satchel—overflowing with everything from leftover programs and netting to a few cans of hair spray—and climbed out of my Nissan Cube. It wasn't the Beamer of my dreams, but the gas mileage was good and there was plenty of room for the dozens of things I ended up toting to each and every event.

I was halfway up my front walk when I felt the presence behind me. My skin prickled and awareness rippled through me. Along with a teeny tiny sliver of fear.

I know, I know. I'm a big, bad, ballsy demon. Evil is my middle name. I shouldn't spook so easily. But with my hands full and my nerves still buzzing from my up-close encounter with the Legion's top demon hunter, I was uncharacteristically jumpy.

All right, so I'm a wuss.

"I have Mace," I breathed. "And I'm not afraid to use it."

"Easy, Dirty Harry," came a familiar voice.

Relief swept through me and I turned to find myself face-to-face with a tall, leggy brunette in three-inch designer pumps, hot-pink shorts, and a white *I Heart Justin Bieber* T-shirt.

Lucy Damon was my mother's youngest sister and my favorite relative of all time. Forget murder and mayhem—Aunt Lucy used her powers to design the most amazing shoes and accessories. She was cool and trendy and didn't give a fig about the power trip Down Under. Even more, she didn't scare the crap out of me like my other two aunties.

Usually.

I arched an eyebrow and eyed her fitted tee. "Isn't he a little young for you?"

Her brown eyes danced. "Maybe, but he's sooooo cute, dontcha think?"

"In an underage, jailbait sort of way," I reminded her. I tightened the grip on my satchel. "Shouldn't you be in New York right now? Dressing models for a runway or something?"

"My show is next month. Listen, I popped in as soon as I heard the disastrous news." She reached into the leopard-print Coach slouch hanging from one shoulder. "And I brought reinforcements." She held out a silver purse attached to a single wrist strap. "Part of my new spring line, launching in thirty-six days and counting."

The smell of designer handbag called to me, and my shitty day melted away as I cradled the coveted clutch in my hands. "I love it."

"I know it's not much compared to what you're going through, but I was hoping it might cheer you up."

Mission accomplished. I couldn't stop smiling for the next nanosecond. Until I felt the uneasy ripple up my spine and the churning in the pit of my stomach. Something bad was brewing, and I couldn't shake the feeling that I'd been plunged right in the middle of it. And that I was sinking.

My smile faded and I gave my favorite aunt a desperate look. "What am I going to do?"

"You're going to stay strong. You can't let one jackass screw up your entire existence."

I glanced overhead, fully expecting to see the star-studded sky crack open. "Um, maybe you should keep your voice down so said jackass doesn't hear you."

"Hey, I call 'em like I see 'em." She touched a comforting hand to my shoulder. "You're stronger than this, Jess. Don't be intimidated. Hold your head high and walk away."

"I can't."

She shrugged. "Then get a vibrator." When I opened my mouth to blurt *been there, done that* she held up a hand. "I know you're really busy with your career, but sometimes we have to slow down and enjoy ourselves. We're talking survival, and we females have to do whatever it takes to get through the tough times. That, or I can arrange to have his head chopped off. Or any other body part."

O-kay. "What, um, exactly are we talking about?"

"The whatshisname who dumped you last week." She patted my shoulder. "It's nothing to be ashamed of. We've all been there, honey."

"No one dumped me last week."

"But I got a text this morning saying there'd been a bad breakup." She seemed to think. "Come to think of it, maybe it was your cousin Tess." She shrugged. "She was probably texting while driving again. Last month I got a message that she was rescheduling her well-woman appointment. Meanwhile, the Women's Health Group over on Louisiana got an invite to a Slutty Susie party she was having at her apartment." She eyed me, her dark eyes soft and concerned. "So if it isn't a man who has you looking like you want to throw yourself into the nearest carton of ice cream, who is it?"

"Ma." I lowered my voice, ready to deliver the devastating news. "She's getting married."

Lucy rolled her eyes. "Tell me something I don't know."

"She wants total control."

"More power to her." She shrugged. "I barely have time to eat, much less worry over a bunch of greedy demons who don't listen anyway."

"That's not the worst of it. She wants me to plan the wedding, which means"—I swallowed, desperate to push down the lump rising in my throat—"we'll be spending a lot of time together. Practically every day."

Horror flashed in her gaze and a strangled cry escaped her full lips.

No, wait, that cry came from *me*.

A second later, I found myself smothered by Justin Bieber as Aunt Lucy pulled me close for a fierce hug. "I'm so sorry," she said, and meant it. That was the thing about Aunt Lucy. She hugged and she cared. Two things my mother and my other aunties would never understand. Not that Aunt Lucy bothered explaining herself to her sisters. She didn't care what they thought. She did her own thing and, more importantly, she was happy doing it.

Her phone beeped and the hug ended.

"Sorry sweetie, I have to take this." She spent the next thirty seconds reading a very long text before sliding the phone back into her leopard-print bag and giving me an apologetic smile. "I've got to run."

I cradled the cute little clutch for a few moments before forcing myself to hand it back over. "Don't forget the purse for Tess."

She waved me off. "You keep it. I think you need it a lot more than she does."

I grinned and watched her body shimmer and fade into the surrounding darkness.

Most demons utilize the usual modes of transportation in this realm because zapping in and out requires a lot of power that they simply don't have. Demon juice is a cumulative thing that grows over the years, meaning the older the demon, the more gas in the tank. Since my aunt Lucy is older than dirt, she cashed in the frequent flier miles in favor of popping in every now and then.

I drew a deep, steadying breath, turned, and headed for my front door.

I *could* do this, I told myself. I had a good friend in my corner. A terrific aunt pulling for me. And even more, I had my very own new preseason, couture clutch.

I could pull this whole thing off *and* get my mom off my back.

The confidence lasted for a few minutes, until I walked into my bathroom. Then doubt screamed in my head. Literally. My gaze hooked on the mirror and the words smeared in red.

You're in over your head,
Back off now or you're dead.

The air rushed from my lungs and cold horror slid through me. A sharp, pungent scent tickled my nostrils. Blood. The message was written in *blood*. AB negative, to be specific.

I quickly became aware of the closed shower curtain behind me and the possibility that whoever had scribbled the worst poetry I'd ever read (and I'd been a huge Walt Whitman fan back in the day) could still be here.

Yeah, and you just ran smack-dab into her.

Aunt Lucy?

I drop-kicked the thought as soon as it struck. She would never, *ever* do such a thing. Forget death and destruction. She was the anti-auntie. The one shining light in the darkness. The demon of designer handbags.

Threats? Not her style. Especially when it came to her favorite niece.

Aunt Bella was a totally different story. Her claim to fame was physical anguish. Think the Spanish Inquisition. The Salem witch trials. The Saw flicks.

Even more, she hated all her nieces. Yours truly especially, since I'd given her a bouquet of flowers for her birthday last year instead of the expected body part. She'd been waiting for an excuse to come after me with her arsenal of toys, i.e., knives, whips, chain saws, the Jackass movies on DVD.

I knew then that it wasn't a coincidence that Portia had called earlier tonight. She'd probably been spying for her mother to find out the truth. And now Aunt Bella wanted to throw a wrench into my ma's plans by taking me out.

AB negative *was* her favorite blood type.

Ba-bom. Ba-bom. Ba-bom.

My heart beat a frantic rhythm as I turned, my gaze riveted on the closed shower curtain. I inched backward one awkward step at a time.

One. Two. Easy—yikes!

I banged into the doorframe and whirled. Panic bolted through me and I raced down the hallway and into the kitchen. Rummaging in the drawers, I searched for the biggest knife I could find. Not that I intended to use it. The sight of blood and guts made me queasy, and I was already batting one for two at the moment.

My hands trembled. Talk about a wimp—but my auntie didn't know that.

If it *was* Aunt Bella.

My mother wasn't my only bride, after all. For a split second, I considered the possibility that maybe, just maybe, the threat stemmed from one of my other clients. I was sure there were a few jilted exes out there who might want to stop a wedding.

But enough to break in and write a bloody death threat?

Doubtful.

Either way, I desperately needed a weapon.

A few frantic seconds later, I realized that the one detriment to having my own business was that I had little time to cook, which meant that my arsenal of weapons consisted of three plastic sporks left over from yesterday's Italian takeout, a pair of chopsticks, and a monogrammed cake server from three weeks ago. The bride—Margaret—had ditched the groom—Jim—during their Jamaican honeymoon when she'd caught him cheating with a cabana girl. Needless to say, she hadn't wanted a souvenir from the wedding.

I grabbed the cake server and tried to calm my pounding heart. When that didn't work, I reached for the cookie jar and the mountain of Oreos stuffed inside. I shoved two Oreos into my mouth. Did I mention that demons have a superfast metabolism?

Which meant the three slices of cake and their soothing powers were long gone.

I chewed the mouthful and by the time I swallowed, I felt loads better.

Okay, so *loads* was stretching it a bit. But I felt calm enough to face my no-win situation—me and my cake server vs. crazy, bloodthirsty Aunt Bella should I go through with the wedding from Hell. Or me and my cake server vs. crazy, bloodthirsty Mother should I back out. While Aunt Bella was a card-carrying sadist for sure, my own mother had founded the club and written the handbook. Aunt Bella could hurt me, but my own mother could *hurt* me. As in calling me back to Hell and keeping me there for all eternity.

On the other hand, if I went through with it and pulled off a successful wedding, I would bank enough money to move my business into an actual storefront. Even more, my mother would be so busy controlling everything and everyone Down Under that she would have zero time left over to keep tabs on me.

And if she did, by some crazy twist, eventually discover that I'd gone legit, she would still be so grateful that I'd pulled off such a fabulous event that she would show a teeny tiny ounce of mercy and leave me alone.

What can I say? Sugar not only boosts my mood, it also makes me slightly delusional.

I held tight to the crumb of hope, stuffed another Oreo into my mouth for an added rush, and marched back into the bathroom. After ripping aside the curtain and checking every nook and cranny of my apartment, I headed back to the kitchen for a dishrag and some Palmolive.

A few minutes later, I'd washed all the evidence of the threat off the mirror and out of my head.

Kind of.

I still had the cake server in one hand (just in case) when I walked into my bedroom. I pulled off my skirt and blouse and climbed into some comfy sweats. While I had a thing for designer handbags, my weakness didn't stretch to my wardrobe. I much preferred comfort over couture. My favorite outfit? A pair of pink Costco sweatpants and a Hello Kitty sweatshirt. Pinky swear.

Back in the living room, I collapsed on the sofa and reached for the remote. I was just about to pull up last night's episode of *My Fair Wedding with David Tutera* when a strange sense of awareness crawled through me and I felt a prickly sensation on my bare foot.

I screamed and jumped, and the spider scuttled under a nearby chair.

My cousin Aylena had a great recipe for a mean tarantula omelet, but big or small, I hated anything with more legs than me.

Which explained why I was still standing on my couch a full fifteen minutes later, cake server in hand, eyes frantically searching for the MIA spider, when I smelled the sharp scent of sulfur.

I knew even before I turned around that there was a demon standing behind me. What I didn't know was which one had decided to pay me a visit.

With my luck at an all-time low, I had no doubt it was Aunt Bella herself, chain saw in one hand, DVD in the other.

I drew a deep breath, held tight to *Margaret & Jim 4-ever*, and turned to face my nemesis.

5

"It's a little kinky, but I can work with it."

The deep voice rumbled through my head and relief washed over me, followed by a wave of irritation. Turning, I found myself face-to-face with the hottest-looking pirate I'd ever seen—and trust me, I'd seen plenty in my line of work.

He had the whole romance-novel-cover-model thing going on, with long dark hair, tight black pants stuffed into knee-high black leather boots, and a flowing white shirt.

Mr. Tall, Dark, and Ahoy Matey was the male version of my kind: an incubus, with mucho sex appeal and enough charisma to make any woman rip off her clothes with nothing more than a glance. Like all demons, his name was something ancient and pompous and impossible to pronounce—Argagiorasmosisarath, for the record. But everybody in this realm called him Gio because, let's face it, long-winded and older-than-dirt didn't up his score on the lust-o-meter.

I'd known Gio since I was eighteen (that's year number eighteen out of my whopping one thousand in existence). We'd both been wet-behind-the-ears virgins back then. Surprising as it might be, I wasn't born knowing every position in the Kama Sutra. I'd had to learn it all like every other sexual demon in the universe. Enter Signorina Camellia and her academy of carnal delights. Gio and I had met on our first day of class. He'd had a fondness for scratching his butt, belching, and talking about his bug collection every five seconds until Signorina Camellia had nixed his bad habits *and* taught him a zillion different ways to please the opposite sex. Ditto for me.

After graduation, Gio and I had joined forces (i.e., bodies) a time or two. Or three. Or more. In the spirit of continuing education, of course. We'd been study buddies. The proverbial friends with benefits.

Until my epiphany.

Since then I'd been avoiding him like the plague, which hadn't been all that difficult because he'd been busy wooing and wowing an Italian socialite whose upcoming wedding was going to unite two nations and end a thousand-year-old feud. No feud, no fighting and killing. Hence my ma and aunties had sent Gio in to seduce the bride and stop the wedding.

I stepped down off the couch and set the cake server on my coffee table. "What are you doing here?"

"Syra's winging it to New York via private jet to meet her mother for a week-long shopping trip. Her mother doesn't know about me, so I needed to get lost for a little while." He collapsed on the sofa. "I had Syra drop me off on her way to the Big Apple. Told her I was going to hang out with some old college friends." Syra wasn't privy to Gio's demon status. "I'm staying at the Hilton."

"Shouldn't you be conserving your energy instead of popping in?"

"I couldn't get a cab. There's a dental convention going on downtown."

"Syra still marrying the prince?" I sank down next to him.

"Technically, yes. But I've just about got her where I want her. She's *this* close to calling it off." A strange glimmer of unease flitted across his face, and I had the fleeting thought that he wasn't half as sure as he wanted to be. "She just hasn't figured out how to break the news. A few more nights like last night, however"—the expression faded into a knowing grin—"and she'll be updating her status on her Facebook page."

"Don't you think you should have changed before getting off the plane?" I blurted, desperately trying to divert his attention from the lavish wedding blazing across the screen and the fact that I was watching said wedding instead of the latest *Guys Gone Wild* video. "You look like Johnny Depp."

He shrugged. "Syra wanted to play a mile-high version of *Pirates of the Caribbean*. Listen, I'm glad I caught you off duty. I really need to talk."

Talk was incubus code for *I want to jump your bones so that I can perfect my bone-jumping technique.*

A sexy vision rushed into my head and I saw myself stretched out on the sofa, a man leaning over me, touching me, wowing me. A man with short, dark hair and piercing green eyes.

A man who looked a lot more like Cutter Owens than like the hot demon standing in front of me.

Uh-oh.

"Off duty? Me?" I bolted to my feet. "I'm not off duty. I'm just getting started." When his gaze swept me from head to toe, drinking in my sweats, I added, "He's into Hello Kitty. My date, that is. He's a huge collector. He's got the Hello Kitty popcorn machine, the waffle maker, phone case, screen saver—you name it. And you know me, I aim to please. Speaking of which"—I did an exaggerated neck roll as if I were about to climb into a WWE ring—"I hate to cut our reunion short, but he'll be here any minute and I'd like to get some stretching in first. He likes his women flexible."

Gio gave me a hurt look, and I fought down a pang of guilt. As much as I hated lying, I knew I had no choice. Friend or not, he was still a demon, and therefore unlikely to understand me wanting to find my One and Only. Even if he did, I still couldn't risk him mentioning it to any of his incubus buddies. My mother was going to find out the truth soon enough, and I was determined to get myself into her good graces before then. "If he sees you here, he's liable to run the other way, and I can't risk that. I've been working on this guy *forever*." I motioned toward the door. "You should go."

"But I really want to talk."

Um, yeah.

"I'll call you," I heard myself say as I grabbed his arm and hauled him off the couch.

"But I want to talk face-to-face," he protested as I pushed him toward the door.

"We'll do it face-to-face." I yanked open the door and nudged him out onto the front porch. "We'll do it missionary and doggie and any other way you want to do it." *Not.* While I didn't want to mess up my karma with a lie, my back was flat against the wall. Better to tell a teeny tiny fib than rip off my clothes and screw things up in a major way. "We just can't do it right now." I slammed the door shut in his face.

I wasn't going to sleep with Gio.

And I certainly wasn't going to sleep with Cutter Owens. I wanted more than sex from a man.

My head knew that, but damned if my body had gotten the message just yet.

I waited, my heart beating a frantic rhythm, for the next few seconds until I heard the soft *poof!* The smell of sulfur faded, and as quickly as Gio had dropped in, he was gone.

I let out the breath I'd been holding and headed back to the living room and the forgotten remote control. I'd just upped the volume on the TV when my nose twitched with the familiar scent, although it was much more subtle this time.

Foreboding rippled through me, followed by a rush of relief when I turned my head to find Blythe standing behind me.

She was tall and voluptuous, her long blonde hair pulled back into a ponytail above a pair of double-D breasts barely contained in an itty-bitty pink tank top that read *Limos Are Luscious.* Tight jeans and strappy stilettos completed her party-girl ensemble.

"Doesn't anyone knock anymore?" I frowned at her. "I thought you were a bloodthirsty demon."

"One out of two." She whistled. "Not bad. And I would have knocked, but my hands were full." She made a beeline for the kitchen and set her grocery bag down on the counter, then pulled a bottle of champagne from inside, followed by a carton of orange juice and three bags of peanut M&Ms. "I had a twenty-first B-day celebration that got cut short tonight because the birthday girl turned out to be preggos, which totally killed cocktail hour. She was craving all-you-can-eat pancakes, so I dropped them off at an IHOP and brought the party favors here. I figured you could use some cheering up, i.e., alcohol." She popped a few candies into her mouth as her gaze dropped to my clenched hand. "What's with the cake server?"

"Spiders and horny demons." When she arched a brow, I gave her a quick rundown of my day, including the brief encounter with Cutter Owens.

"I've heard about him. He took out one of my second cousins a few years ago. Sliced his head clean off before he realized that Apopyr—that was his name—wasn't the demon he was looking for."

"Who was he after?"

"Azazel."

"Why do I know that name?"

"Everyone knows that name." She popped the champagne top and took a long swig of the bubbly. "He's one of the oldest demons in existence," she added when she finally came up for air.

"That's right." I'd heard stories about how smart and cunning and elusive he was. There were even a few who claimed he'd been the one to tempt Eve in that garden so long ago instead of my ma. Not that anyone said that to her face.

"Why does he want Azazel?" I handed her a champagne glass from a nearby cabinet. "I mean, I know why he wants him—he's a demon slayer and Azazel's a demon—but why this demon in particular?"

"He stole Cutter's soul." Blythe mixed the orange juice with the champagne and handed me a mimosa. "Azazel is a collector. He travels this realm, imprisoning as many souls as possible. He's supposed to hand them over to your gramps, but rumor has it he's been keeping some for himself."

"Gramps would never allow that."

"He would if he's too busy worrying about your ma and aunties. He doesn't have the time to micromanage every ancient in existence. Sure, they bow down to your gramps because he led the way, but they don't do it because they *have* to. It's their choice. Your gramps knows that, so maybe he looks the other way on purpose. To keep the peace."

"How do you know all of this?"

She shrugged. "My great-great-great-great-uncle is the chief demon of gossip, remember?"

Duh. I knew that. I'd just been too freaked out by recent events to remember that all-important fact. "So tell me more."

"Well, it seems Cutter has been hunting Azazel forever. He's pissed and he wants revenge."

I didn't blame him. I knew how much I loved my favorite pair of shoes. I could only imagine how it would be to have your very essence ripped away.

"He almost caught him." Blythe sipped her drink. "Cutter actually narrowed down Azazel's location to some ancient castle in Rome a few years back. He goes there for the final showdown, only to get sidetracked by a bunch of lower-tier demons Azazel had gathered as a distraction. Cutter got busy slaying his way through the crowd, which gave Azazel a chance to slip away. Again."

"So Cutter wants revenge against Azazel." She nodded. "Then why is he after my mom?"

"Who knows?" She shrugged. "Maybe his priorities are changing. Maybe he's given up on revenge and he's more interested in prestige. Taking out your mother would push him all the way to the top of the Legion. Maybe even into Gabriel's seat."

"I doubt Cutter could go that high. Gabriel's an archangel."

"True, but even archangels retire. Look at your gramps."

"Maybe." Still, Cutter hadn't struck me as a power-hungry kind of guy. I remembered the glimmer in his eyes. The longing.

Okay, so he was hungry. But not for fame.

For me.

Down, girl.

I took a huge gulp of the mimosa.

"Somebody's thirsty." Blythe eyed me as she mixed her own drink. "Tell me something. Is he as hot as everyone says?"

His image materialized in my mind and my nipples pebbled. I shrugged. "He's all right." When she raised a brow, I added, "Okay, so he's more than all right. He's kind of hot."

"Kind of?"

"Okay, so he's smoking hot. He's the sexiest man I've seen in a long, *long* time. Not that it means diddly. He's completely off-limits." I took another drink and watched her watch me. "I'd be crazy to be interested under the circumstances, right?"

She nodded. "One hundred percent certifiable."

"Seriously. It's not like we're talking about some regular guy. He kills demons for a living. And he has no soul." Which made him the ultimate hard-ass. Cold. Unfeeling. Incapable of love.

Nix any happily-ever-after—which was all I was interested in. Even if my hormones were humming an entirely different tune.

"On top of that, he's after my mom. I might not be the most loyal daughter, but I could never associate with someone who wants to off my very own mother." I took my mimosa, grabbed a bag of candy, and headed into the living room. Blythe followed. "I mean, really," I added as I settled on the couch. "What kind of daughter would I be if I consorted with the enemy?" I was already dealing with a steaming side of guilt served up by my conscience for turning my back on my birthright. I didn't need another heaping spoonful on top of that. "Satan or not, I couldn't do that to my ma."

"Family first." Blythe sank down next to me. "I hear ya."

I popped a handful of candy into my mouth. "Damn straight," I mumbled around a mouthful. "A girl's got to have her priorities."

"Amen."

"No way am I actually going to call him." I punched up the DVR and bypassed David Tutera in favor of a *Jersey Shore* episode. "Even if he did give me his card."

No *effing* way, I reminded myself later that night after Blythe and I had fist-pumped our good-byes and I'd double-checked the locks on all the doors and windows. After looking at the crumpled business card about a trillion times, of course.

I wasn't doing it. That's what I told myself as I climbed into bed. No punching in his digits. No talking to him and betraying my ma. No reaching out and betraying myself.

I clamped my eyes shut and there he was. Teasing. Tempting. Tantalizing.

I'd made a vow. No mindless, meaningless sex.

As for a mindless, meaningless fantasy…

I smiled and snuggled into the pillow. What could be the harm in that?

6

I'd had about a zillion wet dreams since climbing onto the No-More-Mindless-Sex-until-I-Find-the-One Express, so it didn't really surprise me when I woke up to feel a trickle of sweat at my temple. Moisture pooled between my breasts. My favorite Hello Kitty tee clung to me. The damp sheets stuck to my skin.

I smiled as I remembered the way dream-Cutter had touched me. Soft and slow at first. Then strong and purposeful. The man had great hands. And a great mouth. And a really great—

A face full of water smacked into me, cutting off my oxygen supply and drenching my hair. I bolted upright, sputtering and gasping for air.

My eyes flew open, wildly registering the woman standing next to the bed before I clamped them shut again.

No.

No. No. No. No. *No.*

I was used to the texts. The phone messages. The e-mails. The penis-shaped cookie bouquet for my last birthday. All constant reminders from my mother of who I was and what was expected of me.

But two actual visits from her in less than twenty-four hours?

Forget waiting to be damned. I was already in Hell.

"Again." Her voice echoed in my head and my eyes popped open in time to see my mother's ever-faithful assistant step forward with a half-full pitcher in her hands.

"Stop!" I held up my hands to ward off Cheryl and her liquid attack. "I'm awake. Seriously." I scrambled from the bed. The floor tilted for a split second as I struggled to get a grip. "I'm up. All the way up."

"It's about time." My mother flicked a piece of invisible lint from her tailored red suit. She'd pulled her hair back today, which accented her sculpted cheekbones and her full, red lips. "We've been standing here *forever*, haven't we, Cheryl?"

"Actually it's been four minutes and fifty-three seconds," Cheryl offered.

"Exactly." Lillith Damon glanced at her diamond-encrusted Rolex. "I'm late for an appointment. We're working on a new downtown condo development. I'm doing the decorating. Now." She eyed me, and the rings around her pupils fired the same shade as her designer suit. "Show me what you've put together so far."

I was trembling with anxiety. Soaking wet. And suddenly there didn't seem to be enough oxygen in the room. "You just commissioned me yesterday," I pointed out.

"And?" My mother arched one perfectly tweezed eyebrow. "Surely you've put some plans together by now. The wedding is in two weeks, after all."

"Two weeks? But you said next month."

"I've changed my mind. The news has spread fast and there's a lot of dissension. Two weeks is all I can spare."

My heart did a double thump and my stomach bottomed out. "But it takes longer than that to get the invitations printed."

"Then I guess you'd better get moving." She must have noted my loss of color, because she frowned. Her eyes glowed again. "Surely that won't be a problem."

"Of course not," I managed, desperately trying to swallow the golf-ball-size lump in my throat. "The sooner, the better." Don't freak. Just breathe. In. Out. In. Out. Easy. Calm.

"Good, because time is of the essence. Bella and Levita are probably already plotting a way to stop me."

And I knew just how they planned to do it.

Back off now or you're dead.

"And I'm sure Lucy will be in on it when they do. That I-could-care-less-about-the-family-biz is just a front. She's a Damon, which means she's as power hungry as the rest of us."

I debated telling my ma about the bloody message all of a nano-second before nixing the idea. Hey, we're talking the Devil. She wasn't exactly known for her calm, rational thinking. She was sure to want to know who had called and/or paid me a visit last night. And that was the thing. I had suspicions, but I didn't *know*. Sure, the AB negative was probably a dead giveaway that it was Bella, but it could also have been one of her daughters. Maybe Portia. Or Hester. Or one of the others.

Not that my mother would waste time finding the guilty party. She would take them all out, and I didn't want any innocents— even one of my mean cousins—getting hurt in the cross fire.

"It's imperative that we move swiftly." My mother flicked some lint off her jacket. "But not too swiftly. I don't want them to think I'm worried that they'll succeed, which I most definitely am *not*. Even so, the less time they have to plot, the better. Did you call Landon Parks to officiate?"

I remembered her mention of the demon judge yesterday. "Not yet, but—"

"Do it ASAP. He's the only one who can officiate. Now," she went on, "we'll do it the Saturday after next, around sixish. Also, I was thinking we might include Cerberus in the ceremony. You know he's always been such a faithful hellhound, and Cheryl here, being the animal lover that she is, suggested he could be the ring bearer—" She stalled in midsentence and gave me the evil eye. "Shouldn't you be writing this stuff down?"

I spent the next ten minutes jotting down a ton of notes that my mother had forgotten to give me yesterday, including Cerberus as ring bearer and the Four Horsemen of the Apocalypse as ushers.

"Oh, and I'm going with thirteen bridesmaids instead of the original twelve because thirteen has always been my unlucky number."

A sliver of hope blossomed inside me. Crazy, right? I was the wedding planner. I didn't have time to be a bridesmaid. At the same time, she was my mother and I was her daughter, and it would be sorta, kinda nice for her to at least ask. "Who did you have in mind?"

She shrugged. "Whoever. Just plug in some of your cousins and we'll be good to go."

My chest tightened. Not because I was, you know, upset or anything. I barely got a birthday gift from the woman. A heartfelt invite to be a bridesmaid would have been stretching it way too far.

"Maid of honor?"

"Cheryl can stand in. She'll be in charge of most of the duties anyhow. And that's it," Mother finished with a quick glance around, as if seeing the apartment for the first time. "This is where you live?"

"For the past two years. I know it's a little rough," I rushed on when her nose wrinkled in disdain, "but I've been fixing it up. I painted last month."

She eyed the walls. "If I were you, I'd shoot whoever sold you this horrific color." And then she disappeared in a sharp staccato of heels on hardwood, Cheryl following. The door slammed and I was finally alone.

Not that it would last. My voice mail was full and it was just a matter of time before more demons started popping in.

Or popping me.

I thought of the threat scribbled in blood and my hands trembled. Someone was really and truly trying to scare the bejesus out of me, and they would try again, particularly since I had no intention of backing off. I was going to see this thing through.

In the meantime...

I changed into clean clothes, powered up my laptop, and spent the rest of my Sunday morning lining up venues for the wedding from Hell.

* * *

Five hours later, I'd made twenty-three phone calls, left eight voice mails, and withstood two up-close-and-personal visits from my cousins Marjorie and Gregoria, who just happened to be walking by my duplex.

Um, yeah.

I'd *so* had my fill of nosy relatives.

When it came to warding off evil spirits (that's PC for The Cousins), I should have been an expert. I was an evil spirit, after all, so I'd learned early on about salt, sage, and horseshoes. They were Demon 101. The thing was, I knew that stuff worked when humans used them to ward off a spirit. I wasn't so sure they would be effective for one demon to use on another demon.

And I *had* to use something.

I decided enough was enough after my cousin Portia just happened to drop in. And my cousin Millicent. *And* my cousin Janna.

I needed some expert advice on the situation, which was why, after fifteen minutes on Google, I found myself near the Galleria, in the old, revamped Montrose area. A row of houses had been turned into a shopping mecca not too long ago, complete with a coffee shop, an Italian bistro, a gift boutique and...bingo.

Above a white house with bright-pink trim, a neon sign glowed in the window: Bliss, Bling & Otherworldly Things.

Yeah, baby.

I headed up the small walkway and pushed open the door. Forget Scottish folk tunes or indie rock or any other spiritualist-type music—eighties hit "Girls Just Want to Have Fun" vibrated from the speakers. Instead of sage and herbs, the sweet, sugary smell of pink cupcakes drifted from a candle in the corner (shaped, of course, like a pink frosted cupcake).

The entire place looked like the hot spot where zebras went to die. Girly zebras, that is. There was black-and-white *everything*— from lampshades edged with pink crystals to the love seat sitting against the far wall to the swag curtains outlining a door that led to an adjoining room to the welcome mat under my feet.

There wasn't a yak's tongue or a voodoo doll in sight. Rather, dozens of rhinestone flip-flops lined the opposite wall. Sequined handbags in every color hung from hooks overhead. What looked like faux Pandora jewelry filled the cases at the counter. Behind it stood a fortysomething woman with lots of curves, a zebra-tipped manicure (no, really), and a distressed pink rhinestone T-shirt that read *Sassy*.

I was so filing a complaint with Google.

"All of our Fandora is ten percent off today," Sassy—complete with eighties hair to match the song pounding in the air—informed me in a rich Texas twang, motioning to the display in front of her. Her pale-gray eyes twinkled, and I glimpsed Sassy's dream man— Toby Keith in a black cowboy hat. "I've got toe rings two for one. And we've also got this divine bracelet." She motioned to a silver-looking charm-type bracelet hugging her thick wrist. "It's not the real thing, but it's half the price."

"I'm afraid I might be in the wrong place." *Ya think?*

"Well, what is it you're looking for, sugar?"

"Not really flip-flops or costume jewelry." I glanced around before giving her an apologetic smile.

"I've got T-shirts too," she added, pointing a zebra-tipped finger at the doorway leading to the next room, which was filled with clothing racks and jeweled cowboy boots.

"Sorry." I backtracked toward the door.

"There are a few pair of faux designer jeans," she added. "And belts. And against the back wall there's an entire display of amulets to ward off all those evil buggers."

I put on the brakes and turned so fast I gave myself whiplash. "What did you just say?"

"They're on sale. Our potions too. A bottle of our Lover's Delight is half off. So is our top seller—the Ballbuster. It's for SOBs who don't pay their child support. A few drops on a pair of his old boxers and Mr. Happy will shrivel up quicker than a banana in a dehydrator." She grinned. "It works on cheating boyfriends too."

"Do you have anything to help with unwanted demons?"

"Right this way." She rounded the counter, her flip-flops smacking the floor. She led me into the adjoining room, past the clothing racks to a bookshelf set up against the far wall. The top row had—surprise, surprise—horseshoes. There were also amulets and jars filled with all sorts of creepy-looking contents (bingo on the yak's tongue). Below that were several rows of books that included everything from *How to Embrace Your Inner Demon* to *Ghouls Are from Mars and Zombies Are from Venus.*

Sassy might be a human, but she knew her supes, too. Then again, most witches did.

I noted the silver moon-shaped ring—a symbol of one of Houston's largest covens—on Sassy's hand as she pulled out a particular book with a bright-yellow cover.

She flipped through a few pages of *The Idiot's Guide to Demons* until she seemed to find what she was looking for. "Here we go. There are several possibilities. You can burn sage throughout the house and recite a cleansing ritual."

"I think that might violate my building's fire code." And screw me royally on account of I'm a demon and I live in the duplex. I wasn't about to find myself supernaturally evicted because of a little herbal bonfire.

"You can protect the place with holy water."

"I don't do holy water either."

She arched an eyebrow. "Agnostic?"

"Claustrophobic." Liquid would seep into the woodwork and carpet and be impossible to get out. My ma and cousins wouldn't just be locked out. *I'd* be locked *in.*

Had I thought about this stuff or what?

"Don't you have something that's more here today and gone tomorrow?" I asked. "I'm leasing."

Her brows drew together and I knew I'd screwed myself with the *claustrophobic* comment. She'd picked up on the fact that I wasn't just a hot, vivacious human with a nasty demon problem.

Rather, I *was* the nasty demon.

I held my breath as I waited for her to start chanting an Eject spell or wag a yak's tongue at me. Luckily, she seemed more interested in making a buck than casting me out.

She shrugged. "Many believe that a mixture of salt and various powdered herbs can form a barrier against demons." She grabbed one of the numerous jars that lined the top shelf and unscrewed the lid to reveal a bright-pink powder mixed with white crystals. "You could try sprinkling this around the doors and windows, and then just suck it up the next morning with a DustBuster."

"I'll take it." My gaze shifted to the display case at the front and my weakness for faux chic gripped me. "How much did you say that Fandora bracelet was?"

1

"Hi, everyone. My name is Jess and I'm a sex addict."

I'd like to say that I had loads of self-control and had kicked the lust bug by sheer willpower alone. But the truth was, I'd needed a little help to climb onto the wagon and to stay on the wagon, particularly after last night's fantasy starring Cutter Owens.

I'd thought about him and how I shouldn't want to call him and how I really, *really* did want to call him on account of he was so hot and I was so horny.

It was a good thing for me it was Sunday. Because Sundays meant one thing—the weekly meeting of the southeast chapter of the Circle of Love.

Note the word *love* rather than *lust*.

We were a fourteen-step group (we sex addicts needed two more than the usual twelve) committed to supporting one another by sharing stories, advice, and the occasional recipe. I'd contributed my infamous Chocolate Chip Nirvana cookies last month, which had met with rave reviews and three marriage proposals. Obviously sexual demons weren't the only ones who needed a little sugar in the tank to stay on the straight and narrow.

I'd brought a dozen everything-but-the-kitchen-sink brownies tonight. Which had been a generous two dozen before three more cousins had stopped by to interrogate me about the upcoming wedding—I'd yet to use my demon dust. I'd been weak and hungry and, well, at least I'd made it here with something.

"I've been riding the good-girl train for two years, four months, and twenty-two days," I went on. *And twelve hours and fourteen minutes*, my deprived hormones added silently.

Sherrie, a real-estate agent and mother of three who'd started the group several years ago, beamed at me and shifted her attention to the man seated to my right—a bald accountant with a pocket calculator and a Snickers bar. She motioned for him to keep the intros moving and he stood up. "My name is Alex. I'm a CPA and I'm a sex addict too."

The intros rolled on around the circle, one after the other.

"My name is Trish LaFleur. I'm the head pastry chef at Belle Venue and I'm a sex addict."

"My name is Kevin Martinson. I own Perfectly Fit, a nearby fitness club. I can do five hundred sit-ups, four hundred chin-ups, and two hours straight of cardio without getting winded, and I'm a sex addict." Kevin had all the muscles to back up his statement and a pair of dimples that made my stomach tremble when he smiled.

My mouth watered, and I counted down the minutes until I could tackle the dessert table and the last of the brownies. Why, oh, why hadn't I slipped one into my purse before sitting down?

"...name is Frank and I'm a sex addict," said the guy sitting to Kevin's right. "I also sell car insurance on the side, so if anyone needs a quote just see me after the session."

Sherrie frowned, and middle-aged Frank slid back into his seat as if he'd been whacked with a ruler. She shifted her attention to the next person, and the introductions went on for the next few minutes until we reached the last person, the woman sitting just to my left.

Her blonde highlights had been cut into a stylish bob. She wore a petal-pink tracksuit, white running shoes, and a massive handbag that actually wiggled as she shifted it to the side and stood. "My name is Tammie Mae Hutchinson. I don't actually work, but I *am* president of the Kingwood Estates Home Owners Association." When Sherrie gave her a look that said *and?*, she added, "Oh, I'm also vice president for the Fairchild Elementary School PTA and secretary for the Kingwood Little League Association." She started to sit down, but Sherrie cleared her throat. "I'm also an s-e-x addict," she added before sinking back to her chair.

"It's okay." I smiled. "I was nervous my first time too."

"Oh, it's not my first meeting." She waved a hand. "I used to belong to the Kingwood chapter, but all of our members graduated, so I've merged with this group. I've been to fifty-nine meetings including this one. I'm just uncomfortable saying the word out loud."

"Religious issues?"

"Toddlers."

"Now that everyone knows everyone," Sherrie announced, "it's time to share. Please remember. This is a safe place. No judgments. Just acceptance and understanding. And then refreshments." Heads bobbed around the group, and she added, "Now would anyone like to tell us about any experiences since our last meeting that might have tested your progress in the program? Any instances where you wanted to slide back down the proverbial ladder? Or perhaps you slid and you're ready to own up to your mistake so that you can shed the baggage and start climbing again?"

Frank's hand slid into the air. "I met this pretty hot waitress over at this diner out in Clear Lake last weekend. I was giving an insurance quote to the owner—I managed to save him fifty percent off what he was currently paying—and she smiled at me. That was all it took for things to go south. I started having thoughts..."

Frank the insurance guy went on with several descriptive images before Sherrie cut him short, much to everyone's dismay (hey, it's the doing that's off-limits, not the hearing about it).

"So what did you do about those urges?" she asked. "Did you act on them?"

"I almost propositioned her, but then I pictured my wife, Julie, and I ordered a slice of apple pie with two scoops of ice cream instead."

Go, Frank.

"I've got something even more powerful that doesn't pack on the pounds," said the PTA mom next to me. "I've been on the wagon for over a year now and it's all because of my poochies. See, my therapist suggested I try nurturing something instead of feeding my own desires and, what do you know? It worked. The only problem is, Candy and Molly—they're my babies—turned out to be Candy and Mitch, so now I've got puppies." She hefted the bag, which I then realized was one of those chic dog purses, and opened up the top to reveal a half dozen squirming balls of fluff. "They all need good homes if anyone is interested."

"Well, now, what a lovely offer," Sherrie said. "I think we should break now and give everyone a chance to check out these adorable puppies."

The group crowded around Tammie Mae, but yours truly, being the typical dog-fearing demon, headed for the refreshment table.

I was stuffing another brownie into my mouth and trying to ignore Kevin flexing in my peripheral when Tammie Mae came up behind me.

"Rough night?"

"Something like that," I mumbled around a mouthful.

"Well, I have just the thing to cheer you right up." She reached into her massive handbag, which I'd thought was now empty. No such luck. She pulled out a miniature black Yorkie with loads of hair and a black-and-white polka-dot bow on top of its head.

The canine version of Snooki took one look at me and started yapping frantically.

"She's my last one," Tammie said.

"I'll have to pass."

"Come on. She's a cutie, and if I come home with this dog, my husband will shoot me. He says our house is too full as it is, what with the kids and four dogs."

"I thought you had two dogs."

"I had to keep a few puppies for myself. Anyhow, she's nine weeks old and guaranteed to keep you so busy you don't have a second to think about all the nooky you're giving up."

I had no doubt. She was sure to raise such a ruckus on account of my demon vibe that the only thing I would be thinking about was smothering myself with a pillow.

I shrugged. "I'm not much of a dog person."

"I wouldn't be so sure. Go on and hold her. She likes you."

"She's growling at me."

"She just needs to warm up to you a little."

"My building has a no-pets policy, but thanks anyway. Have a brownie." I shoved a piece into her mouth when it dropped open to argue and beat a hasty retreat to the other side of the room just as Sherrie called the meeting back to order.

No way was I getting stuck with a dog. Even if it was the last one. And kind of cute.

And sitting in a cardboard box on my front seat when I walked out of the building and opened the door of my Cube.

She'll be the best thing that ever happened to you.

I read the note sitting on my dash before my head jerked around the parking lot, searching for Tammie. But I'd stayed a few extra minutes to gather up my brownie plate, so the parking lot was all but empty.

Just yours truly and a yapping Snooki, who eyeballed me as if she fully expected my head to do a three-sixty.

"You don't want to go home with me, do you?"

She growled and barked that much louder.

"I didn't think so."

Which meant I had to call animal control.

Problem solved, I told myself as I reached into my purse for my phone. I punched in the digits for information. The experts would come and pick her up.

And possibly send her to a shelter where she would be the smallest and most vulnerable among a cage full of big, starving dogs who would rather eat her than look at her.

"You have to come home with me," I heard myself say as I killed the phone and stuffed it back into my purse.

I fought down a thousand years of instinct that told me this was a bad idea and pushed the box over onto the passenger's seat.

Demons and dogs were like water and oil. They just didn't mix, and to even try would be a major catastrophe. Besides, I had stuff to do. I still had hours' worth of venue details to work on before tomorrow. Add to that the demon-proofing job that lay ahead of me courtesy of Sassy and her magic powder, and the last thing I had enough time (or nerves) for was a yapping dog.

But as busy as I was, and as loud as she was, I still couldn't let her end up a midnight snack for some depraved Doberman. Talk about screwing up my searching-for-true-love mojo.

It was one night.

I could figure something else out tomorrow.

Holding tight to the thought, I slid into the front seat, glared at Snooki until the yapping faded into a low growl, and headed for a nearby twenty-four-hour Walmart for doggie supplies, including a pink ceramic Diva Pooch bowl, a bag of high-protein dog food, a doggie gate, and the cutest rhinestone collar.

What?

She was destitute, and I wasn't equipped to play hostess, even for one night.

Or two.

8

I'd read a news poll once that claimed Monday was the most hated day of the week.

The big M meant the tragic end of the weekend and the start of another grueling work fest. It marked the slowest and most painful eight hours of the proverbial forty plus. It was also the busiest day for suicide prevention hotlines, depression clinics, and Krispy Kreme bakeries.

All right, so I'd added that last one based on the forty-five minutes I'd just wasted picking up a dozen glazed, but still.

Bottom line—Mondays sucked, and no one in their right mind would think otherwise.

I topped off my second cup of black coffee and stopped whistling the chorus of "We Found Love" (barely audible above the constant yapping coming from the bathroom) long enough to take a drink and snatch up my briefcase. A few seconds later, I skipped downstairs to my office, a smile on my face and Rihanna belting it out in my head.

After the weekend I'd had—not one, but *two* visits from my *madre*, various demons popping in to poke their noses in my business (not to mention the one threatening my existence), and an entire night of high-pitched barking—even the most dreaded workday seemed like a dream come true.

A chance to throw myself into a great big vat of normal for a few hours and forget the totally abnormal state of my crappy existence.

That, and I was just this side of punchy after only forty-seven minutes of sleep. While Sassy's powder had done the trick last night and I hadn't entertained any unexpected visitors, I hadn't *known* it would work. I'd found myself wide-awake most of the night (thank you, Snooki), either surfing the Internet for possible venues for my ma or scarfing cookies and staring in abstract paranoia at the windows and doors. The little bit of shut-eye I did manage had been riddled with superhot fantasies starring a certain demon hunter with amazing eyes and buns of steel.

And a really big sword, I reminded myself, determined to keep my head and not let my hormones go gaga. Big, effing *sword*. And I wasn't talking metaphor, though I'd be willing to bet his other, ahem, *sword* was pretty impressive as well.

Solid silver. Sharp. Deadly.

It wasn't the Legion members themselves who were so deadly to a demon. It was the weapons they used. Magical weapons blessed by the head honcho, Gabriel, himself.

One swift stab and—*poof!*—g'bye, demon.

I tried to conjure several images of such a weapon pressed to my throat, but the only thing I could see was Cutter's face and those green eyes and, well, have I mentioned that it's been two long years since I've had sex with anyone other than a vibrator named Big Buck?

I pushed open the door to Happily Ever After Events and walked into the modest but tastefully decorated interior. The living room served as the lobby, complete with framed issues of *Southern Bride* magazine lining the walls, two plush white sofas, and a glass coffee table stacked with more wedding mags, along with an eight-by-ten digital photo frame that flashed images of my work.

The main room opened into another area set up with three small tables depicting the latest in tablescape and centerpiece trends. A small hallway led to another room that served as a work hub with two desks, a large bookcase, a ginormous filing cabinet, a small round table covered with invitation books, and an anxious Burke Carmichael.

He looked as hot as ever in fitted jeans, a distressed black T-shirt that fit his P90X bod like a glove, and an expression that said *It's about freakin' time.*

"I've got good news and not-so-good news." He pushed up from his desk and handed me a stack of phone messages. "Pick your poison."

I set the box of doughnuts on a nearby desk and glanced through the slips of paper. Cousin Laura. Cousin Bernice. Cousin Hester. Cousin Mary. Cousin Susanna. Cousin Millicent. Cousin Andromeda. The list went on and on.

With each name my stomach churned and the cryptic threat on my bathroom mirror flashed in my head. It could be any of them.

All of them.

Maybe I didn't have to worry about just one bad guy. Maybe there was a bona fide conspiracy to kill the wedding planner and put a crimp in my mother's plans to rule the Underworld.

I clamped my fingers around the slips of paper, stuffed them into my pocket, and forced myself to relax. Conspiracy or not, it didn't matter. It didn't change my game plan. It was all about keeping my focus, watching my back, and planning the wedding of my career.

Tamping down on the niggling doubt that told me it wasn't going to be that easy, I tried to focus on the all-important fact that, as of this moment, I was alive and breathing and neck-deep in wedding nirvana. "I like to start the day off on a positive note," I said to Burke. "Hit me with the good stuff first."

"You've got two new brides coming in later today. High profile. Three hundred plus guests for each. Impressive budgets."

Okay, so maybe my immortal life didn't suck quite that much. I perked up and the smile turned genuine. "That's awesome."

"Don't get too excited. You'll have to take the plunge into the depths of misery first. *She's* here"—his voice dropped into the hushed register reserved for the biggest bridezilla in the Bayou

City—"and she's kicking ass and taking names. She even made Andrew cry."

As if on cue, a sobbing Andrew appeared in the doorway that led to the adjoining kitchen. "I offered her the usual latte and/or espresso," he said in between sniffles, "and she told me to take a flying leap." Andrew, waving his gay-pride banner in a pink polo shirt, white linen shorts, and boat shoes, bit back another sob and cut a path straight to the doughnut box.

"Don't do it," Burke warned as his brother flipped open the lid and grabbed with both hands. "No woman is worth ruining a six-pack and some serious guns, bro." He flexed for emphasis.

"I don't care." Andrew devoured half a glazed from one hand, another doughnut poised and ready in hand number two. "I'm upset." He gulped. "And I need a pick-me-up."

I knew the feeling.

I debated wrestling the box out of his hands, but I suspected he needed the sugar more than I did. Besides, I'd already had two, and I was armed and ready with the usual roll of Life Savers tucked into my pocket.

"I'll talk with her, and whatever it is, we'll work it out."

"This is Delaney," Burke reminded me. "*Houston Elite* magazine's Most Likely to Pitch a Fit and Pop an Aneurysm in Public."

"I thought she was voted Wealthiest Oil Brat."

"Same thing."

"Where is she?"

He pointed to the closed door that led to the one and only bedroom, aka my private office. "I didn't want to get any blood on the lobby couches. Especially since we're still paying for them."

"Your faith in my negotiating skills is overwhelming." I popped a cherry-flavored Life Savers into my mouth and fought down the sudden urge to turn and run the other way. I wanted normal, and nothing could be more matter-of-fact than yet another catastrophe à la Delaney Farris.

Delaney had hired me three years ago to plan a huge, extravagant affair befitting the daughter of one of Houston's top oilmen. But three changes of venue, four different bands, and six wedding dresses later, she still hadn't managed to get everything perfect enough to walk down the aisle.

We were in the home stretch, however. The big day (rescheduled a record five times) was only three weeks away, which meant that whatever problem had brought her to my office before eight a.m. on a Monday morning had to be taken care of.

And fast.

Grabbing the doorknob, I pasted on a huge smile and walked into the room to find the tall, leggy blonde seated on a small settee, the latest issue of *Houston Brides* open on her lap.

She wore a white poet's blouse and a pair of Seven for All Mankind jeans stuffed into brown leather boots with three inch-heals. A six-carat emerald-cut diamond ring lined with side baguettes caught the morning sunlight streaming through the windows and temporarily blinded me.

I blinked and held up a hand as I made my way to my desk. "How's my favorite bride doing this morning?"

"Terrible," she declared, waving her hand and sending a shower of prismatic light across the soft pink walls. "We need bridesmaids' dresses."

"We already have dresses." I sank down into my chair and set my purse in the bottom drawer. "I was at the final fittings myself on Friday."

"The color is all wrong." She shook her head. "They're orchid and I distinctly requested grape." She held up a sales slip from a local bridal salon. "See? It says right here. *Orchid.* I was so freaked when I saw them yesterday that I couldn't even sleep last night. I had to take a Valium just to calm myself down."

Easy. Calm. Breathe.

I recited the silent mantra and willed Delaney to pick up my soothing I'll-handle-everything vibe. Unfortunately, I'm a succubus, so the only vibe that anyone ever picked up from me was *Let's get naked.* And that only worked on the opposite sex.

Delaney's eyebrows pinched together. "This is a disaster."

"I know the paperwork says orchid, but the color is really a much deeper hue." I reached for the file sitting on the corner of my desk. "I matched the swatches myself." I found the two scraps of fabric and set them on the tabletop. There. Exactly the same. Even in the bright light of day.

"But I want grape dresses," she whined, still as stubborn as ever. "I want them to *say* grape. I want them to *be* grape. Not orchid. Or amethyst. Or eggplant. Or aubergine. Or acai."

Or any of the dozen different purples we'd debated over for months before she'd finally settled on one.

"The groomsmen's vests are grape," she went on. "And they even say grape. The dresses have to match them exactly. They just *have* to."

"I'm sure if we take a look—"

"That's all I did was look. I stared at the colors all night and I can clearly see a distinction." She leaned forward and touched the identical swatches. "Can't you see? It's wrong." She shook her head. "All wrong."

Forget a Valium. She'd obviously been smoking some serious crack.

Not that I was going to point that out. I was here to make her dreams come true.

I fantasized for a nanosecond about pulling an *Exorcist* on her (think head spinning and a pea-soup shooter) and scaring her into submission. Seriously. We were three weeks away from the big day.

No way could I scrounge up a dozen new custom-dyed bridesmaids' dresses in that short an amount of time.

But I was determined not to mess up my good-girl-searching-for-love aura. Even more, I couldn't really blame Delaney for being so picky. Not when I knew her heart simply wasn't in it. Her fantasy man? Vin Diesel. Meanwhile, her groom looked like Zach Galifianakis from *The Hangover*.

I know, right?

Anyhow, Stuffalumpalous was a colleague of her father's who headed a rival oil company. The marriage was more like a merging of two corporations, with Delaney a perk in the contract.

I didn't miss the flash of desperation in her gaze. I knew that more than worrying about the dress color, she was really freaked over the notion of spending the rest of her life with a man she didn't love.

My chest hitched. "If you want new dresses, we'll get new dresses," I heard myself say.

I know, I know. I was such a sucker.

"Really?" The desperation faded into hope, and I could almost hear her telling herself that everything would be okay. The dresses. The flowers. The cake. The wedding. The honeymoon. The future.

I smiled. "Whatever you want."

"Great." She beamed, and hope faded into determination. "And since we're changing the color," she went on, "I'd like to rethink the style too. I want something with more of a *Sex and the City* feel. You know." She waved a hand. "Something fun and flirty and cocktailish."

Was *cocktailish* even a word?

"I want short," she announced, morphing from worried, vulnerable Delaney back into the be-yotch who had traumatized Andrew and landed her on the front page of the local newspaper's *City Beat* section for punching a waitress who'd served full-fat vinaigrette on her salad instead of low-cal. "And skimpy."

"But full-length ball gowns are much more appropriate for a black-tie affair," I reminded her. "You wanted an Audrey Hepburn feel, remember? That's why we put together a formal ceremony, followed by a grand reception with a full orchestra, an eight-course sit-down dinner, and tableside flambé."

"About that..." She shrugged. "I'm not really feeling the whole flambé thing. I still want a vintage feel, so I was thinking we could do a *Sex and the City* theme instead."

Forget vintage. Delaney was going for total cliché.

"I want a salsa band and a buffet," she rattled on. "Oh, and one of those mashed potato stations with the giant martini glasses so that you can add your own toppings and Cosmos for the signature drink and..."

Anxiety rolled through me and my brain reeled with the magnitude of changes that I was about to face and, even more, with the possibility that we might have to postpone the wedding yet again if I couldn't pull off said changes in a timely manner.

Which meant I could be dealing with Delaney for another three years.

I went for the Life Savers in my pocket, peeled off four, and stuffed them into my mouth. It was going to be one hell of a long day.

* * *

Long turned out to be an understatement. Since Delaney insisted I tend to her personally, I spent an hour on the phone with her dress designer, who finally agreed to help us find a new look, and another six hours trying on new dresses with Delaney's twelve bridesmaids, who were already in love with the old dresses. Then another two hours getting the measurements right and the dresses on order. Then several more hours back at the office making phone calls to catch up on all the work I'd missed—namely booking Judge

Landon Parks as the demonic officiant for my mom's big event and working to secure a venue.

Luckily Burke and Andrew had met with my two prospective brides, otherwise I would have been even more stressed. As it was, I spent a total of twelve excruciating hours hard at work, but I managed it all without a three-sixty head spin or any projectile upchucking.

I was *so* going to find the man of my dreams.

I powered off my computer and popped my last Life Savers into my mouth. I'd been crunching them all day long, and while the sugar had helped, what I really needed was to kick back and savor the sweet treat for a few peaceful moments. I settled into my chair and closed my eyes. And then I heard my mother's voice.

"Let's make this quick. I've got another meeting and the car is running."

I gulped. And swallowed.

Bye-bye, my sweet, sugary friend.

My eyes snapped open to find Lillith Damon standing in my office, wearing a tailored navy suit and an impatient expression. "I thought we were meeting at the museum," I said. My gaze went to Cheryl, who stood next to her. "I left you a voice mail specifically stating that we're meeting first thing tomorrow for a tour."

"Cheryl told me. But I've been thinking about this museum business and it won't do. I need something bigger. It's not just about joining forces with Samael. It's about making a statement. A big statement."

Such as *I'm Satan. Bigger than you. Badder than you.*

"But the museum can accommodate up to eight hundred guests. Even more, it's available two weeks from now." Which was a huge thing given the short notice. "I really think you should consider it."

"And I think you should find something else." She glanced at the file folder sitting on my desk, and the edges sparked. "Think big. Huge."

I grabbed a nearby magazine and slapped at the licks of fire until the paperwork was nothing but a smoldering heap. "There's always the Chase Bank building."

Her face lit up. "Perfect."

"I was joking." Her eyes turned a brilliant crimson, and she glanced at a nearby file cabinet. Clearly she wasn't amused, and before I could stop myself, I blurted, "But maybe I could work something out."

Her eyes cooled to a chilling blue. "Do whatever you have to do, dear. You're a succubus, for Pete's sake. There isn't a man alive who can resist you. Strip naked. Flaunt your feminine wiles. Seduce someone. Anyone. But make it happen. And fast. I'm losing my patience for all of this."

"We've been at it less than twenty-four hours."

"Exactly. My time is being sucked away as we speak." She shook her head. "Cheryl will keep tabs on you and report your progress back to me."

Cheryl gave me an apologetic look as she scurried after my mother. The slam of a door followed, and I barely resisted the urge to burst into tears.

I damned myself for not sprinkling my No Demon powder downstairs too, but I'd mainly been concerned about being caught off guard in the privacy of my own apartment. Not at my place of business.

Drawing a deep breath, I nixed the museum idea and e-mailed every contact I could find for the Chase Bank building, including a security guard whom I'd hired to handle crowd control for one of my weddings last year.

Not that I was going to get up close and personal with Dougie Cooper (said guard) or anyone else, for that matter, despite my mother's suggestion. Rather, I was going to be my übercharming self and try to talk my way in. That, or fork over a few Benjamins.

Hey, money talks.

I ignored the sliver of doubt that told me I might as well call it quits and hop the nearest train straight to Hell.

Easy. Calm. Breathe.

I recited the silent mantra yet again and focused on dashing off one more note to a fellow wedding planner. Karla St. Charles was her name and big weddings were her game. She was everything I aspired to be. Except that she was pregnant with twins.

Since jumping on the mommy train, she'd gone from being a royal bitch to a cordial acquaintance. Lucky for me. We now shared know-how and the occasional vendor. I pleaded my case to her via voice mail and finished with the promise of unlimited babysitting for six months if she could hook me up. Of course I didn't know the first thing about babies, but if I could put up with Snooki's yapping all night, I figured I could cope. I would have taken on quintuplets if it meant finding the inside track into Houston's tallest building.

And that was it.

I was out of ideas and Life Savers.

I rummaged in my top drawer, desperate to find a few ancient butter mints left over from the Morrison wedding last spring. My hand closed over one monogrammed package just as the bell on the door tinkled.

"It's only been twenty minutes," I told Cheryl as I ripped open the package and popped the stale mint into my mouth. "I need at least twenty-five to get naked," I said around a sugary mouthful. "And thirty to launch a full-on seduction."

"I could leave and come back." The deep voice slid into my ears and brought every nerve in my body to pulsing awareness.

My heart stalled as I glanced up to find Cutter Owens, star of last night's fantasy, standing right in front of me.

9

He looked even sexier than I remembered. Hard, muscular body. Broad shoulders. Sensuous lips. Brilliant green eyes. A five o'clock shadow that made the insides of my thighs tingle in anticipation—

The thought stalled as the mint took a nosedive and my throat slammed shut around it. My eyes burned and a strangled sound spurted past my lips.

I know they say your life passes before your eyes in those few moments when you face your mortality, but I've been around for a lot of years, which meant there wasn't nearly enough time for a recap. But the one thing that did rush through my mind was *WTF*? I'd existed a thousand years only to be pushed out of my favorite body and tossed back to Hell because of a stale mint and pure stupidity.

Seriously?

The man was a *demon* slayer and I was a demon. I should be running the other way instead of standing here thinking about his five o'clock shadow rubbing against the insides of my desperately deprived thighs. But in pure succubus fashion, my thoughts flashed from mortality to sex, to really great sex—*huuugh*.

The sound echoed in my head as strong arms closed around me and a pressure punched the middle of my chest. My mouth fell open. The mint went flying. And suddenly I could breathe again.

I slumped backward, gasping for air for a long moment before my lungs filled enough for me to form a coherent thought. I became acutely aware that Cutter's arms were still around me and I *really* liked it—and so did a few choice body parts.

"I, um, thanks," I rasped, my throat burning and my eyes watering. "But you can let go of me now."

He loosened his grip and I swayed, and his hold tightened again. "You sure?" he asked after a long, heart-pounding moment.

No.

Yes.

I don't know.

The only thing I was sure of was that I enjoyed having him close, and that wasn't good. Not at all.

"I'm, uh, fine. Really." I gathered my strength and shrugged away. Unfortunately, I had a small office, which didn't allow for a safe retreat. I could still feel the heat from his body. Smell the potent scent of warm male and massive sex appeal. Hear the frantic beat of his heart.

No, wait. That was my heart. Keeping time with the frantic rush of adrenaline.

"I, um…" My voice faded as I turned to find him staring at me with those incredible green eyes. If I hadn't known better, I would have sworn I saw a flash of surprise in his gaze. As if the full-body contact between us had startled him as much as it had startled me.

As if it had turned him on.

"What are you doing here?" I blurted, eager to distract myself from the lust slamming through me.

"You're welcome," he murmured, reminding me that he hadn't been feeling me up, but saving my life.

Fever rushed to my cheeks, and suddenly they were on fire like the rest of my body. "Thank you for doing the Heimlich. So, um, what's up?"

"You didn't call me." His gaze narrowed, and I knew he knew that my mother had paid me another visit.

"You've been watching me," I said accusingly.

"You said you would call if she made contact with you."

"I was going to," I started, but then he arched an eyebrow. "Really. I just haven't had a chance. She just hired me today."

"For a wedding?"

"Nah, for a birthday party."

"Gwyneth was right then." The words were muttered under his breath, but I heard them anyway because as a succubus, my senses were fine-tuned. That, and my office really was atrociously small.

Which was why I desperately needed to make it through the next two weeks in one piece, pull off a successful wedding, and snag my very own storefront. That, and I so didn't want to be sucked back Down Under.

No more happily-ever-afters. None. Nada. Zip.

I stiffened against the overwhelming desire to throw my arms around Cutter and press myself up against his hard body. I forced a deep, calming breath. "Gwyneth?" I repeated the familiar name of a lower-tier demon who ran the spa frequented by my mother. "Gwyneth Dolmari? She works at my spa," I rushed on, eager to explain how I knew her without blowing my cover. "That is, she works at the spa where I send a lot of my brides to get pampered. I've been there once or twice myself. It's supernice."

Recognition lit his gaze before nose-diving into those dark-green depths. "You should have called me."

"Why are you so interested in my client?" As if I didn't know. But he didn't know that I knew, and I wasn't letting on that I knew that he knew that I knew.

I *so* needed another Life Savers.

"Your client is a very powerful woman who uses that power to do very bad things."

"What is she? Con artist? Embezzler? Ponzi schemer?"

"The Devil." His gaze locked with mine. "And you're the demon who's planning her biggest power play to date."

Busted!

Panic bolted through me, and my first instinct was to run, but then his hand shot out and strong fingers closed around my wrist.

The skin-to-skin contact flipped on my lust switch. My face flushed and my nipples pebbled and my breath caught. His gaze darkened and he shook his head, seeming surprised by his own reaction.

"You're a demon, all right."

"No." I fought to drink in some oxygen, but it was no use. My voice came out soft and breathless and I knew denying it would be pointless. Besides, Cutter Owens hadn't made a name for himself by going after the little guys. He was more interested in the big boys (or girls, in this case) and a third- or fourth-tier demon—even a member of the Damon clan—wouldn't warrant a blip on his radar.

Or so I hoped.

"I mean, I am a demon, but not a bad one. I'm one of those pesky fifth-tier demons, more irritating than evil. But even so, I'm trying to change my ways. I use my power for good." I pointed to the photo album on the corner of my desk. "I make bridal dreams come true." When he looked skeptical, I added, "I know it sounds far-fetched, but being a demon slayer, I'm sure you've run into a few demons who've broken ranks. Gwyneth, for instance. She's your source, right? She isn't so bad."

He regarded me while he appeared to think. "If you're telling the truth, then you won't mind helping me stop this wedding and ending your boss's sorry existence."

"Trust me, I would love to—really—but I'm seriously trying to make it in the wedding biz. Sabotaging my own event would be a major conflict of interest." Not to mention we were talking my *mother*. My kin. My blood.

Not that he knew that.

At least I didn't think he did, otherwise he wouldn't be hearing me out. He'd be chopping off my head because—not to toot my own horn—I was pretty sure Satan's daughter equaled mucho brownie points for a slayer, even one with little interest in climbing the Legion's corporate ladder. A fifth-tier demon, not so much.

"On top of that," I rushed on, "if I help you, she's liable to take me back to Hell with her. I want to, but I can't—" My words stalled as he pulled out the biggest knife I'd ever seen. "What are you doing?"

"If you're not going to help me, then I might as well kill you."

My stomach bottomed out. "Y-you can't do that."

"Sure I can." A grin played at his sensuous lips. "I'm a demon slayer, sugar, and you're a demon."

"Who just so happens to be your only connection to Azazel," I blurted, remembering the 411 from Blythe. Sure enough, his gaze hardened and I knew the Internet rumors had to be true. "That's right." I pulled my shoulders back and stood my ground. "I know Azazel."

His words came out a growl. "Where is he?"

"Well, I don't, um, know at this exact moment, but I can find him. That is, if you're interested in striking a deal."

"I spare you and you lead me to Azazel?"

"That, and you leave my newest client alone."

"Now why would I do that?"

"Because you want Azazel more than you want Lillith. I know she's the Devil and a bitch to work for, but Azazel stole your soul." He stiffened and I knew Blythe had been right on the money. "You want revenge and I want to stay in this realm. You back off Lillith and let me do my job and I'll give you Azazel. A win-win for both of us."

He didn't look convinced at first, but then he slid the knife back into his waistband. "You deliver Azazel and I'll abort the new mission."

"And let me go through with the wedding?"

"*If* you deliver Azazel before then. Otherwise, there won't be a wedding, because there won't be a Lillith." His somber expression said he meant every word. "And there won't be a you."

I swallowed past the lump in my throat. "You've got yourself a deal."

* * *

"You did *what?*" Blythe's hand stalled on the ice cream carton she'd just pulled from her shopping bag. She'd arrived at my apartment five minutes ago after a voice mail plea for help.

"I promised Cutter I'd help him find Azazel."

"But you don't know where Azazel is," she pointed out. She still wore her work uniform—a pink *Luscious Limos* tank top, skinny jeans, and a pair of to-die-for leopard-print stilettos. "You don't even know if he's in this realm. He could be Down Under." She retrieved a spoon and handed me the carton of fudge brownie nut. "Why would you make a crazy deal like that?"

"Maybe because Cutter pulled a knife on me and threatened my existence." After he'd saved said existence from a stubborn mint. That little bit of FYI had stuck in my brain and niggled at me for the past half hour as I'd tried to write Cutter Owens off as a cold-hearted demon hunter who would sooner kill me than look at me.

The thing was, he'd saved me *before* I'd announced that I could lead him to Azazel, but *after* he knew what I was. Which meant that Cutter wasn't half the ruthless hunter he made himself out to be.

Because of my *do me* vibe, of course. He was picking up on it. Responding to it. All men did, and while Cutter was a badass hunter, he was still human. Susceptible.

But if he had been head over heels because of my carnal vibe, he surely would have tried to hump my brains out instead of doing the Heimlich.

"You'll never find him," Blythe said, pulling me away from my thoughts. Thankfully. The more I went over it in my head, the more confused I became.

And turned on.

"Azazel is elusive," Blythe went on. "That's his thing."

"Somebody somewhere has to know where he is. It's just a matter of finding that someone who can lead us to him—"

"You mean you. Finding someone who can lead *you* to him, because I am not getting pulled into this."

"But I need your help. I've got work coming out of my ears. I can't look for Azazel *and* plan my mother's wedding in two weeks. You have to help me. At least ask around. Put out some feelers. Talk to Agarth. He's an ancient like Azazel." Hope blossomed and my adrenaline pumped faster. "Surely those guys keep in touch."

"Why don't *you* talk to Agarth?"

"Because I'm not the one starring in his baby mama fantasies," I pointed out, a grin teasing my own lips. "He wants you for the mother of his demon spawn." When she didn't say anything, my smile faded and desperation crept into my voice. "Please. I would do it for you."

"No, you wouldn't."

"Yes, I would."

"Yes, you would," she finally admitted. She shrugged. "Fine. I'll talk to Agarth and see if he knows anything. But you owe me. Big-time."

I beamed. "Don't worry. When Agarth finally talks you into a wedding, I'll do all of the planning for free."

"Very funny. First off, I won't even go on a date with him, much less waltz down the aisle, and second, I was thinking more along the lines of a little instant gratification."

I glanced at Snooki yapping away in the corner and gave Blythe a hopeful expression. "How about your very own pet? I guarantee you'll never be lonely—"

"A clutch," Blythe cut in. "The one from your aunt's new spring line."

"My cheer-me-up purse?"

"The one and only." I thought of the custom-made silver and the near orgasm I'd had when I'd held it in my hands for the first time. Smelled it. Cradled it.

"You sure you don't want the dog? I'll throw in the doggie bed and a year's supply of Kibbles 'n Bits."

"I'm sure an ancient demon like Agarth won't have a clue how to get in touch with another ancient demon—"

"It's yours," I cut in, my lust for life overwhelming my lust for designer handbags. "And I'll throw in the dog too, because, you know, this is such a big deal and I want to do everything I possibly can—"

"Why don't you just call animal control?"

"I'm going to." Unless, of course, Snooki warmed up to me and learned to keep her trap shut. "I was thinking we might actually be able to coexist."

Blythe arched an eyebrow. "Seriously?"

I gave the dog a hopeful expression, but she only yapped louder. "Or maybe not."

"Call the pound," Blythe said again. "She's irritating."

"She's just having adjustment issues. Once she gets used to me, she'll settle down." Snooki barked louder, and I shrugged. "All right, all right. I'll call the pound."

First thing tomorrow.

1 0

"These are for a wedding?"

I shrugged as if it wasn't the least bit unusual to order a black vellum invite with bloodred font and embossed silver skulls edging the thick paper stock. I knew it was a bit much, but my mother wasn't known for subtlety. "What else?"

"Oh, I don't know," said the young clerk at the Paper Emporium in River Oaks, "A Halloween party. A Day of the Dead celebration. A funeral." She eyed me as if I was trying to hide something. "But a wedding?"

"You got me," I blurted. "It's a Day of the Dead–themed wedding. We're doing this great big morbid production complete with lots of black candles and edible white chocolate skull favors." The idea struck and I made a mental note to call a chocolatier ASAP.

"I guess it could work. But I'd go with a little more color on the invites if you want true Day of the Dead."

She was actually right. *If* I'd been going for festive Day of the Dead with lots of reds and oranges and blues and yellows. But my mother wanted dark and sinister, and I aimed to please.

"So, um, how soon can you have them ready?" I rushed on before she could press the color issue. "I need them, like, yesterday."

"I need to talk to my manager first, but I don't see why we couldn't do an in-house rush and get them finished in two days, if you can provide me with the venue and address by ten thirty p.m. tonight. I can't very well print without a venue."

"I'll nail that down this afternoon. I swear. So?" I eyed her. "If I get that to you, can you get them done by tomorrow afternoon instead of the following day?"

She stared at me as if I had grown two heads. Which wasn't totally out of the realm of possibility. I was a demon, after all, and at a thousand years old I'd accumulated a little gas in my tank for just such an occasion. But since I was a lover not a fighter, I opted for something more emotional than physical.

I stared deep into Jeanie's eyes, picked up on her dream man, and did my best imitation.

"If you can make it happen by tomorrow, that would be totally fresh. Then we could spend the rest of the time getting our GTL on."

For those not sadly addicted to reality TV, Jeanie's dream man was Pauly D from *Jersey Shore*. I know. There was no accounting for the taste of today's youth.

Myself included—I hadn't missed an episode in four seasons.

A dreamy look came over her face. I knew then that she was buying into the illusion and seeing the image that went with the voice. "Anything for you, Pauly." She licked her lips. *"Anything."*

O-kay.

"I really appreciate it," I told her. "Not the lip licking, but the invitation rush. Of course, if you get them done in time, I'll be down with the lip licking too." *Not.* But hey, the whole point of the illusion was to give her some incentive to get the invites done early. "I'll text the venue address later this afternoon." Provided I could confirm a venue between now and then.

I tamped down the sudden wave of doubt and headed for my car. Climbing inside, I checked off my number two—one thousand invitations—on my Must Do list and moved on to number three—the dress.

"I'm busy," my mother told me when I called her to set up an appointment at a couture salon in downtown Houston. "Can't we do it another time?"

"It's the dress. The most important piece of the wedding. The center of the entire ceremony and all of the decor. We have to have the dress to move forward. Not to mention we need to give the designer as much time as possible. Wedding dresses take time."

"How much time?"

"A lot more than two weeks. Not that I can't get a dress done in two weeks," I rushed on when I could practically feel the coldness of my mother's sigh on the other end of the phone. "It'll be pushing it, but I can totally pull it off. As long as we choose a design and do a fitting now. *Today*."

"Tomorrow," my mother corrected. "That's the absolute earliest I can make an appointment. Talk to Cheryl. She'll set it up." Before I could protest, she handed me off to her assistant and I spent the next five minutes begging Cheryl to juggle appointments so that we could meet first thing in the morning. She promised me nine a.m. and I called the designer to coordinate.

Dress? Almost a check.

I held tight to the hope and turned my attention to the multitude of other things on my plate. I spent the rest of the morning formulating a game plan for each of the two new brides we'd signed yesterday—thanks to Andrew and Burke—and dealing with an endless amount of details for Delaney's upcoming wedding. First up? A problem with her shoes, which she insisted were supposed to be three-inch Swarovski-covered stilettos rather than three and a quarter inches. In between phone calls with a frantic Delaney and an equally upset shoe designer, I worried over finding Azazel.

Until I received a cryptic message from Blythe telling me that Agarth would be happy to help her find Azazel, provided she went out with him first.

I could still hear her final words: "I want matching shoes to go with the bag. And a belt."

The shoes I could deliver. The belt? Let's hope Aunt Lucy had branched out into a wide array of accessories. Otherwise, I was so screwed.

While morning was spent at my desk, the remainder of the day involved me running around like a chicken *this* close to the sacrificial altar. First, I headed to Delaney's photographer to go over the selected photo plan, then to three different cake tastings, then to a fitting for one of my current brides, then to a venue walk-through at the Crystal Ballroom, then to Insanity by Chocolate to look at different skull molds for my brilliant stroke of genius for Mom's favors.

And yes, I had three samples while I was there. Sue me.

Anyhoo, by the time five o'clock arrived, I was slumped over my desk, a Hostess cupcake in one hand and a pen in the other. Burke and Andrew sat across from me, minus the cupcakes, of course. After the doughnut slip yesterday morning, Andrew had jumped into a no-carb plan while Burke cheered him on with his usual banana smoothies and bran muffins.

Health-conscious humans. Blah.

Together (Burke and his bran, Andrew and his carrot sticks, and me with my handful of chocolate decadence), we were doing our damnedest to come up with a specific plan for Lillith Damon's big affair.

Yep, I'd brought them on board to help. There were too many things to accomplish and not nearly enough time. While I was a superfast demon, I was still stuck in a mortal's body, vulnerable to brain-dead-itis and fat ankles after putting in a long day on my feet.

Like today.

Enter Burke and Andrew to share my pain and help me think of something brilliant.

"If we're talking *really* big, nothing says impressive like a photo booth," Burke announced.

Okay, so I couldn't very well give them *all* the juicy details—like the Devil overthrowing Hell via over-the-top affair. They only knew that my momzilla was tying the knot with an outrageous budget and eccentric tastes. That, and said event had to happen *now*.

"We can have lots of props," Burke pushed his idea home. "Like fuchsia cowboy hats and sequined boas and big funky sunglasses. An attendant can monitor the whole thing and fit the finished pics into some really darling frames that the guests can take home as mementos. *Everyone* will be talking about how amazing the wedding was and how brilliant we are. Your mom will love it!"

"Oh, that's simply too cute," Andrew squealed, frantically tapping notes into his iPad. "We are definitely on the fast track to fabulous."

I tried to picture even one of my bloodthirsty relatives mugging for the camera while wearing a pink cowboy hat and matching boa.

Ugh. I sucked down half the cupcake in one desperate bite.

"No offense, guys," I managed once I'd swallowed and chased the sweet with a mouthful of Diet Coke, "but I don't think a photo booth is my mom's cup of tea. We need something impressive. Something grand. Something *memorable*."

Silence descended for a nanosecond before genius seemed to strike. "Glow bracelets," Burke announced.

Scratch the genius.

"My mom was voted Houston's top interior decorator," I hedged. "She's super high profile. Powerful." *Deadly.* "Glow bracelets seem a tad understated."

"You're right. We should pull out the big guns and go straight for the necklaces." I shook my head, and he added, "Too cheesy?"

Too human.

"I've got it," Andrew jumped in, looking as if he'd discovered a supersculpting ab pill that worked regardless of diet and exercise. "A flambé table."

A roomful of demons, fire, and dessert?

"Not bad." My phone picked that moment to buzz. I glanced at the text from Karla St. Charles telling me she had a lead on the Chase building. Hope blossomed and I grinned. "Fabulous, here we come."

* * *

"This is so *not* fabulous," I told the überpregnant wedding planner a few hours later as we walked into the only available rental space in the Chase Bank building.

It was just this side of seven p.m. and the building had long since cleared out of all the nine-to-fivers. Thankfully. I didn't need an audience to witness the meltdown I was about to have.

I glanced around at the blah, empty space. There were so many things wrong with this that I didn't even know where to begin.

Karla, pulling off the professional mommy-to-be look in a clingy blue jersey knit dress, sipped one of those all-natural/organic/gluten-free/supposed-to-be-good-for-the-baby protein shakes that smelled like vitamins and made me want to toss my cookies. (No, really. I'd eaten a handful of Oreos on the way over.)

"If you want the Chase Bank building," she said in between sips, "this is what you get." *Sip.* "The building is owned by a corporation that doesn't lease out for special occasions." *Sip. Sip.* "They only let out for corporate space. But lucky for you, it just so happens a friend of mine works for an insurance company up on four." *Sip. Sip. Sip.* "Since they're tenants, they have access to the one and only party space in the entire building." She swept a hand around the room. "Here you go."

I glanced around the gold-carpeted space with its minimal windows and fake potted plants. My nose wrinkled with the smell of carpet cleaner and stale food. "This isn't really what I'd pictured."

She tossed her now-empty Styrofoam into a nearby trash can and eyed me. "Why don't you give this up and go for the Wells Fargo Bank Plaza? I can get you the lobby area. Lots of windows. Great atmosphere. It's not the tallest building in town, but it comes a close second."

If only. But no matter how big, my mom wouldn't be happy with second place. She wanted this event to be over-the-top and I had to make that happen.

But tallest building or not, it couldn't happen here. "This is terrible."

"You're telling me," Karla echoed, but then she touched a hand to her stomach and I knew she was talking about something other than the space. "I probably shouldn't have doubled up on the B-twelve in that shake. I think the babies are starting their own Zumba group." Her eyes twinkled. "Want to feel?"

Time out. Can someone please tell me why all pregnant women think that the entire world is equally amazed by what is happening inside their bodies? Seriously. I'm not a baby person. I never have been. My cousin Delilah tried to get me to hold her kid at the last family get-together—a birthday party for my second cousin Millicent—and it didn't end well. There were lots of tears (baby) and spitting up (me on account of said baby was actually a toddler who punched me in the stomach and, well, I'd just eaten four brownies). Needless to say, I'd never been into the whole mommy thing.

I *so* didn't want to get up close and personal with any kicking babies.

"Here." She grabbed my hand and pressed it against her tummy before I could make up an excuse. "Feel."

"I've really got to run—" The words stalled as I felt the tiniest thump against my palm, and then another and another.

All right, so it *was* sort of cool.

A smile played at my lips. "Do they move like that all the time?"

She nodded. "Especially when I listen to the Black Eyed Peas. The twins absolutely *love* Fergie."

We spent the next few minutes oohing and ahhing over the joys of impending motherhood and the hotness of Fergie's significant other, aka Karla's fantasy man, Josh Duhamel. Then her cell beeped and she had to leave to make it to her natural water birth class.

"Just leave the door open when you've finished looking around," she said. "The security guard will lock up."

I nodded and waved good-bye. Then I spent the next few minutes walking the perimeter of the room and beating my brain for some way to make the space work.

Better lighting. Great tablescapes. A bulldozer.

The hope that had sprung when I'd gotten Karla's text took a nosedive, and I blinked against the burning behind my eyes. I was so screwed. If I wanted invites by tomorrow afternoon, I had to secure a space today. *Now.*

I wallowed in self-pity for the next few moments until my cell beeped me back to reality and the all-important fact that I was an optimist. I had been ever since I'd turned my back on my birthright and latched onto the dream of finding my own happily-ever-after.

If I could believe there was a Mr. Perfect out there somewhere for me, I could damn well believe that I could nail down a venue in less than three hours and pull off a wedding that would meet with my mother's approval.

I just needed to get really creative.

That, or run like hell. I'd surely wind up living in an igloo in Antarctica.

"What are you doing?" Blythe demanded when I picked up the phone a few minutes later; she'd called after I didn't immediately answer her text.

"*Not* living in an igloo," I said with all the courage I could muster. "What's up?"

"Agarth. Literally. I called him for information and he asked me out. I said I'd think about it and the next thing I know, he's standing on my doorstep. Either he's got his sword in his pants or he's *really* glad to see me. I'm betting number two, which is why I've locked myself in the bathroom. I don't care how important this is, I'm not boffing him for information."

"So he's a little excited. He's wanted a date with you *forever*. Just get back out there, go to the movies, and ignore whatever he's got working below the waist. Pretend like you don't notice it."

"We're not going straight to the movies. It's dinner *and* a movie."

"That's good. The table will be in the way so you don't have to actually make eye contact with his lap."

"You're not making me feel any better." She grew silent for a long moment, as if weighing her options. "But there is one thing that might help." Her voice took on a desperate note. "Come with?"

"A date usually means two people."

"So meet us there. We'll pretend like it's a chance thing."

"I don't want to piss him off. He's our only lead to Azazel."

"He's in love with me. If I act like I'm superworried about you because you're so stressed about this wedding and that it would make me extremely happy to at least invite you to eat dinner with us, he'll go along with it. Please," she added when I hesitated. "I would do it for you. I *am* doing it for you. It's not my head on the chopping block, remember?"

"I've got two hours and fifty-two minutes left to secure a venue for my mom or it won't matter if Cutter chops off my head. I'll be dead anyway."

"I once partied in the backseat of my limo with the manager of the Bell Tower on Thirty-Fourth. I could give him a call."

"It's not nearly big enough."

"It accommodates one thousand people."

"I'm talking height. The Bell Tower is only two stories."

"True, but it's got a water wall. The *only* water wall in the city of Houston."

If she'd been talking flowing blood, we'd be in business. But while it wasn't my ideal, I was getting desperate. Two hours, forty-nine minutes, and counting. "Is it available?"

"I'll give him a call and tell you at dinner."

"You could always text."

"But then you wouldn't have any incentive to help save my ass."

"I'm sure Agarth means no harm to your ass. He worships it."

"That's the problem. I don't want any *worshipping* tonight."

I weighed my options all of five seconds. "All right. Where?"

"Cabo Bar and Grill in the museum district. Be there in twenty." She hung up before I could protest.

Not that I would have. Blythe was putting herself out there for me. She'd gone on exactly one previous date with Agarth that, in her opinion, had ended in disaster. Unfortunately, Agarth wasn't too savvy when it came to dating, and picking his teeth during dinner hadn't seemed like a deal breaker to him. He still lusted after her, and she'd done her best to avoid him like the plague.

Until tonight.

She was doing this for me and the least I could do was help her out.

That, and we're talking a wall built entirely of flowing water.

I sent Cheryl a quick reminder about the dress appointment first thing tomorrow, texted the venue address to the Paper Emporium, and then left the depressing party space to head out to my car. The garage had been full, so I'd parked a block over.

It was almost eight o'clock and the sun had already dropped behind the massive buildings in downtown. Dusk crawled through the streets, eating up the light, leaving a trail of thick shadows in its wake.

Goose bumps whispered up my spine as I rounded the corner and made my way to my Nissan, parked near an almost expired meter.

Just as I reached my Cube, a strange sensation crawled through me. I felt the presence directly behind me—a fierce coldness followed by a whisper of air against the back of my neck.

My entire body froze. My keys plummeted from my suddenly limp fingers.

Someone was there.

The same someone who had left the cryptic message on my bathroom mirror?

Maybe. Probably.

I whirled, desperate to face my fear and catch a glimpse. "You're so busted if I tell my—" I started, but the street was empty.

A jingle of metal cut through the pounding of my heart, and I glanced down in time to see my keys rise up off the ground. They rose higher, higher, until they dangled right in front of my face.

I forced myself to swallow past the lump in my throat. Evil thrived on fear. It drew power from it. The worst thing I could do would be to let on that I was freaked.

Which I wasn't, because I knew that my aunties would never really hurt me.

Or would they?

We're talking total control Down Under. They'd been at each other's throats *forever*, always arguing and fighting and backstabbing. This past year alone, Bella had set my ma's hair on fire at the Fourth of July celebration and chopped off her hand over the last piece of apple pie. My mom had regrown both, but still. Bottom line? Bella hated my mother. Aunt Levita too. She'd been the one to spike Lillith's mimosa with rat poison at my cousin Alice's baby shower a few months back. After my ma had upchucked for about thirty minutes, she'd retaliated by dousing Levita with gas and setting her on fire.

I know, right? Stabbing a set of keys into the forehead of little ole me seemed petty in comparison.

I shook away the possibility and focused on the fact that this was my family we were talking about. Sure, they were crazy. Power hungry. Deadly. But I was immortal. While they could screw up the good thing I had going with this body, it wasn't as if they could get rid of me forever. They knew that and so did I.

They were just trying to shake me up, to upset my mother's plan by forcing me to back out of the wedding. It was petty and stupid, and it certainly wouldn't stop my mother from tying the knot if she truly wanted to. But it would piss her off. And my aunties loved pissing off one another.

"Seriously?" I fought to keep my voice from shaking. "Is that the best you can do? Talk about Demon 101."

The keys stalled then and, just like that, they crashed to the ground at my feet.

Jess Damon: one. Crazy demon stalker: zero.

I drew a much-needed breath, snatched up the keys, and climbed into my car. I was just about to crank the engine when the hair on the back of my neck stood on end again. The coldness whispered around me. As if a heavy breath were rushing at the windshield, it clouded and then an invisible fingertip traced the words:

I warned you.

The coldness pressed in, and icy fingers tightened around my throat.

I was choking.

The realization peeled back the layers of shock and jump-started my survival instincts. Adrenaline pumped through me, pushing out the denial until the only thing I could think of was escaping. I grappled for the door handle. Just as my fingers closed around the slim metal, a loud click slid past the panic beating at my temples. Whoever was inside the car with me had locked the door.

Desperation flooded through me. I was going to die. Right here. Right now. No more wedding planning. No more searching for my prince charming. My human body was going to die, which meant I would be sucked Down Under for who knew how long. While my mom and aunties could grab another body at will (they were in charge, after all) everyone else was doomed to get back in line and wait their turn.

And you thought the line at the DMV was long.

I searched blindly for the lock button. There. It clicked, and I made a mad grab for the handle, only to have it wrenched from my hand. The door swung open and strong hands reached for me. In the blink of an eye, my feet hit the pavement and the supernatural noose snapped. I gasped for air as muscular arms cradled me close and a familiar heat zipped through my body.

"What the hell is going on?" Cutter's deep voice rumbled past the thunder in my ears.

"I..." I croaked, drinking in huge drafts of air until my burning lungs eased. "Couldn't breathe," I finally managed. As the dizziness passed, I became acutely aware that I was leaning heavily on a certain sexy demon hunter. I could feel the hard planes of his body, the ripple of his arms as he tightened his hold.

Oh, boy.

A wave of lust overtook my terror.

"What happened in there?" His warm breath close to my ear distracted me from my traitorous body. I inhaled and exhaled calmly.

I considered telling him the truth—that I was being targeted by one of my crazy aunties, most likely Aunt Bella, who was undoubtedly desperate to throw a wrench into my ma's plans. But then he would know that I wasn't just some lowly demon wedding planner, but a direct descendant of the soon-to-be head honcho herself.

"Asthma attack," I heard myself say. "I probably should have checked medical history before I hopped into this body, huh?"

He looked doubtful. In fact, he looked downright pissed, and ready to tear apart whoever had trapped me inside the car.

Then again, I was his ticket to Azazel. Of course he wanted me safe.

"What are you doing here?" I blurted, eager to kill the fierce, protective look in his eyes and ignore the desire rippling through me. A feeling that made me want to curl into his arms even more than I wanted to jump his bones.

He stared at me a heartbeat longer, as if he felt the push-pull of emotion just as much as I did, but then he seemed to realize that he was standing much too close.

His arms dropped away and he stepped back. "You didn't think I was just going to back off and disappear because you said you'd deliver Azazel?"

"I was hoping."

"That's not the way this works."

"You don't trust me." I wasn't sure why that bothered me so much. If I were him, I wouldn't trust me either. A demon had stolen his soul, for Pete's sake. Definitely a foundation for trust issues. "I meant what I said. I'll find Azazel."

"And I'll lay off your client, *after* you fulfill your end of the deal."

"Meaning I'm under surveillance."

He nodded. "You and your newest client. I spent months tracking Lillith Damon. I'm not backing off until you give me a good reason to back off. Until then it's business as usual. Lucky for you." His gaze caught and held mine. Sparks flared along my nerve endings and I had the sudden urge to rip off my clothes and straddle him right there on the sidewalk.

The way he was looking at me didn't help the situation either. His eyes glittered, hot and mesmerizing, and I knew he was feeling the exact same way. Raw desire. Fierce need.

My breasts ached and my thighs trembled and…

This was so *not* good.

"I could have opened that door by myself," I pointed out. "I am a badass demon, after all." *What the hell are you doing? That's like reminding the deer hunter that you're the prizewinning buck.*

But I had to do something. He looked too good and I wanted him too bad and he was obviously falling under my succubus mojo, because I knew he wanted me too.

The blaze in his eyes faded into a hard, glittering light. "It's getting late. You should go."

The statement jump-started my brain, and I glanced at my watch. "I'm fifteen minutes late." Shit. Blythe was going to kill me.

"Hot date?"

"Something like that."

Cutter stiffened and I had the insane idea that he wasn't all that happy about my response.

I should be so lucky.

The thought struck before I could remind myself of the all-important fact that Cutter and I were at opposite ends of the supernatural spectrum. Human there. Demon here. A giant, demon-killing sword in between.

No way was he jealous. And even if he was, no way did it actually mean anything except that my demon mojo was alive and well and spilling over in abundance.

The notion sent an unexpected burst of disappointment through me. "I really should go."

And then I climbed into the car, keyed the ignition, and left Cutter staring after me.

* * *

Agarth was from an ancient era of plagues and idols (that's golden calves, not the superpopular gig with Randy Jackson). He was a throwback to a time when demons were big and bad and ferocious. Forget trickery and manipulation. The bad boys of ancient times were in-your-face with their power. They were fierce, barbaric, and aggressive. Qualities that hadn't been lost just because times had changed and people had become more civilized. While Agarth occupied the body of a thirty-two-year-old construction worker with a decent face and great abs, his old-school personality was still front and center via a foot-long beard, a piercing black stare, and a fondness for sharp things.

It was no surprise I found him wielding a butter knife when I walked into Cabo a half hour later.

Blythe sat across from him looking slightly desperate, particularly when he reached over, stabbed her roll, and proceeded to devour it in one bite (minus any chewing). He burped. She cringed.

O-kay.

Pissing off a crazy eccentric with a weapon was not the way I wanted to spend my Tuesday night. I was just about to rethink the whole date-crashing thing when Blythe spied me out of the corner of her eye. Her head whipped around and relief flooded her expression, followed by a hard edge because I was late.

"Jess," she called out, waving an arm and beckoning me over. "What a surprise seeing you here. Agarth"—she motioned to the man sitting across from her—"you remember Jess?"

Agarth turned his hard stare on me and ice sank into the pit of my stomach. Suddenly I was sitting in my car, the cold fingers slithering around my neck, cutting off my air.

Was I insane? I already had one demon after me. I so didn't need to piss off another.

"I..." I swallowed and fought for my courage. Blythe was in this mess—aka a date with Agarth—because she was trying to help me. The least I could do was hold her hand and try to ease the pain. "You did the ice sculpture for my last wedding," I reminded him. "It was awesome."

He grunted his recognition, and I spent the next few moments going through the whole chance meeting spiel that ended with Blythe insisting that I join them. Agarth looked as if he would sooner stab me in the heart than share his date. But when Blythe batted her eyes at him, he shrugged and growled, "Sit, woman."

"I know she wishes not to be here with me," he said when Blythe headed for the little girls' room a few minutes later. "It matters not. I am simply happy she is here."

Agarth definitely put on his big-boy boxers today. He was actually interested in pleasing my best friend. Even if it meant putting up with a third wheel when he would much rather be alone with Blythe.

Too cute.

"Blythe's really picky," I heard myself say. "Maybe you'll grow on her." He gave me a steely-eyed stare and I added, "Maybe not. But you'll still help me, right?"

When he didn't answer, I continued, "Blythe falling head over heels for you isn't part of the bargain. You wanted another date with her, you got it. Now I need to know what you know about Azazel."

"I know not of his whereabouts."

"But?" I prodded.

"I shall look into it."

"Before Friday?"

"Ye have my word. Now stop all this yapping and eat." He motioned to the turkey sandwich the waitress had set down in front of me.

"I'm not very hungry..." Before I even finished my reply, he leaned over, stabbed a slab of turkey with his knife, and popped it into his mouth.

I spent the next few minutes avoiding Agarth's butter knife as he stabbed more of my food and then proceeded to order a double-decker for himself.

"Old-school demons obviously like meat."

"'Tis an appetite for the flesh I cannot forget."

Ewwwww.

"I'm back." Blythe slid into her chair.

"Thank God," I blurted. Agarth gave me a sharp look, and I added, "Sorry."

"'Tis the problem with demons these days. They are so settled in with the humans that they forget where they came from. Back in my day"—he waved the knife at me—"we would skewer a demon for uttering such sacrilege." Agarth launched into a thirty-minute story about the old days, and I did my best not to grab his butter knife and stab myself.

I became acutely aware of Cutter Owens about halfway through the sacrilege story when I had the sudden thought that the air unit had gone out in the crowded bar. But then the hair tingled on the back of my neck and I knew.

I half turned, my gaze catching sight of him sitting at the bar. He wore the usual black jeans and a matching T-shirt that outlined his broad shoulders. One bicep rippled, and a slave-band tattoo played peekaboo beneath the edge of his sleeve as he lifted a mug of beer to his lips. Our eyes locked and my stomach fluttered, followed by a rush of coldness when I noticed the crook of his sensual lips.

He was smiling at my predicament. The rat.

Agarth stabbed another roll and Cutter's grin widened as if to say *priceless*.

I stiffened and glared. Seriously. If he had an ounce of compassion, he would waltz over and save me from the most boring night of my life.

But slayers weren't compassionate and his presence had nothing to do with looking out for my well-being. He was keeping tabs on me. Nothing more.

Okay, so he was laughing too. Particularly when Agarth threatened to impale a flirty accountant who offered to buy me a drink.

"I think I can handle things myself," I told the ancient demon.

"Nonsense. Ye be a mere woman."

Blythe gave me an I-am-*so*-getting-you-back-for-this look, and I busied myself ignoring the blistering heat from Cutter's gaze and the yawning hunger inside of me. I sucked down the chocolate banana daiquiri I'd just ordered and set it aside. "Wow, would you look at the time? I really need to go and leave you two lovebirds—"

"You can't run off," Blythe cut in, her fingers closing around my wrist in a vise grip that made me wince. "They're having a Greek warriors festival over at the Palladium. It's a double feature tonight—*Clash of the Titans* and *300*." She smiled, her eyes pleading. "I'll buy the popcorn."

"Bite your tongue, woman," Agarth growled. "I'll be buying ye popcorn and any other nourishment ye require. And ye, too."

He pointed at me with his knife. As opposed as he was to having a third wheel, he knew it was the only way he was going to get a few more minutes with Blythe.

I thought of Cutter and how he'd held me after my near-death experience, and how I'd liked it. And how I'd felt so alone when I'd driven away from him, even though, realistically, I knew there could never be anything between us.

"Throw in a box of Jujubes," I told Agarth, "and I'm there."

1 2

Someone was in my apartment.

The thought struck as I pulled into my driveway. I stared through the windshield at the light edging the drapes in my living room. After the evening I'd just had—near-death experience followed by dinner and a double feature with Blythe and Agarth—I'd figured my luck had already tanked and there was nowhere to go but up.

I'd been wrong.

The front door of my duplex trembled and my flight mechanism kicked in. I debated my two options—shift the car into reverse and hightail it out of there or kill the engine, fling open the car door, and race toward the black Land Rover parked a half block down the street.

I'd throw myself into Cutter's arms and he would hold me close. Then I'd kiss him and he'd kiss me. I'd slip my hands under his shirt and he'd slip his hands under my shirt. I'd touch him and he'd touch me. I'd lick his nipple and he'd lick mine.

If I managed to find Azazel.

Otherwise, I'd be just another kill on his résumé.

My hand tightened on the gearshift and my foot poised over the gas. Just as I slid into reverse, my front door opened and I let out a huge sigh of relief at the mega-hot cowboy framed in the doorway: black *Cowboy Up* T-shirt, worn jeans, fringed leather chaps, and boots. A black Stetson sat low on his head.

Gio gave me a look that said *what the fuck are you sitting out there for?*

I slipped the car back into park, killed the engine, and climbed from behind the wheel.

"Don't tell me Syra has a Roy Rogers thing going on."

"Ty Murray. She flew to Vegas after New York and caught the pro bull riding finals. It was lust at first sight."

"Where is she now?"

"Dinner party with the groom-to-be and his parents. I'm meeting her later for a little after-hours fun. I had some time to kill, so I thought I'd stop by."

I knew exactly what he was thinking.

What he was always thinking.

"I can't. I mean, I would, of course. If I didn't have to save my energy for later. I've got a hot date. I've got the libido of a demon, but it's all wrapped up in a human package."

"I know what you mean. Syra's insatiable, and it gets a little exhausting." A smile touched his lips. "If I didn't know better, I'd swear she was a demon herself."

"If I didn't know better, I'd say you really like this girl."

Longing glimmered in his gaze before diving deep into the bright-blue depths. "Yeah, right. She's my assignment. That's it." At least that's what he was telling himself.

Sheesh. I really was tired, otherwise I wouldn't be thinking such crazy thoughts. Gio falling for a woman? Nah.

"I'm hungry," he announced. "For food," he added when I summoned a yawn.

"Seriously?"

He nodded. "Something sweet."

Now here was a man after my own heart. Cutter was parked out front, watching, waiting, and the knowledge was playing havoc with my self-control. My own stomach grumbled. "I've got Twinkies," I told Gio.

"That'll work."

* * *

"Where's Mom?" I asked Cheryl the next morning when I walked into one of Houston's top bridal salons and found her flying solo.

"Foot massage."

"But I thought she was meeting me this morning."

"She was, but then she had an emergency."

"A foot massage emergency?"

"Bunions," Cheryl mouthed because, apparently, even Satan wasn't immune to icky feet.

I had a quick mental image of myself huddled inside a ridiculously cold igloo after fleeing for my existence. "But she's the bride," I said, doing my best to keep the shriek out of my voice. It crept in anyway. "And this is a fitting for the bridal gown. She *has* to be here." I touched Cheryl's hand. "Please."

Cheryl gave me an odd look, as if she couldn't quite believe I was related to her boss. I didn't blame her. Demons weren't the sort to appear so openly rattled. Rather, they did the rattling. They were cool, calm, collected, vicious.

I glanced down at my fingers clasping the woman's arm. Everything about me screamed desperate.

Cheryl seemed hesitant, but then she caved. "I could call her and tell her we really need her." She pulled out her cell. "Of course, the last time I bothered her during a bunion extraction, she zapped me and gave me hemorrhoids." She gathered her courage and punched a button. "Pebbles has obedience class tomorrow night. We're learning how to sit and I really don't want to use one of those doughnut pillows—" Her voice cut off as my mom picked up the line. "Miss Lillith?" She drew a deep breath and summoned her courage. "We have a little bit of a prob—"

"You have to get over here," I blurted, snatching the phone from Cheryl's hand. What? She couldn't very well teach her dog to sit if she couldn't take a load off herself.

"Jezebel?" my mother demanded. "What is the meaning of this intrusion?"

"You're the bride. You have to pick the dress."

"But that's what I hired you for."

"You hired me to plan the wedding. This is different. This is the *dress*. Time is of the essence. We have to choose something today. Now."

"So choose one."

"I can't choose your wedding dress. That's something special. Personal." What was I saying? Lillith wasn't the typical blushing bride. This wasn't a declaration of love. It was a show. A statement. A coup to overtake the big H, which my mother had made perfectly clear. And even if she hadn't made it perfectly clear, I was supposed to be in business to spoil big days. I should have welcomed the chance to pick someone's dress. Talk about a prime opportunity to throw a wrench into what should have been the most wonderful day of a girl's life. I was a spoiler. A deceiver.

At least that's what my ma was supposed to think.

"What I mean is," I rushed on, "I would so love to pick the dress if this were any of my other weddings. But it's yours, so I want things to be perfect, and I'm not a stylist. I don't know what looks good on you."

"I look good in everything." So sayeth the most vain woman in the universe.

"True, but I'm sure you want to look *really* good. To show up the aunts, of course. That's why I wanted you to model a few dresses. To see what looks the best. An A-line? Empire cut? Mermaid svelte? Strapless or sleeves? Ruching or ruffles?"

"Yes."

"To which one?"

"All of the above."

"But it has to be fitted specifically to you."

"Cheryl has my measurements."

"But—"

"Just pick something that screams dark and powerful," she snapped and then hung up.

I blinked back a rush of hot tears and put on my most professional face as Devon Diamond, owner of Designs by Devon, floated from the back room. She looked as pristine and professional as ever in a white fitted suit with a pink rose pinned to her lapel.

"Welcome!" The woman made a beeline straight for me and did the proverbial kiss-kiss on each cheek. "You must be our bride," she said, turning to Cheryl and taking both of her hands.

"Actually, I'm—"

"Nervous," I cut in. Devon was the most sought after bridal dress designer in the South. I'd had a hell of a time getting her on the phone yesterday, much less wrangling an appointment on such short notice.

Devon booked months in advance for her custom couture.

But after a lot of pleading and a little bribery, with a spur-of-the-moment rush fee and a promise to set her up with one of my seriously hot incubus friends—she was recently divorced and starting to date again—she'd finally agreed.

Since we were crunched for time, she'd also agreed to take a preexisting sample dress and do the unthinkable—alter to fit. To say she would feel extremely slighted that my demanding bride couldn't find the time to make it to her own appointment would be an understatement. Devon was a prima donna when it came to her work. And a drama queen.

I sent up a silent prayer (our little secret) that the next two hours didn't blow up in my face. "Why don't we get started?" I steered Cheryl into a nearby chair and motioned to Devon. "Bring on the magic."

Devon clapped her hands and motioned to the two clerks standing in the doorway. A model entered the room wearing a vision in white.

"What do you think?"

"Lillith, here, is more of a nontraditional bride." I indicated Cheryl. "She really wants something a bit more, um, colorful."

Devon seemed to think. "I can do color. What are we talking? Ivory? Champagne? Blush?" When I shook my head, she added, "Rose?"

"Deeper."

Her eyebrows drew together. "Purple?"

"Darker." And sinister.

Disbelief fueled her expression. "Don't tell me you want a navy dress."

"Why, that's crazy. Navy for a bride?" While dark, navy wasn't even close to sinister. I summoned a laugh. "I don't know anyone in their right mind who would order a navy wedding dress."

"But you said darker than purple, and if navy is out, the only thing left is brown. Or black." She said it as if she couldn't possibly have heard me correctly.

I smiled. "Bingo."

* * *

Finding a black sample wedding dress proved much more difficult than I'd imagined. So much so that I had a major migraine and a serious craving for cookies by the time the deed was done a whopping six hours later. Not that we'd actually found one. But I had managed to settle on a satin number that could be dyed.

Very, very carefully.

Talk about stress.

Not only that, but I'd had to persuade Devon that Lillith, aka Cheryl, was going to grow three inches and slim down by about twenty pounds in less than two weeks.

Needless to say, I'd had to dip into my demon bag of tricks. I'd hopped into the salon owner's body for all of five seconds and written down my mother's correct measurements. Then I'd taken a hike, leaving her feeling hot and sexy and ready to pounce on the nearest man.

I know, I know. Movies and books would have you think possession is about as fun as a root canal, but it's not the possession itself that's bad. It's the demon. Since I'm the demonic version of Aphrodite, I tend to leave my humans with a heightened sensual awareness and a boost of lust.

"When did you say I could meet your friend?" Devon had asked after assuring me the chosen dress would be altered in time. "Because I'm ready to get back in the game."

What'd I tell ya?

"Do you think she'll like it?" Cheryl asked me for the zillionth time as we walked out of the salon.

"Sure," I said with more confidence than I felt because, hey, that was my job. I was the rock of assurance when it came to nervous brides. Then again, we were talking my mother. "But if I were you, I'd stock up on some Preparation H. Just in case."

"Did you get lucky?" I asked Blythe later that night after a long afternoon at the office nailing down more of the endless wedding details for my mother. While I was making progress and crossing things off my list, I wasn't one hundred percent confident in my choices. Instead of feeling relieved, I felt nervous.

"I most certainly did *not* get lucky." Blythe's voice stirred the anxiety already rolling in my stomach as I propped the phone against my shoulder and opened a can of dog food for Snooki. "But it wasn't because Agarth didn't try when he took me home. He told me how hot I was making him, and then he tried to throw me over his shoulder and tote me to my front door. And *then* he tried to kiss me. It wasn't pretty. The only thing that didn't suck about the whole going-home thing was when he punched my doorman for trying to cop a feel when I walked by him. Seriously, that guy is the sorriest excuse for a doorman. He's always dropping my groceries when he brings them up and he always loses my mail, and just last week he tried to grab my ass. I even reported him, but apparently he's related to the building manager. A nephew or cousin or something. Anyhow, when Agarth threw that punch, I was like *wow*. Not that I'm reevaluating my opinion of him. He's still a total caveman and I'm not interested."

Um, yeah. I could practically feel the sexual tension crackling over the phone line.

"I meant *lucky* as in a lead on Azazel," I told her. "I have to find out if he's here or Down Under."

"Agarth knows this demon over in the Motherland—" i.e., Italy "—who's in charge of keeping the archives on all the ancient spirits. He tracks everyone. Documents, possessions, et cetera. Agarth has a call in to him to see if he knows anything about Azazel."

"I didn't know we had archives."

"*We* don't. The archives were started by this brotherhood of theologians about a zillion years ago. The job's been handed down over the years. The most recent guy in charge choked on a meatball last year, and just as his spirit took a hike a demon by the name of Rathenbubzer checked in. He's been keeping tabs on all the oldies but goodies for the past six months now."

"Including Azazel?" Hope filled my voice as I set the doggie bowl down and opened the gate for Snooki. She yapped (when did she not yap?) and growled at me until I backed away and left her to her dinner.

"Maybe. Rath's still new to the whole record-keeping system. He said it might take him a few weeks to track Azazel through the endless pages of documentation. They're old school and still haven't managed to computerize."

"A few *weeks*?" Panic welled.

Easy. Calm. It's not the end of your life here on earth.

"Or a few months."

Bye-bye, cupcakes and cable TV.

A golf-ball-size lump pushed into my throat, and I reached for a bag of Chips Ahoy sitting on the counter. "But my mother's wedding is in two weeks," I said in between cookies. "If I don't hand over Azazel before then, Cutter will chop off her head."

Blythe grew silent, making the thunderous crunch of the store-bought treats more pronounced. "Maybe you can persuade him to give you more time?" she finally said.

I swallowed with a loud gulp. "I'm totally going down. In flames."

"Maybe not," she said, jumping in to cheer me up in true BFF fashion. "You've been known to work a little magic with the opposite sex. Maybe you *could* persuade Cutter to give you more time."

But while Cutter Owens might be attracted to me, I knew he didn't *want* to be attracted to me. Which meant he had his guard up. Which meant I might as well be a green alien with three eyeballs in the middle of my forehead. "Can't Rath move any faster?"

"He's trying, but the last theologian was so old that he was still writing in ancient Hebrew when Rath took over. He'll have to find a translator to decipher the records." Her voice grew softer. "You might want to think of a plan B."

My plan B consisted of more Chips Ahoy, a box of Kleenex (what? A demon can't cry?), and an evening with Google.

I knew it was a long shot, but I was desperate. I needed something—anything—that might lead me to the ancient demon.

The good news? There were over two hundred thousand references to Azazel.

The bad news? There were over *two hundred thousand* references. Everything from Wikipedia definitions to several black magic spells guaranteed to summon an ancient demon ($9.99 or your money back).

I spent most of the night clicking one by one, soaking up all of the information, however crazy or sparse, desperate for any clue that might lead me to his whereabouts. I spent a ridiculous amount of money purchasing a few spells, complete with a bottle of virgin's blood and overnight shipping.

I know, I know.

The odds that I was forking over money for the real thing were slim to none, but it was the best I could come up with. I couldn't just sit around waiting for Blythe to find me a lead.

Failure was not an option.

That's what I kept telling myself. But when I finally fell asleep, my dreams were filled with dancing virgins, barking dogs, and Cutter coming after me with his giant sword (and I don't mean that in a good way).

I was so screwed.

* * *

I woke up with a major sugar hangover (what's new?), a great big mound of guilt (get thee behind me, Chips Ahoy), eight urgent phone messages from Delaney, who insisted on changing the table linens—all five hundred of them—and my cousin Monique looming over me because I'd been so busy googling that I'd forgotten to spread my No Demon powder across the windowsills and thresholds before dozing off on the couch.

"Do you know that you drool when you sleep?"

"No, but thanks for passing that along."

"You snore, too, and not in a cute, fluffy sort of way. You really let it rip—"

"What are you doing here?" I cut in, scrambling upright. Crumbs flew and the remote took a nosedive to the floor.

"The real question is"—she swept a gaze around at the circle of burned-down candles sitting center stage in my small living room—"what are you doing here?"

"I was, um..." My brain raced for something to say, and not very fast since it was early and I hadn't had a shot of caffeine. "That is, I was just summoning Tylechanezer." The ancient demon's name popped into my head courtesy of the bottle of Tylenol sitting on my nightstand. "For my mom's bachelorette party. She wants to get wild, so I thought we could have him jump out of a cake."

It was a lame excuse, but Monique seemed to buy it.

"Good idea, but wouldn't it be easier to just text him? He's been living in Chicago for the past ten years. Occupying a really hot body from what I understand, so I'm sure your mom will be happy." She gave me an odd look. "A conjure spell only works if a demon is Down Under. You should know that."

Duh. Talk about Demon 101. The thing was, it had been so long since I'd actually sat through Demon 101 that I'd sorta, kinda forgotten a lot of the dos and don'ts.

"I'll e-mail his number." Her mouth drew into a tight line as she eyed me. "Then again, you probably won't open my e-mail because you never open my e-mail. I tried calling you too, but you haven't called me back." She stared at me as if she were about to hand over the fate of all mankind. "I need you to bring the brownies."

"Brownies?" I pushed to my feet and sidestepped a wayward candle. "What? When? Where?" A sleepy fog still gripped my brain, and I did a quick visual for a leftover Diet Coke on the nearby coffee table. Caffeine would be good right about now.

"Brownies," she prodded as I stumbled toward the kitchen. She stalled in the doorway and cast a sideways glance at Snooki pacing behind the doggie fence blocking off the bathroom. The animal barked and growled, and Monique glared. "For the baby shower, remember?"

"I'm sorry. I meant to call. I can't make it this Saturday." I sent up a silent litany of thanks. "I've got a wedding."

"Which is why we switched it to Thursday afternoon. One o'clock." She bypassed a snarling Snooki and walked toward the counter where I stood. "You really haven't been reading my e-mail."

"My server's been down," I murmured, desperately trying to digest this new piece of information. *Moved? To Thursday?*

"Now back to the brownies. Hester positively loves them. And so does everyone else. So we have to make sure we have plenty. I'm thinking a full dozen for each person there. That puts us at"—she glanced at the iPad in her hands—"eighty dozen."

"Thursday?" I mumbled, still stuck on her earlier news. *This* Thursday? Without a major shot of caffeine it was a little difficult to keep up. "But today is Tuesday." My head snapped up and my gaze collided with hers. "That means tomorrow is Wednesday. Followed by Thursday." Anxiety zapped me and blood started pumping even before I popped the top on my Diet Coke. "But that gives me barely forty-eight hours to make a zillion brownies."

She shrugged. "You should have read the e-mail. Or at least checked the Facebook page that I designed for the event." She beamed. "Talk about cuteness."

"I can only imagine." I downed a can of soda while Monique slid into a kitchen chair and chattered on about the baby shower for my cousin Hester. Ugh. It was just so wrong on about a million different levels.

Number one? I couldn't stand Hester—one of Aunt Bella's brood—when she wasn't expecting. Add a bunch of raging hormones and swollen ankles and three solid hours listening to her brag about everything from her shoes to the size of her husband's penis and I could safely say she was my least favorite relative.

If Hester's company wasn't bad enough, a baby shower meant all of my kin stuffed into one location—in this case the penthouse apartment of the Galleria Towers. Which meant my aunt Bella would bring her usual pickled eyeballs and my cousin Dahlia would talk nonstop about her own set of twins and then everyone else would want to know why I didn't have a baby on the way, including my mother, who was sure to be front and center, reminding me that my specialty was the big S and I should have two dozen of my own little illegitimate demons running around by now. And who knew? Maybe I'd be the one to break the curse and finally birth a boy.

Like that was going to happen.

I knew that was next to impossible, and you would think after more than seventy-two female births, the rest of my aunts and cousins would know it too. But obviously optimism is alive and thriving in the Damon clan.

Case in point—Hester had registered for an all-blue layette complete with a miniature cowboy outfit, baseball-themed nursery sheets, and a sterling silver football ready to be engraved with the new baby's name.

Hargathonarazmas. That had been the name listed on the powder-blue invitations.

Welcome Baby Hargie!

"So that's eighty dozen brownies, and don't forget a baby gift," Monique told me. "I'm getting the baby a miniature Dallas Cowboys football uniform, complete with tiny helmet."

"But what if it's a girl?" What can I say? With a demon slayer hot on my tail and my livelihood hanging in the balance with my mom, I was fresh out of optimism at the moment.

"It's not a girl." Monique gave me a narrowed look that promised retribution if I didn't jump on board the XY-chromosome train.

"Did she see the sex on the ultrasound?" What? I was already on the *Demons' Most Wanted* list, being tormented by my big bad aunties. Monique, a lower-level demon who specialized in slow grocery clerks and long wait lines at the DMV, was the least of my worries.

"Everybody knows you can't trust those ultrasound thingies." She waved a hand. "If Hester thinks it's a boy, that's good enough for me. Now about the brownies…" She spent the next fifteen minutes giving me specific instructions on the size she wanted each brownie square and what type of serving platters to bring and how high to pile the plates and what color doilies to use.

"That's *powder* blue," she told me. "Not baby blue. Or cornflower blue. And don't even think about showing up with azure."

Yep, you guessed it. It isn't just optimism that runs rampant in our family. We're also a bunch of OCD pain-in-the-asses.

"Don't forget," she went on. "You need to be there two hours early."

"Got it." I downed the last of my Diet Coke and glanced at the clock. A bolt of panic went through me. I had two dress fittings, three cake tastings, and a meeting with Cheryl to go over the guest list, and I was already forty-five minutes late.

"I really have to get going." I ushered Monique toward the door. "But thanks for stopping by."

"Don't forget the brownies," she blurted before I slammed the door in her face.

As if.

I might be guilty of lots of things. Too many one-night stands. A little creative Photoshopping on my Facebook pic. Slipping a Valium into Snooki's nightly kibble. Okay, that last one I'd only thought about. But still. I made mistakes.

But forgetting a mountain of chocolate?

I was stressed, not crazy.

"Here's the guest list." Cheryl handed me the neatly typed pages when she walked into the office a few hours later, where I was neck-deep in Momzilla wedding details.

I was flying solo that morning since Andrew and Burke were finishing last-minute errands for a vow renewal we had planned for this Saturday, complete with a Friday night dinner party at the Waldorf Astoria. An event that was completely under control. Unlike my mother's extravaganza. Sure, it was taking shape. Slowly. But slow wasn't good enough. I needed fast.

On top of that, I'd spotted Cutter's black Land Rover parked across the street this morning and a box of Krispy Kremes waiting on my doorstep.

Not that it was a gift or anything, even if my heart did skip a few beats. It was a reminder. He knew what I was, and he wasn't going away until he got what he wanted—namely the ancient demon who'd stolen his soul.

If only I didn't keep fantasizing that *I* was what he wanted.

Seriously. I was having some major fantasies starring Houston's hottest demon slayer. Sexual fantasies, I reminded myself, which was to be totally expected since I had succubus flowing through my veins.

But the sun was shining now and it was time to focus on the finished invitations that had been delivered earlier that morning.

A quick glance at the neatly typed pages from Cheryl and I realized it was an alphabetical list of names only. WTF?

"Where are the addresses?"

She shook her head. "No addresses."

"How am I supposed to send out invitations without any addresses?"

"That's what George is for." She motioned to an empty corner. The air shimmered and solidified and suddenly we had company.

George was a black-robed figure with a shrouded face and a pair of impressive wings that looked a little singed around the edges.

"I'm guessing he's not a postal worker."

Cheryl smiled. "He's better. No lunch breaks. No union. Just fast and efficient service."

"Guaranteed or your money back," said a deep, vibrating voice that seemed to bounce off the walls.

"He's part of a new Down Under courier service that your mother started. While she can summon with the snap of a finger, often she only wants to send a message. Do this. Do that. Fry this. Fry that. George here is her faithful delivery guy."

I thought for a second and a memory stirred. "Didn't you bring me six thongs for my birthday last year?"

"It was seven, dear," Cheryl said. "One for each day of the week. I purchased them myself."

"But I only received six."

Cheryl arched an eyebrow at George. A startling slash of white cracked open the blackness of his face. "I thought you were working on the undie fetish?" The shrouded shoulders shrugged, and she shook her head. "Demons. What are you gonna do? Anyhow, you just get them labeled and George will deliver them. No addresses needed." When I didn't look convinced, she added, "A lot of our guests don't actually have a physical address, since half of them are coming from Down Under."

Duh. Unfortunately I'd been planning human weddings for so long that I hadn't actually stopped to consider that all-important fact.

"What about the RSVP cards?"

"What RSVP cards?"

"We need an exact head count for the reception. Guests mail the cards back in with the number attending or their regrets. Will George be bringing those as well?"

"There won't be any regrets. No one is going to miss your mother tying the knot."

"I know that's what most brides think, but trust me, there are always regrets. Things come up."

"Not this time. If your mother invites them, they will come. They *have* to come."

Her words sank in and reality smacked me. We're talking Satan Speak, which equaled the Down Under version of Simon Says. Meaning whatever Mom *said*, they *did*. Otherwise they spent an eternity on shit duty.

No was not an option.

"So they're all coming. Everyone." The moment the word slid past my lips, an idea struck. A brilliant idea.

All I had to do was summon Azazel to the wedding on behalf of my mother and—bam!—he would have to make an appearance. Cutter would have his revenge, and I would keep my ma from losing her head permanently.

If I could get my mother to invite him.

I glanced down at the *A*s and sure enough, no Azazel.

"This seems like an awfully small list," I told Cheryl, my heart pounding and my mind racing. "I thought my mother wanted to go big."

"There are six hundred names on the list."

"This is Texas." I managed a laugh. "Big usually means a thousand. At the very least."

Cheryl seemed to think before shaking her head. "Your mother handpicked the list herself. Everyone who's anyone Down Under will be there. Anyone else is just added baggage."

"But I can think of at least a dozen demons she's missed."

"I wouldn't mess with her list," Cheryl said. "She was very specific about who she wanted in attendance."

Meaning there would be no slipping Azazel onto the list without my mom realizing that something was up. If I wanted him invited, I had to come up with a really good reason to get my mother to change her mind.

"What about a date? Surely I can bring a date?"

"I'm afraid your mother didn't allow for dates."

"But I need him there." When Cheryl arched an eyebrow, I added, "We're serious." When she looked confused, I added, "Semiserious. We still see other people, of course. I *am* a succubus and duty calls. But there's just something extra between us. We have so much in common." Cheryl didn't look convinced, so I threw in a quick, "We walk our dogs together."

I knew I'd hit pay dirt when excitement lit her eyes. "You have a dog?"

I nodded. "Her name is Snooki, and she's a recent acquisition. I was all thumbs when I got her and so I joined a dog-lover website. That's where I met him. We're pet-loving buddies."

"What's the website? Maybe I know it." Because Cheryl was a huge dog lover and knew all about pet-loving sites.

"It's www.luvdoggies.com."

"I don't think I've heard of that—"

"Or something like that," I cut in. "It's on my favorites so I don't actually have to type it in exactly. Anyhow, we both have Yorkies, so we have lots to talk about."

"What's his dog's name?"

I scrambled for a plausible name, but the only thing that popped into my head was, "Pauly D."

"Really?"

"We both love *Jersey Shore* too. We've never met face-to-face, and this would be the perfect time for me to say thanks for all of his great doggie tips. I don't know how I would have made it the past few days without him. He's like the Yorkie Whisperer."

"I suppose I could bring it up to your mother—"

"No," I cut in. "She'll just freak if we ask her and probably set me on fire, and then who would take care of my new little Snooki? Besides, we're talking one measly demon. She'll never even know. She'll be so busy with everything else that she won't have a spare second to scrutinize the hundreds of guests in attendance. Please," I added. "It would mean so much to me. And to Snooki."

She looked doubtful, but then she nodded. "Add him to the list," she said. "But that's it. No one else. And make sure he keeps a low profile. She'll have my head if she notices him."

"We'll keep it very low-key," I promised. "No making out at the reception table." On second thought. "We'll make out all over the place. She'll never notice anything is off."

Cheryl left, and I finished off the invites, adding Azazel's name to the bunch before handing them over to George.

He grunted a garbled *you suck*—the Down Under equivalent of *thank you*—and disappeared in a wisp of black smoke. The sharp aroma of sulfur burned my nostrils.

I lit the Yankee candle sitting on my desk—vanilla cupcake flavor, what else?—and mentally crossed *Beheaded Bride* off my list of upcoming tragedies. I texted Cutter a quick *You can get off my back. One soul-stealing demon en route.* No sooner had I hit *Send* than my phone beeped with a new message. *How?????*

I hit the delete button and slipped my phone back into my purse. The less Cutter knew about how I'd managed to summon Azazel, the better. The last thing I needed was every demon slayer affiliated with the Legion standing in line, begging me to add their next kill to my guest list. I wanted to pull this wedding off without a hitch, not turn it into a Pop That Demon party.

I could deal with the guilt of sacrificing one ancient demon to save my own mother. But a whole ballroom full? Even Dr. Phil wouldn't be able to counsel me through something like that. I was the black sheep of the family, going it alone, dancing to the beat of my own drummer. Not a traitor.

I squelched a wave of anxiety and focused on the all-important fact that I'd done it. I'd saved my mother from the Legion's sword. A feat that called for some serious celebration.

I skipped the next five items on my Momzilla list and grabbed my purse to head over to Cake Creations. I hauled open the door and ran smack-dab into Cutter Owens.

He looked even sexier in the bright light of day. He wore the usual jeans and black T-shirt. A serious expression drew his mouth tight. "Where did you find him?"

"I haven't found him. I mean, I have, but I can't tell you where he is because I don't know exactly. All I know is that he'll be at the wedding. He's on the guest list."

"How do I know you're telling the truth?"

"Why would I tell you he's going to be at the wedding and risk you showing up and getting pissed because I lied to you? If I were lying, I'd send you on a wild goose chase someplace far, far away from this wedding. Speaking of which, I'll have to work out some way to get Azazel off by himself so you can deal with him without interrupting my event. In the meantime, you can stop following me."

His expression eased and a grin tugged at the corner of his mouth. "Not on your life, sweetheart."

That's what I was hoping.

I ignored the last thought and stiffened. "I don't need a babysitter."

"Says you. The car," he reminded me about the incident a few nights ago. The coldness. The noose. "You were choking and I played Superman."

And how. I remembered the feel of his hard body pressed up against me, his strong arms wrapped tight. "Um, thanks." I cleared my suddenly dry throat. "But I'm fine now. I really need to go. I have a cake tasting."

He didn't move for a long, drawn-out moment. Instead, he stared down at me, his gaze hooked on my mouth as if he wanted to taste me as much as I wanted to taste him.

Hello? He wants to kill you. That's what he does. He takes out demons. He needs you right now. That's the only reason he isn't slicing and dicing.

"Are the rumors true?" I heard myself ask. "About you wanting to take out as many demons as possible?"

"Azazel stole *my soul*," he murmured, as if that explained it.

And it did. I saw the flash of torment in his eyes, so quick, but it was there. Deep inside.

"I'm really sorry." I shouldn't have said it, but I couldn't help myself. I *was* sorry. Sorry that he'd suffered because of my kind. Hopeful that I could help him find some peace. And not just to save my own skin, I realized as I stood staring up at him.

No, it went beyond that.

I liked Cutter. I actually *liked* him.

Yeah, right.

You hardly know this guy. It's the hormones talking.

Surprise glittered hot and bright for a brief moment. "Are you sure you're a demon?"

I shrugged. "Nobody's perfect."

He grinned, just a small lift at the corner of his mouth, but it was enough to send a whisper of *yowza* through my already hormone-riddled body. The tension between us thickened, and I became light-headed. Yep, it was the hormones, all right. I licked my lips. He was so close.

Just a little closer. Please.

He stiffened. "You really should go." He stepped aside and motioned me forward, and hope faded in a rush of disappointment.

A kiss? Really? Are you that delusional?

I was. I'd been on the wagon so long that I was starting to imagine things. Like how I actually *liked* him. And how great it would be if he liked me.

Ugh. I *so* needed a big fat bite of chocolate decadence.

I spent the next two hours gobbling down mouthful after mouthful of my favorite, as well as a dozen other flavor combinations, before nailing down both the bridal cake and the groom's cake. With a major sugar buzz sating my craving—for the moment—I managed to turn off the deprived-succubus-trying-to-stay-on-the-celibacy-train and switch on Houston's-upcoming-wedding-planner-of-the-year.

I headed to a nearby salon to check on the dress fittings for the Stout-Fowler wedding, ordered the engraved invites for the Gray-Schneider vow renewal, and talked one of my upcoming brides out of making her pet boa constrictor the flower girl. Daisy gobbling up a few of the 115 wedding guests would surely shoot the modest budget to Hell and back.

I also stopped off at Costco to pick up brownie supplies for tomorrow and headed home feeling calm and hopeful for the first time since my mother had dropped the bomb about her wedding— a feeling that disappeared the minute I saw my mom's black Lexus parked in front of my duplex.

I walked into my office to find her sitting on the white settee in the main lobby area. Andrew and Burke perched in front of her, glazed, adoring looks on their faces as they each held one of her feet and worked the kinks out of her toes.

"Your minions are too cute," she murmured, sipping a glass of champagne with a strawberry floating on top. Cheryl sat to her right, champagne bottle in one hand, iPad in the other. "Isn't that right, Cheryl?"

"Too cute," the woman readily agreed.

"My minions?" *Not.* "Oh, yeah. Mine. And definitely cute. What, um, exactly did you do to them?"

"They started bombarding me with all these questions about colors and music and food, so I zapped them. They're much more tolerable this way. The arch," she told Andrew, who gazed at her with total adoration. "And do it just a little harder. There. That's it." She smiled and apprehension wiggled through me.

"Mom?"

"Yes, dear."

"What, um, are you doing here at my office?"

"I'm here for the bridesmaids' fittings, of course."

"But how can we fit anyone when we haven't decided which cousins to ask? I made a list, but I haven't narrowed it down—"

"No cousins. I've decided to have your aunts. All three of them." A smile lifted her mouth. "I want them front and center for every moment of this event."

My mind riffled back through the past forty-eight hours, complete with the cryptic message on my bathroom mirror and the invisible noose in the car. Both screamed *mad as hell*, and now she wanted said perpetrator in the wedding? "Do you really think that's the best idea?"

"I think it's brilliant. Getting married is a huge coup. But rubbing their noses in it will be just plain fun. I don't want them to miss a minute of this, particularly your aunt Bella. She'll be the matron of honor." She giggled. No, really. *Giggled.* Like a schoolgirl having her first crush. Or the Devil appointing her most detested sister as the matron of horror.

"And they agreed?"

"They have no choice, dear. Your grandfather supports this union and they won't risk pissing him off. Speaking of your grandfather, he'll need a tuxedo. I have no clue as to his measurements because he's off playing some tournament right now and can't be reached, but I have no doubt he'll show up just to make sure that I am, indeed, tying the knot. He won't let me assume sole control without proof."

"One tux," I murmured, still trying to process the latest news. My aunties? In the wedding?

"So where are we going to do this?" My mother's voice slipped past the pounding of my heart. "Give me a location and Cheryl will text the aunts where to meet us."

"But it's almost nine o'clock at night."

She cut a glance at me. "And?"

I wanted to tell her that all the shops were closed because they were all run by humans who actually kept normal business hours.

At the same time, this was my chance to prove to her that I was actually good at something other than seducing men. I was Houston's hottest up-and-coming wedding planner. Translation? I had mad wedding skills and it was time to prove it.

"Give me five minutes."

"I really appreciate this, Summer," I told the chic brunette who opened the glass doors of the elite dress shop in the heart of the Galleria area.

"When duty calls, I answer." Summer Canfield routinely dealt with Houston's rich and famous. She was no stranger to opening after hours—thankfully—and loved getting the scoop on the lives and times of Houston's most prominent VIPs. This burning desire—plus a ten percent bonus commission—had lured her out of bed at nine thirty on a Thursday night. "So who is it?" Her eyes danced with excitement. "Debutante? Actress? Politician?" She finished flipping on the lights, chasing away the last of the shadows, and turned an expectant gaze on me.

"Um, yeah." I glanced around the pristine shop with its plush cream-colored sofas and thick champagne carpeting. The only real color came from bunches of pale orchids situated here and there and the collection of dress magazines stacked on a gold-edged coffee table. A bowl of white Jordan almonds sat nearby. Michael Bolton drifted from the speakers.

Summer's was the perfect scenario for an excited bride to choose fabulous dresses for her wedding party. A not-so-perfect scenario for Satan to torture her hellish sisters.

I sent up a silent plea that the sofas had been coated with Scotchgard. Otherwise, I was screwed.

"So?" Summer's eager voice drew my attention. "Which one is she?"

I did a quick mental tally and blurted, "Politician." What? While my mom fit the bill for the first two (she could throw a temper tantrum and do a crackerjack Angelina Jolie impersonation) false promises were definitely her specialty.

Excitement lit the woman's eyes. "Local or state?"

"Bigger."

"National?" she breathed.

"And then some."

"I knew it." She mouthed a quick *tell me all the dirt later*, clamped her lips shut, and pretended to lock her trap and throw away the key. While Summer thrived on being in the know, she was still a master of discretion. At least until we walked out and she started texting the members of the local women's auxiliary. She gave me a wink before waltzing past me to greet the aunties, who'd just arrived and now stood in the doorway.

"Ladies! Welcome! Can I interest anyone in some champagne?"

"By all means," said my mother, easing into a nearby chair. She wore a black silk blouse, a fitted black skirt, and an expression that said she was really going to enjoy what was about to happen. "This is definitely an occasion worth celebrating."

I barely resisted the urge to grab Summer and run for cover. But that would surely blow my cover as a mad, bad demon. I forced a deep breath and concentrated on not having a major freak-out. Tough, considering all the aunts were here. Right now. Right *here*.

"I'll have a drink." Aunt Lucy slid a hand into the air as she perched on the edge of a sofa. She looked fun chic in a Rihanna concert tee, a pair of pink spandex pants, and a hot-pink pair of retro cowboy boots.

"Me too," said Aunt Levita. She was the picture of cold indignation with blonde hair, stormy gray eyes, and an expression that said she would rather have bamboo shoved under her fingernails than sit down. "In fact, make mine a double." She eyed a nearby sofa as if it were going to jump up and bite her. "It's really pale in here."

"It's called eggshell." Summer beamed. "It's the latest in the *in* color palette."

"Peasants," Aunt Levita snorted and slid on a pair of sunglasses before forcing herself down next to Lucy. Meanwhile, Summer turned to Aunt Bella. "How about you, dear? A glass of Cristal?"

"I'd rather have fresh-squeezed virgin's blood." Aunt Bella was the oldest of the bunch and the most traditional. She was the least superficial, too, and preferred a more motherly approach to deception. Translation? With snow-white hair and a black dress, she looked more like a grieving widow than a demonic princess. "That always gives me a nice kick."

"Virgin's blood," I snorted. "What a joker." I gave Aunt Bella a pointed stare that said *Hello? Human alert.*

A chilling smile curled her bottom lip. "I suppose a glass of AB negative would do just as well."

Her words conjured an image of the bloody mirror and my stomach contracted.

"Bella's such a riot." Lucy's voice pushed past the noise and snagged my attention. She laughed and gave me a look that said *get it together, and fast.* "The champagne will do just fine," she told Summer, who rushed off, a strange expression on her face.

I gathered my courage and gave myself a mental ass kick. I might be quaking inside, but I wasn't going to give Aunt Bella the satisfaction of knowing it. I met her icy stare with one of my own. "Seriously?"

She shrugged. "Back in the old days, we drank a dozen virgins anytime we felt like it."

"Virgins are so last season," Lucy told her, "but then you wouldn't know that because you live under a rock."

"It's a cave, and there was a time when all demons lived in one, including you."

"About a zillion years ago," Aunt Levita said. "In case you didn't get the memo, Bel, we've evolved since then."

Bella scoffed and gave her sister a pointed look. "Evolution is for peasants."

"You're an eccentric idiot," Levita countered.

"*You're* an idiot."

Oh the joy of a family get-together.

"Why don't we all just relax and enjoy the moment," I cut in. "Remember, we're not here for ourselves. This is all about the bride." I scooted around to position myself in a nearby chair. Close enough to play referee but far enough not to get caught in the cross fire. "Mother? Do you have anything you'd like to say to everyone?"

"Just that I'm happy to have all of you here to share this special time with me. It really means a lot." My mother beamed, and I had the crazy thought that maybe, just maybe, this hasty marriage wasn't solely a power play.

Maybe my mom actually had feelings for Samael.

Maybe she'd realized the error of her ways and the dueling between the sisters was now officially over.

Maybe it was (deep sigh) true *love*.

"Choosing the right bridesmaids' dress is crucial for this event," my mom went on. "I mean, really, I can't have any of you looking better than I do on the one day when I'm trying to show everyone up."

Then again, maybe not.

* * *

"Tell me again why we're adding five thousand dollars to the Momzilla budget?" Andrew asked the next morning when I finally dragged myself into work. After a restless night courtesy of a yapping Snooki and a frisky Cutter.

Not the real Cutter. The fantasy Cutter.

I tried to ignore the ache in my nipples and grabbed the air freshener to mask the pungent smell of smoke that still clung to me. "A few unexpected expenses."

"Bigger centerpieces?" Andrew's brow wrinkled. "Extra cake? More than one photographer?"

"Insurance deductible."

Thanks to Mommie Dearest, who'd stuck the aunts in bright-white dresses. Short, frilly, virginal white taffeta with matching hair bows, parasols, and chunky jewelry.

I know, I know. Virginal white is so anti–dark and sinister, but it was the quickest way to torment her sisters. Needless to say, Aunt Lucy had been slightly freaked (white was *so* last season, and chunky jewelry? *Not*). Aunt Levita had thrown a fit because, hey, it's *white*. And Aunt Bella had thrown not one, but two lightning bolts and a few claps of thunder.

Long story short, Summer's shop was closed for fire damage and she was just this side of deaf but happy thanks to my demon glam skills.

Sure, she'd be wearing a wig for a little while, but the good news was her hair would grow back.

Someday.

"Insurance deductible?" Andrew stared, the question quickly forgotten as he wrinkled his nose and watched me wave around the can. "Have you been barbecuing?"

"You have no idea." I shot another wave of Tropical Breeze into the air and sank down at my desk.

I cleared my still-scratchy throat and he arched an eyebrow. "So why is your mother paying an insurance deductible?"

"We had a bridesmaids' fitting last night and things got a little ugly." Or a lot.

Understanding lit his gaze. "Bad dress?"

"The worst."

"Say no more. I'll give the photographer a heads-up. Photoshop, here we come."

16

"You're off the hook," I told Blythe that evening when she finally answered her cell. "I managed to summon Azazel all by myself."

"Really? How?"

"I have my ways." Or at least George had his ways. Thankfully. "No more Agarth," I reminded her, waiting for her sigh of relief.

Silence ticked by for a few seconds. "That's great." Only it didn't sound so great.

"What's up?" I asked her.

"Nothing. I mean, I was getting ready to go see Coldplay. Agarth bought the tickets because he knows they're my favorite, which was really kind of sweet, or it would be if I was remotely interested in him. Which I'm not." She laughed. "He's such a caveman. It drives me nuts. Not that I can't put up with it a little while longer if you need me to. In fact, it might be a good idea. Just in case your plan A falls through."

"Trust me, it's foolproof."

"Awesome." The word was small and insincere.

"Something else is going on. What is it?" But I already had an idea. "Don't tell me you actually *like* Agarth."

"Are you kidding?" She laughed, a brittle, harsh sound that didn't ring sincere. "I do *not* like Agarth." Her voice softened. "It's just that I had a really crummy day and Coldplay was the one thing pulling me through."

"Crummy?"

"The school district called last night. I went on my first substitute-teacher job today. It's part of a work program for my major. I need at least sixteen hours in the field in order to graduate. It was at Granbury Elementary School. First grade."

"That's terrific." The minute I said the words, I heard a strangled cry on the other end. "Or not."

"Oh, Jess. It was terrible. One kid kicked me. Another threw up on my shoe. And that was all in the first twenty minutes. It was the longest eight hours of my life. Being a teacher sucked. What was I thinking even considering giving up the limo service to be a kindergarten teacher? I should have majored in marketing or something that would help me book more tours. I think I'm in way over my head with the teaching stuff."

"Don't say that. Teaching is your dream."

"It felt more like a nightmare."

"Nothing worthwhile is ever easy." Great. I sounded like an inspirational calendar. "It was your first day. Things happen. You need to cut yourself some slack. Hang in there. Don't quit."

She sniffled. "That's what Agarth said when I texted him earlier." Another sniffle. "Speaking of which, he's supposed to be here in a half hour. I need to catch him before he drives all the way over here for nothing. Later."

She hung up before I could ask the all-important question—why was she texting Agarth the details of her day?

Unless...

The idea danced in my head for a nanosecond before I shut down the party and switched off the music. Blythe hated Agarth. Despised him. Loathed him. She was thrilled that I had saved her from yet another evening with him.

Even if she didn't sound all that thrilled.

Before I could dwell on the notion, my phone beeped with a text from Monique.

Don't forget the brownies. Or else.

All right, already, I texted back.

I powered off my computer, ignored the table full of white favor boxes for the vow renewal and the roll of personalized ribbon just waiting for my mad wrapping skills, and headed out the front door of my office. I could knock out the favors after the shower tomorrow. In the meantime, it was me and eighty dozen Whatever Floats Your Boat brownies.

Or else.

Monique was Aunt Bella's daughter. Maybe the brownies were just an excuse to lure me to the shower so that Aunt Bella could scare the daylights out of me again.

Maybe worse.

The possibility stirred a wave of prickles that raced along my arms. A faint breeze made the sensation that much worse as I headed for the side staircase leading to my apartment. The streetlight cast a dim glow on the front lawn, but otherwise the house was dark. Not quiet, of course. That would be too much to ask for. Snooki yapped away, a sound that did little to ease the goose bumps. My gaze slid to the curb, but other than a small, beat-up Datsun parked a few houses down, the street was empty. Obviously Cutter had taken me at my word and backed off.

I stifled my disappointment and turned back to my door. I hadn't thought to turn on the porch light, so I fumbled for a few minutes with my key.

Finally the lock clicked, and the hinges creaked, and I rushed inside. I slammed the door and locked the deadbolt and started turning on lights one after the other until the apartment blazed and the prickles eased.

There.

Flipping on the TV, I scrolled through the channels until I found a rerun of *Bridezillas*. While a smart-mouthed diva named Cheyenne ranted over the unjust fact that her maid of honor refused to bow down and give her a foot massage at the bridal shower, I walked into my bedroom, changed into an oversize University of Houston T-shirt and shorts, and headed to the kitchen to feed Snooki.

A few minutes later I was clearing off the counter and pulling out my mixer. Soon brownie pans covered the countertop along with the batch of ingredients I'd picked up earlier. It was a tight fit in my small kitchen, but I could make it work. I had eighteen hours to make eighty dozen brownies. At two dozen per pan, four pans an hour, I could do it in ten with enough time left over for a quick shower, a few Red Bulls, and the usual just-go-and-get-it-over-with pep talk that preceded all family functions.

Soon the smell of rich chocolate filled the air, dispelling any lingering angst and bumping up my mood considerably. Snooki's yapping faded into the sound of the bridal march when bridezilla Cheyenne finally walked down the aisle, albeit in a turquoise dress that was totally unsuitable for a wedding. But every good wedding planner knows, what the bride wants, the bride gets...

I even felt a tiny bit sad when her maid of honor refused to walk down the aisle after Cheyenne slapped her with the bouquet preceremony and called her a skanky ho.

Where do they find these people?

Anyhow, I was on batch number sixteen when it first hit me that something wasn't quite right.

First off, there was no demon-hating dog yapping in the next room. Maybe Snooki was getting into the latest bride— Lakwanda—and her fierce temper tantrum because she wanted a lime-green limo instead of the traditional black. Maybe Snooki liked lime green, too.

And maybe it was just wishful thinking, because I knew in my gut that something was terribly wrong. Even before the doorknob started to shake.

A split second later the front door blew inward. A fierce gust of icy wind spiraled into my apartment, whooshing through the living room, straight into the kitchen. The bag of chocolate chips I'd just picked up sailed to the floor and scattered at my feet. A ringing filled my ears.

No, wait. That was a scream. My scream.

As quick as it had stirred, the wind died. Snooki started barking again and I clamped my mouth shut. I drew a shaky breath.

It's almost over, I reassured myself. I would not be scared off. That's all this was. A scare tactic. And it wasn't working—yikes!

I glanced down at the spilled chocolate chips around my feet. Only they weren't just lying there. They were moving. Walking.

Spiders.

Pans clattered as I scrambled onto the counter, yanking my knees up to my chest, holding tight. I hated spiders, and I hated being afraid of spiders, and I really hated whoever was messing with my head.

They're just a trick. A trick to scare you off the wedding track and possibly punish you for last night's bridesmaids' fitting.

A scary, dangerous, possibly poisonous trick.

A tear slid down my cheek. Followed by another and then another.

Stop it. They're harmless and they'll go away. Eventually. Just hold tight.

Yeah, or maybe I was going to die right here without ever finding the man of my dreams. Or kissing the one man who haunted my fantasies. I was going to die hungry. Deprived. And then I'd be back in Hell. Still hungry. Still deprived. *Forever.*

I made a mad grab for the monstrous bowl of brownie batter, shoved my hand inside, and scooped up a mouthful. Sugar danced across my taste buds and sent a rush of *ahhhhh* through me.

I was going back for more when I noticed the smear of chocolate on the counter next to me and I froze.

Because it wasn't just a smear. It was a warning.

I'm coming for you.

As I read the words, I felt a sensation on my arm. Glancing down, I shrieked. The bowl went flying as a single spider sank its tiny fangs into my flesh.

Get off. Get off. Get off.

I slapped at my arm, scrambling off the counter as fast as my legs would carry me. My foot landed on something soft and squishy and—*ick!*

My legs sailed out from under me and the floor slammed into my backside. The air rushed from my lungs. Pain gripped every nerve in my body and sent off tiny flutters of light behind my eyeballs. Through the thunder of my own heart I heard the sharp, shrill barks of a frantic Snooki and the deep, sexy voice of the demon hunter who'd haunted my sleep for the past few nights.

"Jess?"

In that next instant, I didn't just hear him, I saw him. Tall, dark, and mesmerizing as he hovered over me. He wore black jeans, a black T-shirt, and a concerned expression. As if he actually cared that I was sprawled on the floor.

As if he liked me as much as I liked him—

Stop it. You don't like him. He doesn't like you. And this is just a hallucination.

I was having one final imaginary moment before I kicked the bucket for good and spent the next eon Down Under, waiting in line for my chance at another body.

I savored the moment, forcing my blurry eyes to focus, desperate to drink in one long look at Cutter Owens before I went south.

Oddly enough, he didn't just look real.

He felt real.

Strong fingers closed over my arms, and before I could think about what that meant, everything shimmered and shook, and then—bam!—it all went eerily dark.

17

"Jess?"

The rich, masculine voice peeled back the layers of nothingness and yanked me back to my tiny kitchen and the all-important fact that Cutter Owens loomed over me. No, really.

"Wake up, sleepyhead."

"I'm not sleeping." I cracked one eye open to see Mr. Hot and Incredibly Sexy hunkered down next to me on the floor. "I'm dead."

"Overdose?" He arched an eyebrow and I became keenly aware of the chocolate covering my hand. And my chin. And oh, no, my cheek too.

"Don't judge." I wiped my face and only succeeded in making it worse. When I tried to sit up, the room started spinning and I slumped back down.

"Take it easy." One strong finger reached out and touched my chocolate-smeared cheek. He licked the sugary goodness off the tip of his finger and his eyes smoldered. "Not bad."

"Thanks. Brownies are my specialty." *Among other things*, a voice whispered.

Bad voice.

"With that much sugar swimming in your system, you're going to be a little shaky," he murmured as I struggled into a sitting position, my back against the cabinet.

"It's not the sugar. It's the venom. I was bitten."

"By what?" He glanced around. "A brownie?"

"There were spiders…" My voice failed as I drank in the scattered chocolate chips surrounding me. "There *were* spiders. They were here just a second ago. Everywhere. One of them bit me and then I saw you but I thought it was just the venom and you weren't real and then I felt you and then I lost it for a few seconds and then…" The words trailed off as my mind snagged on what I'd just said. "I didn't think you were actually here. I didn't see your car outside."

"I had a meeting this evening, so I had one of our rookies keeping an eye on you. I was relieving him when I heard you scream."

And, of course, Cutter had come running to check on me because I was the most beautiful woman he'd ever seen and he couldn't shake his undeniable attraction to me.

That, or I was his one and only link to Azazel and he couldn't afford to let his chance at revenge slip through his fingers.

I held tight to the second explanation and tried to ignore the lust making my thighs tremble.

"It was the spider. It creeped me out." I struggled to my feet, shrugging off his hands as I reached for the counter. My gaze zigzagged to the spot where the warning had been smeared in chocolate, but there were no words now, just a swipe of batter. I'd imagined it all. Hadn't I?

Real, my gut insisted. I knew it. I felt it.

Even if the feeling wasn't as frightening with Cutter beside me. No, his nearness stirred an entirely different feeling. "Stop stalking me and go home," I said, desperate for some air that didn't smell like chocolate and hot, hunky demon slayer. "I've got it covered."

He pushed to his feet and simply stood there, towering over me. Disbelief glittered in his green eyes. "You're really that freaked out by spiders?"

"Why is that so hard to believe?"

"You're a demon."

"Yeah, well, I'm also a Pisces, and I'm allergic to fish. Go figure."

A grin curved his lips and I felt a funny flutter in the pit of my stomach.

I scooted around the counter, desperate to put as much distance between us as possible. I needed to keep my head, and that meant keeping my hands busy.

Busy hands couldn't reach across and grasp the soft cotton of his T-shirt and pull him close.

My fingers closed around the flour and I started pouring. "You really should leave. I'm totally fine."

"A spider bite isn't fine." His gaze narrowed as he looked around, and I knew then that as unbelievable as my story was, he believed it. "What happened before the spiders?"

My mind did a quick rewind and I replayed the last few moments before slamming into the floor as I mixed up a batch of dry ingredients. "A gust of wind. A roaring in my ears."

"Did you smell anything?"

"Just chocolate." I eyed him. "Why? Should I have smelled something else?" He shrugged, and I added, "Did you see something when you came in? Someone? Maybe a little old lady in a black dress?"

"What?"

I shook my head. "Never mind." So what if he didn't actually see Aunt Bella? It didn't mean it wasn't her. She was the only demon I knew who hated chocolate. Violating a bunch of chocolate chips with her demon mojo would be right up her alley.

My hands trembled as I reached for my wet ingredients. Eggs first.

"You might need this." His voice sounded a heartbeat before he stepped up next to me. One hard, muscular bicep kissed my shoulder and a shock wave vibrated through me.

"Thanks." I took the bottle of vanilla extract and tried to pretend that his nearness didn't affect me. Fat chance, but I was giving myself an A for effort.

"Oil?" He held up the bottle of Mazola.

I shook my head. "I use butter instead, but you can hand me a set of measuring spoons." I motioned to the other end of the counter. "It looks like somebody knows his way around a kitchen," I said when he handed me the plastic spoons.

"I manage." He shrugged. "I used to help my mother every now and then back when I was a kid. She made the best chocolate pie, with melt-in-your-mouth meringue."

"How high was the meringue?"

"Six inches or so."

I let loose a whistle. "Impressive." I added the vanilla to my mixture. "Fluffy meringue is hard to come by. I still haven't found a good recipe, and believe you me, I've looked."

"I'd share hers, but it's long gone now. She and my dad passed away in a car accident when I was nineteen."

"I'm sorry."

"It's okay. It was years ago." He retrieved several sticks of softened butter from a nearby plate and placed them next to my bowl. "What about you? Any family?"

"My mom." I unwrapped the sticks and added them to my wet ingredients. "I never really knew my dad, but I do have three sisters." I slid a sideways glance at him. "You?"

"I was an only child. I have a cousin, but otherwise I'm flying solo."

Silence descended for a few moments as I added the dry ingredients to my wet mixture and turned on the mixer. Whirring filled the air as we stood there, side by side.

Oddly enough, the sexual tension radiating between us seemed to morph into something as comforting as it was stimulating. I had an oddly domestic vision of us whipping up a mountain of pancakes the morning after.

I killed the mixer along with the crazy thought and retrieved a cake pan.

"So you like to bake brownies," he murmured as I poured the batter into the pan.

"Actually, I like to eat brownies." I spread the dark chocolate with a spatula. "Baking them is the evil necessity."

"I always liked grilling, myself. Ribs, brisket, chicken—you name it, I grilled it."

Glancing over at Cutter leaning against one end of the counter, I imagined him standing outside in the hot summer sun, wearing nothing but a pair of blue jeans and a smile as he flipped hamburgers. Sweat glistened on his shoulders and muscles rippled as he worked the spatula.

I swallowed against my suddenly dry throat and fed the brownie pan into the oven. "That makes sense."

"How so?"

I set the timer for twenty-five minutes. "You look like the outdoorsy type."

"I did know my way around a tent." A grim expression covered his handsome face as he took the mixing bowl and set it in the sink. "I used to go camping and hiking every weekend. I'd set up camp and cook out over an open fire. It was nice."

"Was?"

"I was camping in Palo Duro Canyon about ten years ago when I met Azazel. One minute I was pouring a cup of coffee and the next I was facing off with an ancient demon. My parents had just died and I was in a bad way, and there he was. He told me he could take away all the pain if I would just give him my soul. I said no, and then he just took it." Pain twisted his features. "One minute I was telling him to get lost and the next I was hunched over. I couldn't move. I could only feel." His shook his head angrily. "My priorities shifted then. Azazel was all I could think about. I saw him in my sleep and every waking moment in between."

"That's understandable. You want revenge."

"It's not just about revenge." His gaze collided with mine. "I want my soul back. That's why I'm after Azazel. He took everything that was good from me."

As I stared into his eyes, I saw exactly what he was talking about. Rage swam in the deep, dark depths. Torment. Loneliness. And lust. I saw that too. But nothing softer.

"Is that even possible? To reclaim your soul?"

"Some of the higher-ups in the Legion think so, but no one's ever actually done it before."

"So it might not work."

He nodded. "But maybe it will." For a second, I saw a spark in his eyes. Hope? No, there was little hope left in Cutter now. More like determination. And the lust. The lust simmered and bubbled as he looked down at me. "And if it doesn't, at least he'll die for what he did. What he's done a thousand times over."

"I hope it works," I said softly.

His gaze widened as if I'd just confessed to being an alien. "You know you just violated about a zillion different demon laws by saying such a thing?"

"I know, but it's the truth."

"Demons don't tell the truth. You know that too, right?"

"What can I say? I like breaking the rules."

He stared at me for a long, silent moment, his face dark and unreadable. The air seemed to sizzle around us as the tension wrapped tight and refused to let go.

He wanted to kiss me.

And I wanted to kiss him.

And how.

Heat sizzled from the tips of my toes, working its way through my body until I felt as if I were suspended over an open flame. Erogenous zones tingled. My stomach fluttered. My lips twitched.

I knew even before he leaned down that he was going to kiss me. And as many times as I'd promised myself no more dead-end trysts, I licked my lips anyway. Realistically I knew there could never, ever be a future between us, but old habits died hard. I leaned up on my tiptoes. My eyes closed. I felt his breath on my lips and smelled the intoxicating scent of dark desire and wild intent.

Yum.

"This is the worst idea I've ever had," he murmured.

"Terrible," I breathed. And then his tongue swept my bottom lip.

Excitement thundered through me as I struggled to remember every reason why I needed to put a stop to this right now. *I* was the sexual demon. *I* controlled the situation. And that's what I fully intended to do. Just take the bull by the horns and put an end to this.

Pull away. Pull. *Away.*

But you know how when you're watching one of those B-grade horror flicks and you're screaming at the heroine *not* to go into the house? Because you know it will end in disaster? Well, just call me Jamie Lee Curtis.

I knew I needed to stop. Common sense told me to put on the brakes. Self-preservation told me to run like hell. This was so totally bad and there would be no coming back from it. No escape once I'd crossed the threshold.

But then he deepened the kiss and I opened the door and marched straight into the House of Lust. His tongue pushed inside and tangled with mine and it was like being struck by lightning. Fierce. Electric.

All rational thought faded as the hunger I'd been stashing down deep came welling up inside me like a tidal wave. Desire drenched every inch of my body.

He tasted like hot, potent male and forbidden secrets and a sweetness that drew me like the dessert tray at my favorite restaurant.

I drank him in, relishing the taste. My hands slid up his chest and my fingers caught the soft dark hair at the nape of his neck.

And surprisingly that's all I focused on for those next few minutes. Not the very detailed fantasy I'd had last night or the fact that I wanted to strip off my clothes and add some full-on rubbing to the equation. For a succubus, it wasn't so much about the journey as the destination. The orgasm. Every moment was a mad rush to get to the finish line because nothing—repeat, *nothing*—felt as good as an actual orgasm.

Except maybe this. Him.

The silky feel of his hair and the warm, strong column of his neck and the sweet, intoxicating scent of leather and male.

His arms closed around me. Strong hands pressed against the base of my spine, drawing me closer, until I felt every incredible inch of him flush against my body—the hard planes of his chest, the solid muscles of his thighs, the growing erection beneath his zipper.

Ugh. Who was the moron who invented zippers? What happened to the old days when drawstrings were king and access was merely a flick of the wrist away?

A flush spread from my cheeks, streaming south and stirring the naughty girl that lived and breathed inside me. The fierce burn traveled at the speed of sound, sweeping through and making my nipples throb. Wetness flooded between my legs, and I was so deliciously close to coming right then and there.

The truth registered and reality swept through me. I was about to explode and all because of a kiss. One measly *kiss*.

One thousand years and I'd never been that quick on the trigger.

Then again, I'd never met a man quite like Cutter.

Wait a second. Wait. Just. A. Friggin'. *Second.*

It wasn't *him*. I'd been on the wagon for two years now, so any member of the opposite sex this close, this hot, would press my buttons.

Any man.

Breathe, I told myself. Just *breathe*. "I..." I jerked away. "That is, we..." I shook my head and tried to get a grip. "This is wrong. I mean, you and I..." I shook my head again. "It can't happen." There. I'd done it. I'd put on the brakes like the controlled succubus that I was.

Had I just used *controlled* and *succubus* in the same sentence?

Before I could dwell on the thought, Cutter's gaze caught and held mine and the air stalled in my already deprived lungs. If he touched his lips to mine again or said even one of the seductive things running through my mind, I was a goner, my reclaimed virginity history.

I want you.

I need you.

Let's do it.

"You're right." His voice echoed in my head and lust pounded my senses.

I *was* right. We should just do it. Get it over with. Right now—

"This is all wrong." He stepped back, as if he needed the breathing room as much as I did.

"It is? I mean, yeah, it is. Seriously, I'm a demon and you're a slayer and, well, I'm sorta, kinda attached to my head."

"I'm not going to kill you, Jess."

Not unless he knew the truth.

But he didn't and he wouldn't because I wasn't going to let him get that close. Even if he did reclaim his soul, it didn't mean that he would stop slaying. Reclaiming his soul might make him that much more determined to annihilate all demons on behalf of the thousands of others who'd fallen victim to the dark side.

No, better to forget any foolish hope of a future with Cutter.

Rather, I was going to give him Azazel, sign up for an online dating service, find my real Mr. Right, and end my celibacy once and for all.

"I wasn't talking about you," I rushed on. "My cousin Monique will throw a fit if I don't finish these brownies." My gaze snagged on the empty bowl to my left. "For a baby shower. Tomorrow."

"I didn't mean *wrong* as in not happening." He touched the curve of my cheek with his fingertip and a shiver went through me. "I meant wrong because I've got a new recruit on standby outside your front door." Reluctantly his hand fell away. "I'd rather not have an audience when we do this."

I swallowed the sudden lump in my throat. "You mean *if* we do this."

"I mean *when*, sugar." He shook his head as if he couldn't quite believe he'd said it. "I don't know what it is. There's just something about you…" His green eyes glittered. "It's hot between us and I like it. I like it a hell of a lot."

"But doesn't that violate about a million different rules of the Legion?"

"Probably."

But it didn't matter because he wanted me.

I knew anything long-term was out of the question, but I still couldn't help entertaining the possibility of the two of us in the near future. Him. Me. Minus lots of clothing.

His lips crooked in a grin. "Besides, you're about the sorriest excuse for a demon I've ever seen."

"Thanks a lot." I scrunched up my nose. But truthfully, it was the nicest thing anyone had ever said to me.

At that moment, his cell phone beeped and he glanced at the display. "I've got to go." He returned the phone to his pocket and his gaze caught mine. "But I'm coming back. And next time, I'm not going to stop."

Promises, promises.

* * *

The baby shower was exactly what I expected. A room full of hormonal demons trying to one-up each other.

Worse, my three aunts were front and center, Aunt Bella brazenly nursing a glass of AB negative. As if I hadn't already gotten the message that she was guilty.

My sisters were there too. Tracey, Jill, and Camille. All older than me. All a million times more obnoxious. Tracey loved talking about herself. Jill loved talking about everyone else. And Camille encouraged both. Which explained why I spent my time hiding out in the kitchen, refilling the brownie platters and trying not to think about Cutter and the kiss and his parting words—darn it.

I scooped up the brownie that had fallen from my trembling fingers and tossed it at the nearest trash can.

I wasn't going to think about him. Or what he said. Or what he did. Or what I *wanted* him to do. I wasn't—

"What's taking you so long? We need more brownies," Monique called out when she ducked her head in the doorway. "Stat."

Ugh. Demanding demons.

Speaking of which, I checked my phone for the twentieth time to find yet another text from my mother asking about some wedding detail or another. Not that I was complaining. I much preferred a text to a one-on-one, particularly after the run-in with Cutter the night before. My mother had a way of noticing things... rosy cheeks and sparkling eyes and why, oh, why did he have to kiss so good?

You're deprived. You could have kissed a monkey and it would have been good.

That's what I was telling myself.

I just wasn't so sure I believed it.

I punched in a quick response about the menu—plenty of raw meat and lots of Bloody Marys (literally)—and slid the phone back into my purse. The only saving grace of the entire afternoon was that my mother had been too busy doing a remodel on a wealthy banker's condo to make the event. Instead she'd sent a six-foot basket overflowing with onesies and blankets. Pink onesies and blankets.

What can I say? My ma had never been much of an optimist.

I pushed all thoughts of Cutter from my head, or at least I tried, and finished piling the brownies.

I walked out with the mountain of chocolate goodies just as my cousin Devinah screamed, "Baby Bingo!" and waved a blue bingo card. "It's me. I win!"

I hauled butt straight to the dessert table, careful to keep a low profile and avoid making eye contact with my sisters.

"She won again?" I heard my sister Jill say as I set out the overflowing platter and picked up several empty ones. "She probably cheated. You know, I heard she cheated last year on her significant other with a third-tier demon from Down Under..."

Jill rattled on while Monique spent the next ten seconds checking Devinah's numbers to make sure she hadn't fudged before handing over a baby bottle filled with powder-blue M&M's.

"It's time to move on." Monique held up a stack of index cards and a handful of pencils, and I started for the kitchen. "Next we're going to play a guessing game."

I know what you're thinking. Guess the number of M&M's in the bottle. Guess the baby's weight. Guess the number of stretch marks. *Wrong.*

We're demons, remember? So it came as no surprise when Monique shouted, "Guess the number of limbs!"

Okay, here's the down-low on demon procreation. Spirits can't just multiply on their own. We need a human body for that. When a demon mates with a human, no problem. Human genes are dominant when it comes to physical traits, so the baby looks like any other adorable bundle of human joy. But when a possessed human—aka a demon—mates with another possessed human— aka a demon—the result is a pure demon child.

In other words, anything was possible. An eye in the middle of the forehead. A tail. A forked tongue. An overabundance of junk in the trunk.

You didn't think Kim Kardashian came by that ass on her own, did you?

"I say three," cousin Portia chimed in.

"Five."

"Nineteen."

"Great answers, people. But you have to write them down." Monique started dealing out cards and pencils. "And when you're done"—she waved an ultrasound pic—"I've got the proof right here. Everyone who guesses the right answer will go into a drawing for the big prize." She beamed. "A yearly membership to the Cheesecake of the Month club!"

I paused an inch shy of the kitchen, slid into a nearby chair, and grabbed a card and pencil.

What? We're talking *cheesecake.*

* * *

I didn't win the membership. To make matters worse, I got stuck talking with Jill and Tracey and Camille. And I'd been forced to refill Aunt Bella's glass of AB negative not once, but four times.

And we ran out of brownies. And petits fours. And cupcakes. And truffles.

The latter thanks to Cutter Owens and his seductive promise that had me so worked up, so desperate for another kiss, that I'd been hell-bent on drowning my sorrow in lots and lots of sugar.

Unfortunately, instead of forgetting Cutter, I'd found myself replaying our encounter over and over every time one of my relatives asked me when I was going to squeeze out a little demon of my own. Needless to say, I was worked up and extremely turned on by the time I pulled into the driveway of my duplex later that evening.

It was already dark out and I damned myself for again forgetting to leave a light on. I gathered my purse and the empty platters I'd used for the brownies and climbed from behind the wheel. I was just about to mount the stairs when the hair on the back of my neck prickled.

Here we go again.

I smelled the overpowering scent of Chanel No. 5 and Reese's Peanut Butter Cups, a telltale sign that there was a demon on my heels.

Awareness skittered up the back of my neck, and my hands squeezed the platters.

Because this wasn't just any demon.

No, this was the most evil, most vile demon to ever walk the face of the earth and ruin my one and only slumber party while growing up.

Yep, that's right. We're talking my oldest sister, Camille.

18

"Camille," I said as I turned. "What a nice surprise." *Not.*

Camille Damon looked like a life-size Barbie. She was taller than me, her blonde hair longer and silkier, her boobs bigger, her waist smaller, her smile brighter. *Perfect.*

And, of course, she had well-manicured nails to go with the rest of her perfection.

I balled my chewed nubs—shorter than ever thanks to my escalated anxiety level—and tried for a smile. "What brings you here?"

"I never got a chance to talk to you at the shower." She pointed an accusing finger at me. "You snuck out right in the middle of the gifts."

We'd run out of brownies and I'd wanted to miss the inevitable World War Three when everyone found out. That and I'd been really desperate for a candy bar. "I had a work emergency. I've got a vow renewal this weekend."

"And here I thought you ran out early to miss the catfight when Charlotte and Hes threw down over the last brownie."

Big Brother had nothing on Big Sister.

"They ran out of brownies? Why, I thought we had plenty. So, um, what is it that you need?"

"I wanted to know if you want to go in on the group gift for Mother. Everyone knows how much she loves Mexico, so Tracey, Jill, and I thought we'd give her a mariachi band for the wedding."

"But I've already booked the music." I'd gone with the gloomy organ despite my instincts, which screamed for a harpist. *Dark and sinister,* I reminded myself. *Otherwise your mom is going to be pissed.*

"No, silly, we're not hiring them to perform, we're *giving* her a mariachi band." She held up a blue bound contract with several signatures in vivid red. "Five souls. Signed, sealed, and delivered. So should I add your name to the card?"

"I'm actually already getting her something for the reception. I do it for all my brides. But thanks for asking."

"Have it your way." She shrugged. "But don't get all sulky when she likes our gift better."

I thought of the ice sculpture that I'd had Agarth make for last week's couple and the fierce heat in my ma's eyes whenever she got really mad. "On second thought, I'm in." I was this close to eternal damnation as it was. I needed all the help I could get.

Help with a capital H, I realized when Burke called an hour later while I was trying to relax despite Snooki and her barking.

"Promise you won't freak," he said the minute I picked up the phone.

This was so *not* good.

"I won't freak."

"Yes, you will. You'll freak sideways when you hear this."

"Then why are you making me promise?"

"Because I can't just blurt it out without warning you first."

"Just get it out."

"Maybe you should mix up a margarita first."

"I don't need a margarita." I had Oreos. 'Nuff said.

"What about a piña colada?"

"*Tell*," I growled around a mouthful of cookie.

He paused as if trying to find the words, and then the dam broke and everything spilled over in a mad rush of frantic syllables. "The cooler went out at the florist and we lost the two hundred violets for Saturday's reception, not to mention the centerpieces for the rehearsal dinner tomorrow night and the bridesmaids' bouquets and the bridal bouquet and—"

"Maybe a margarita wasn't such a bad idea."

"Told you so." He paused to take a breath. "This is bad, isn't it? Sort of like the first hit of the *Titanic*. It was all downhill from there."

"This is not the *Titanic*. That was a lost cause. We can fix this." While my ma wasn't much in the optimism department, I kept coming back for more. "Maybe we'll find a florist with two hundred violets sitting in a cooler somewhere and it'll turn into the best three days of our lives."

"And Brad Pitt just knocked at my door. This is a disaster," he moaned.

"Calm down. We can work it out if we stay calm, cool, and collected."

"This sucks. My life sucks. I ate four doughnuts."

"There, there. It's not the end of the world. Just go an extra hour on the treadmill."

"That was four doughnuts earlier before I got the news. I've had three more since."

I made a mental note to make sure Burke wasn't possessed by one of my fellow brethren. "So you do three or four hours on the treadmill. Or take a few extra spinning classes."

"I should have seen this coming," he wailed. "I knew when I opened that fortune cookie at lunch today that something was going to go wrong. I had the noodles, and Martin—he's this cutie that lives in my apartment building—had the fried rice. His fortune was fabulous, but mine said that hard times were ahead. What kind of fortune cookie predicts hard times?"

"Eat another doughnut and call me in the morning."

"You think that will help?"

"It can't hurt." Besides, I needed to get off the phone in the worst way. I killed the connection. I'd had enough pessimism for one night. I'd dealt with wedding calamities before and I could deal with this one.

Holding tight to the positive reinforcement, I prayed for a big hole to swallow Snooki, who barked madly from the next room.

"You're just lucky I haven't had time to take you to the shelter," I told her when I saw her prancing behind the doggie door that separated the bathroom from my bedroom. "Just as soon as things calm down, you're history."

But with the next three days not looking so good and my mom's wedding right on its heels, I had the uneasy feeling that I was the one who was going to be history. My career over. My dream of a happily-ever-after gone in a puff of smoke.

And my dream of kissing Cutter again?

Well, that wasn't a dream so much as a fantasy that haunted me the rest of the night as I tossed and turned and tried to forget the intense attraction between us and the fact that I liked his smile and the sound of his voice almost as much as his magical lips.

Uh-oh.

* * *

Thanks to a faulty cooler (the flowers), a severe thunderstorm (the venue), and two teens fighting over a paintball gun (the dress), the next few days passed in a frantic blur.

A bad omen of the week to come and proof that my aunties were hard at work, trying to ruin my life and, ultimately, my ma's big day.

That, or payback for running out of brownies.

Sure, I managed to work it all out. I found a substitute florist, took the garden nuptials inside the reception ballroom, and talked a local designer into loaning a couture gown to replace the ruined one (and I even talked my cousin Hester into zapping the teens with a bad case of jock itch).

All in all, there was still a happy ending. Even more, the bride and groom loved the lemon tree that I had planted in their honor (my special gift since they were eco fanatics) at Buffalo Bayou Park.

So why didn't I feel the usual sense of relief and delight that came once the last bag of birdseed had been thrown? Instead, I walked into my apartment late Saturday night feeling uneasy. Nervous. Freaked.

Even a leftover piece of groom's cake and the latest episode of *Say Yes to the Dress* did little to calm me down. By the time I climbed into bed, I still felt like crying.

And killing Snooki.

Seriously, my nerves were shot and I really needed her to lose the attitude.

Just for a little while.

My gaze swiveled to where she stood behind her doggie gate. Her shrill barking filled the air and grated across my nerves.

"I can't deal with this tonight. Give it a rest, otherwise I'm going to duct-tape your mouth shut." She barked again and I narrowed my gaze. "I'll do it. I will."

Okay, so I wouldn't, which she quickly figured out after several more barks. What? She looked a little freaked herself, running back and forth behind the doggie gate. As if she expected the big bad boogeyman to jump out at any moment and she needed to be on her guard.

I knew the feeling.

I glanced at the line of demon-busting powder surrounding my bed. A little extreme, but I was sick of being caught off guard.

The barking continued and I tried stuffing my head under the pillow. When that didn't work, I climbed out of bed, determined to do a little bodily harm.

I was just about to choke her (really), or at least shut the bathroom door, when she whimpered and licked my fingers. Okay, so it couldn't hurt to pick her up and sit her at the foot of the bed.

So she can keep you up all night?

She was doing that anyway.

Besides, I really didn't think I was going to manage any sleep. Not after the past few days of chaos, not to mention the knock-down, drag-out with the chocolate-chip spiders and the startling and surprising kiss with Cutter. And the promise.

But I'm coming back.

As excited as the notion made me, it was also equally depressing, because he never would have said such a thing if he knew my true identity. And wasn't that the point of searching for The One in the first place? To find someone who would love the real me?

The questions pushed and pulled, making me even more stressed than usual.

On top of that, I was starting to feel a little bad about keeping Snooks cooped up in the bathroom all day. The last thing I needed was animal control knocking on my door.

I ignored the tiny voice that reminded me that would be a good thing. I wanted her gone, didn't I?

Damn straight. She was noisy. Annoying.

And soft, I admitted when I scooped her up and climbed back into bed, holding her close. I snuggled closer and surprisingly enough, she stopped growling after a few minutes and settled down against me.

When I closed my eyes, I had the fleeting thought that maybe all the yapping wasn't because she was prewired to hate my demon guts.

Maybe there were exceptions to every rule. The biggest, baddest demon hunter in the Legion had kissed me. *Me.* Satan's own. Sure, he didn't know I was the daughter of Hell's numero uno, but that was just a minor detail. The point was, he'd still done it, which meant that maybe all the rules weren't written in stone. Demons and dogs didn't have to be enemies, just as demon hunters and demons didn't have to be on opposite sides of the fence.

We could get along.

Be friends.

Fall in love.

Yeah, I knew it was a stretch, but I was tired and desperate, so I latched onto the small thread of hope and fell into a restless sleep.

I quickly came to my senses the next morning, however, when I woke to find Snooki chewing a hole through my favorite pillow.

"You are so going to the nearest shelter," I told her.

She growled.

I glared.

And just like that, my small thread of hope faded in the overwhelming realization that I had exactly six days to pull off the wedding of my career.

The countdown had officially started and I still had a million and one things to do.

"Hell, here I come."

19

If I hadn't already had the heebie-jeebies about the coming week, Sunday would have stirred every apprehensive bone in my body. It was a day straight out of a *Twilight Zone* episode.

It started out with a phone call from Cheryl telling me that she had the guest list ready for Thursday night's bachelorette party. Yeah, I know. My mom and my aunties and my sisters and the cousins all in one room. Together. In just four short days.

Oh, joy.

As if that wasn't doom and gloom enough, I headed over to Bliss, Bling & Otherworldly Things for more demon-busting powder, only to find that they were out. Apparently with my mom's big event just days away, there was an overwhelming amount of demon activity in Houston and the stuff had been flying off the shelves.

"I just sold my last case," Sassy told me, "but I've got some antivampire deodorant on sale if you're interested. Spring meadow or baby powder scent?"

"I'll pass."

"Werewolf flea powder at a ten-percent discount?"

I opened my mouth to decline when a thought struck. "Does it work on Yorkies?"

"Sure, but don't use too much, otherwise you might have a big problem on your hands." When I flashed a questioning look, she added, "The stuff has growth hormones. It's deadly to fleas, but I'm afraid your Yorkie might end up a Great Dane."

"Just put me on the waiting list for the demon-busting powder."

"Will do. You sure I can't interest you in something else?"

Anxiety rolled through me and my stomach jumped. I desperately needed something to ease my nerves, and there was only one thing powerful enough to do that. My gaze shifted to a new Vera Bradley hipster purse hanging on a nearby wall. *Come to Mama!*

I forked over my credit card for the purse and left my name and number on Sassy's waiting list. Then I hightailed it to a nearby restaurant (demon doth not live by cookie alone) for omen number three—Blythe, who showed up for our lunch date with Agarth in tow.

"It's not like I could just up and leave," she told me when I hauled her behind a nearby potted plant under the pretense of going to the ladies' room, "not with him sitting on my couch."

"And why, pray tell, was he sitting on your couch?"

"Actually, he was sleeping. What?" she asked when I arched an eyebrow. "We had a late night. I couldn't let him drive home at four in the morning. You know what kind of crazies are out at four in the morning?"

Talk about preaching to the choir. "I thought you weren't going out with him again?"

"He bought Maroon 5 tickets for my birthday."

"Your birthday isn't for another three months."

"It was an early present." Another eyebrow arch and she shrugged. "You know I love Maroon 5. I couldn't let them go to waste. Besides, Agarth really behaved himself at the Coldplay concert so I thought, why not? It's not like I actually *like* him. Seriously"—she motioned toward where Agarth was sitting several tables away—"what's to like?"

My head pivoted in time to see him swipe a platter of hot wings off a passing waiter's tray. He popped one into his mouth, bones and all, chewed, and swallowed.

"I rest my case," she murmured before heading back to the table.

I followed and slid into my seat just as Agarth gulped down another hot wing. "So, um, Agarth, I was hoping to talk to you about doing another sculpture for me."

He paused, buffalo sauce on his lips, another chicken wing in his hand. "Is Blythe part of the bargain?"

"I'm afraid not—"

"I'll do it," Blythe cut in.

I slid her a sideways glance. "Do what?"

"You know." She shrugged. "Whatever you need me to do. One more date. Three more dates. Whatever it takes for Agarth to cooperate."

"What might ye be in need of?" Agarth waved a knife at me. "Another ice lion? Or maybe a dragon? A two-headed serpent?"

"Not exactly. See, I was thinking…" I spent the next fifteen minutes giving Agarth my vision for my mom's special wedding surprise. Not that it fit with the dark and sinister she was going for, but it was as close as my conscience would allow. I gave something special to all of my brides, and Satan's own would be no exception.

After bargaining a half dozen Blythe dates for Agarth's agreement, I spent the next hour stuffing my face with not one, but two desserts—after a grilled chicken salad, of course. Then I headed back to my apartment to order place cards for the reception.

To go with the Day of the Dead theme playing in the back of my head, I wanted to use miniature hand-painted skulls for place cards, which meant I had to find (a) six hundred miniature skulls, and (b) an artist to paint them.

Frustration clenched my hands, but I flexed my fingers and took a deep breath. How hard could it be? One could find anything on the Internet.

Except six hundred miniature skulls.

I figured that out five hours later, after a full afternoon spent looking at every website that even mentioned the word *skull*, including a voodoo headshrinker at www.itsybitsyheads.com who promised the real thing.

And the problem was?

My mom wanted dark and sinister and frightening. *Voilà.* But I couldn't silence the voice that kept telling me I was violating my principles. This was a wedding. A happy occasion, or it should be.

Which meant I was going to find ceramic skulls rather than the real deal if it killed me.

"I can't make it tonight," I told Circle of Love president Sherrie when six thirty rolled around and I was still shit out of luck.

"But Sherman Meister cheated on his wife a few nights ago with the fry girl at the McDonald's and I was counting on your red velvet cupcakes to calm everyone down after they listen to the details. You know how worked up we can get."

Boy, did I ever.

I had a quick vision of my own fall from grace last week with Cutter and the kiss and...whew, was it hot in here or was it just me?

I drew a deep breath and tried to find my suddenly scratchy voice. "I'm so sorry. I had two dozen ready to go, but I just can't give up the extra few hours. I've got a big wedding this weekend."

"What about fifteen minutes? Surely you can spare fifteen minutes to drop them off."

"I could do that." If I hadn't already eaten some of them, that is. The rest I was saving for tonight. "I could definitely do that, except I don't actually have them. See, I left them sitting on the counter and Snooki got into them. Not that she ate them, because chocolate is really bad for dogs, but she made a huge mess and now I have to clean it up and, well, I *really* need to go." *Click.*

I stifled a pang of guilt and made a mental promise to bake a full four dozen for the next meeting so everyone could have extra.

In the meantime, I grabbed another cupcake and plowed back into my mad search for skulls. I had a feeling it was going to be a long night.

* * *

"She's going through with it," Gio told me when he popped in later that night.

Literally, since Sassy had yet to call with the new batch of demon powder.

"I still can't believe it."

"Who? What? When? Where?" The questions poured out of my mouth as I tried to shift off my internal wedding planner and switch on loyal friend with zero benefits, because I wasn't sleeping with Gio no matter how good he looked in black leather chaps, biker boots, and a tight black tee.

Sure, he wore it well. But not quite as well as a certain demon slayer.

I'm coming back. And next time, I'm not going to stop.

Yeah, right.

I hadn't seen him in the four days since. Not even his black Land Rover.

Instead, I was playing cat and mouse with the Legion's newest rookie in the now familiar beat-up Datsun parked a few houses down.

"…said they were eloping."

"That's great."

"Are you shitting me? She can't elope."

"Of course she can't. Why, that's the worst idea I've ever heard. It's a disaster. Isn't it?"

"Damn straight. She can't go running off with that guy. He's all wrong for her."

"Completely wrong." I swallowed. "Um, who exactly are we talking about?"

He stared at me as if I'd just confessed to being celibate (which I totally was, but I wasn't about to blurt it out). "Syra. The Italian princess that I've been on assignment with for the past three months?" He shook his head, and I didn't miss the pain that flashed in his expression. "She doesn't even love the guy and he sure as hell doesn't love her. He couldn't. They've spent all of ten hours together making public appearances. Forget sex, or even kissing, for that matter. He doesn't even know who she really is. I bet he can't name her favorite color, which is fuchsia, by the way, or that she likes her eggs poached in the morning or that she's ticklish behind her left ear."

But Gio knew. He knew it all.

Because he loved her.

The realization hit as I watched him pace the floor and completely ignore the six remaining cupcakes sitting on my coffee table. Cupcakes weren't going to ease the anxiety eating him up from the inside out. He was head over heels and he didn't even know it.

"Have you told her you've fallen in love with her?"

"Hell, no." He shook his head. "I don't love her. I just think she's making a mistake marrying someone she hardly knows. It's a recipe for disaster."

"And you care because...?"

He shrugged. "She's a good person. She's really smart. And sweet. She works with disadvantaged children every Saturday and she goes to see her grandmother every Sunday. She's loyal and the kids love her like crazy." The minute he said the words, he came to a dead stop. Every muscle in his body went deathly still and I knew he'd come to a very important conclusion. "I love her like crazy too." Sheer desperation creased his face. "I *love* her and she's eloping with that asshole. What the fuck am I going to do?"

Love? Gio loved Syra?

Sure, I'd suspected. Actually, I'd hoped. I mean, here I was searching for my own true love. It only stood to reason I'd want one of my brethren to find the big L, if for nothing else than to prove that it existed for someone like me. But the real deal? "Are you sure? Maybe you're just feeling jealous."

"I'm feeling that too."

"That's it, then. You're superjealous and you're mistaking it for love."

"I love her, Jess. I know it sounds crazy, but that's how I feel."

"Did you tell her that?"

"No." He shook his head frantically. "I couldn't."

"Yes, you can. You just put on your big-boy underwear and tell her."

"I really can't." His gaze locked with mine. "She told me she never wanted to see me again."

"And why would she tell you that?"

"Because I sort of told her how stupid she was for marrying such a womanizing idiot."

"You didn't?"

He nodded. "Right after I forbade her from marrying said womanizing idiot."

"You *didn't*."

He nodded. "I told her she couldn't marry him, that I wouldn't allow it, and she told me that I had no right to tell her what to do, and I told her that someone needed to because she obviously couldn't make good choices for herself, and then she said she never wanted to see me again, and I said fine because I never wanted to see her again. But I didn't mean it. I was angry." He shook his head. "I really screwed up, didn't I?"

"In a major way, which is exactly what you're going to tell her."

"Don't you understand? She doesn't want to see me, Jess. She hates me." He collapsed onto my sofa. "I was just trying to protect her." He put his head in his hands. "I'm such a jerk."

"No, you're not. You're a man. And men sometimes say things they don't mean."

Like Cutter and his *I'm coming back. And next time, I'm not going to stop.*

The heat of the moment. That's what it had been. He'd been worked up. I'd been worked up. And so he'd made a promise he never intended to keep.

"Jess?"

"Um, yeah."

"Yeah, I can stay here?" His face lit up before I could open my mouth. "I knew you wouldn't let me down. You're the best!"

"You want to stay here? For the night?"

"Actually, it's more like a few days. I need to get my head together. It's either here or a hotel, and I really don't want to be alone right now."

Translation? *I need a little mattress dancing to help me forget.*

"Gio, we really need to talk—"

"Can I take a rain check?" He ran a hand over his face and stifled a yawn. "All of this emotional stuff has me really wiped out." He reached for the hem of his tee and pulled the shirt over his head. "I'm ready to crash." He stretched out and crooked an arm under his head.

"You're going to sleep here?" Disbelief fueled my voice. "On my sofa?"

"Look, Jess, don't take this personally, but I really love Syra. I know you and I go way back, but it just can't happen between us."

A grin tickled my lips as I watched him snuggle down into the sofa pillow. "You just might be in love, after all."

2 0

After a sleepless night (half spent listening to Gio cry—so loudly he'd drowned out Snooki's barking—and the other half listening to him roar—I mean snore), I barely dragged myself into the office by nine.

Andrew was already halfway through a latte, while Burke was on the phone with Delaney, who wanted to change her signature cocktail from a chic Cosmo to a banana daiquiri.

"Don't tell me." I held up a hand as he slid the phone into its cradle. "She's through with the sexy urban theme."

Burke shrugged. "She saw a come-to-Jamaica commercial and she thinks fun and tropical is a better fit for her personality."

I thought about the enormous amount of time and energy that had already been wasted and the mountain of work that still waited should she switch themes yet again.

"I think I'm going to be sick," I murmured as I sank down at my desk and reached for the Life Savers in my drawer.

"Well, I have something that will cheer you right up." Andrew set a large brown envelope in front of me and beamed. "Couriered over from the publisher first thing this morning."

I opened the clasp and slid the contents from inside. My gaze riveted on the glossy cover of the upcoming issue of *Texas Brides*, complete with my picture and a caption that read *Meet the wedding genius behind Houston's wildly successful Happily Ever After Events.*

"The editor wanted you to see it first," Andrew said, "before it hits the stands next week."

Dread churned in my stomach.

I'd been so frantic that I'd actually forgotten about the magazine article touting me as the fastest-rising star in Houston's wedding biz. And the cover shot of me surrounded by stacked wedding cakes. Proof beyond a doubt that I'd gone legit.

But it was real. And it was hitting the stands in just eight short days for all the world—and the Underworld—to see.

"Now I know I'm going to be sick." The cherry candy suddenly felt strange on my tongue. My hands shook. My stomach hollowed out.

"I know what you mean." Burke waved a hand. "They should have put you in green instead of that awful pastel. Everyone knows redheads can't wear pink."

My fright level shot to DEFCON 1 and I hyperventilated for the next few moments while Burke raced around searching for a paper bag.

"Try this." He shoved a handful of plastic at me.

I stared at the Ziploc baggie. "I don't think this will work."

"Well, it's the best I could find. I dumped my carrots out so you could at least try."

I nixed the baggie and focused on not freaking out. What the hell was I doing? Even if I managed to pull off Mom's wedding and help Cutter reclaim his soul, there was no way I was getting away with *this*. My mother would see it, the ruse would be over, and my chance at my own happily-ever-after would be lost.

Dead.

Because I'd be dead.

I ripped open the Ziploc and shoved the baggie over my nose and mouth.

In. Out. In. Out.

Easy. Calm. Breathe.

The room started to spin, and I spent the next fifteen minutes in the bathroom wishing with all of my heart that I had skipped the three doughnuts I'd scarfed earlier that morning.

My mother was going to kill me when she saw the magazine. *If she saw the magazine.*

As it was, she was scheduled to cruise the Caribbean next week for her honeymoon, which meant there was a slim chance she would miss the issue. Unless I failed miserably, the wedding was called off, and she stayed in Houston.

All the more reason I couldn't fail. I wouldn't fail. I was Houston's hottest up-and-coming wedding planner and it was high time I started acting like it. Forget all the anxiety and worry. I was taking control. Starting right now.

I walked back into the workroom. "You." I pointed at Burke. "Call Delaney and tell her to meet me in a half hour at the bridal salon. And you"—my gaze shifted to Andrew as I snatched up the magazine and shoved it at him—"burn this."

I might be going down with a sinking ship, but I intended to tread water for as long as possible. Some things I couldn't control— hurricanes, my favorite candidate getting voted off *The X Factor*, my mom killing me when she saw the magazine article. But Delaney Farris and her indecisiveness?

That I could fix. I could reason with her.

And if that didn't work?

Head spin, here I come.

* * *

I didn't have to resort to a three-sixty. Not that Delaney capitulated on the Jamaican theme, but she did cry. And scream. And kick.

My shin still ached by the time I got back to the office a few hours later and called the florist.

"I need to order five hundred birds-of-paradise."

"No problem. When's the event?"

"Two weeks."

Laughter rumbled over the line and I blinked against the burning behind my eyes.

Okay, so Delaney wasn't the one who'd cried. Rather, she'd done the kicking and screaming and yours truly had turned on the waterworks.

I fought back another wave of tears and stiffened. The one thing about crying? It made me feel better. Stronger. Determined. And less likely to slit my wrists.

I wasn't going to accept defeat, no matter how bleak the future seemed. I was going to give Delaney the wedding of her Jamaican dreams.

But first, I was going to pull off an even more hellacious wedding and help a certain demon hunter reclaim his soul. And I was going to do it without having a bona fide meltdown first.

"I'll pay extra," I told the florist. "Double."

"How about triple and the extra shipping to get everything here in time?"

"Done. Now tell me what you can do about supplying two thousand roses for Saturday."

"It's no problem getting the flowers. It's storing them that's impossible. My cooler is already full for a wedding I'm doing Saturday morning. The only extra space I have is my back storage room and I'm afraid it's not air-conditioned. In this hot temperature, they'll be shriveled and half dead in less than a few hours."

"Perfect. I'll take them."

* * *

The rest of Monday went a little smoother. After securing the roses (and a few hundred other variously colored flowers to feed into my Day of the Dead theme), I managed to find my ceramic skulls and a local artist to do the hand painting. I also secured a photographer that Sassy turned me on to when I called her about the demon powder. No, she hadn't gotten a shipment in, but she did know a guy/werewolf who worked construction by day and moonlighted as a paranormal paparazzo by night. For an indecent amount of money, he agreed to cover the wedding and not get all fanged and furry if some drunk demon made doggie noises.

While I had a few misgivings about having a werewolf in attendance—demons and werewolves didn't exactly get along—I had to swallow my trepidation and hope for the best.

Then again, demons didn't get along with any paranormal entity. Rather, they tended to be outrageously snobbish. Which wouldn't have been so bad except every other supe out there (vamps, werewolves, shifters, etc.) tended to be outrageously snobbish too. Bottom line, supernaturals kept to their own kind.

At the same time, just because of the segregationist mentality of my demon brethren, I couldn't very well have a human photographer at my mom's event. That would be like leading a lamb to slaughter. Talk about bad mojo.

Bottom line, werewolf or not, I had a photographer who wouldn't be mistaken as an appetizer. I also had a caterer. Luckily my one and only demon food service connection was a sixth-tier demon who hadn't made the guest list. Needless to say, she was itching to rub shoulders with the demon elite. She all but jumped at the chance to cater the event.

"It'll be my pleasure," said Edna of Edna's Edibles. "I can't wait for Lillith to try my marinated brains. I use a habanero sauce that's to die for."

First off, ew. "Sounds yummy. Listen, just make sure you have enough to accommodate everyone. Running out of food would be a disaster of biblical proportions."

"You can count on me," Edna said. "I've got it covered."

Caterer? *Check.*

I breathed a sigh of relief as evening rolled around and I'd managed to knock out over half my Momzilla list and most of Delaney's last-minute changes, including trading in the harpist for a bongo drummer.

I was actually feeling optimistic as I closed up shop and headed upstairs.

Until I caught a glimpse of the Datsun sitting across the street and the young man perched behind the wheel. He looked to be in his early twenties, with blond hair and a clean-shaven face. He dropped the binoculars when he saw me and sank down into his seat.

The kid might have joined up with the baddest slayers in the world, but he was still terrified of a big, bad demon like yours truly. A fact that would have bothered me if I wasn't so busy wondering about Cutter's whereabouts. Or fretting over the fact that he hadn't so much as called. Or texted. Or—*hell*, no.

I was through wasting another second angsting over Cutter. If he'd changed his mind about me, I wanted the truth.

Stepping forward, I crossed the street and approached the young rookie.

He scrambled upright in his seat just as I reached the car. The locks clicked down. "W-what do you think you're doing?"

"My question exactly." I nailed him with a glare. "What do *you* think *you're* doing parked out here in front of my house?"

"I'm just killing some time, w-waiting for my girlfriend and—"

"Bullshit. You're watching me."

He tried to fake a get-outta-here smile. "That's crazy—"

"You're a member of the Legion and you're watching me." He started to protest, and I held up a hand. "What's your name?"

"Smith."

Yeah, right. "Listen up, *Smith*. I know you're part of the Legion and I know you're here for me. What I don't know is why it's you and not Cutter. Where is he?"

He didn't look as if he wanted to answer, but then I stared deep into his eyes and summoned every ounce of demon mojo buried down deep. "Please." I tried for my sexiest, sultriest voice *ever*. I don't know if it was lack of practice or the sheer amount of stress I'd been experiencing, but it came out more as a sad, desperate cry. *"Please."*

He looked uncomfortable, as if afraid I might burst into tears. And where lust failed, good old-fashioned female hormones saved the day.

"Cutter needed to go off the grid for a little while," poured out of his mouth. "He asked me to keep an eye on you and report directly back to him." His voice lowered a notch. "There's a lot of demon activity going on right now. Something big is brewing."

Tell me about it. Satan herself was tying the knot. It didn't get bigger. Or more strange.

"So you've talked to him recently?"

He nodded. "An hour ago. He checked in to make sure you were home safe."

Warmth rushed through me, momentarily easing the coldness that sat in the pit of my stomach.

"Do you want me to get him a message?"

I thought of a half dozen things to say.

I like you.

I want you.

I need you.

Call me, already!

I shook my head. "Tell him I can take care of myself." Then I turned on my heel and headed back across the street to my apartment.

Inside, Gio was sprawled on the sofa, a massive pizza box open on the coffee table in front of him. He picked up a slice dripping with cheese and swallowed half of it in one bite before tearing off a piece of the crust and feeding it to Snooki, who cuddled next to him.

Cuddled. No, really.

The animal lapped at the treat and wagged her tail excitedly, oblivious to the fact that Gio was a vicious, forked-tongue demon himself.

"She likes you," I said accusingly.

"It's called bribery," he murmured as he fed her a slice of pepperoni. "It works every time."

"She really shouldn't eat junk food." I headed for the sofa. "It'll give her a tummy ache. Traitor," I murmured as I snatched her up and deposited her behind her doggie fence.

She barked at me as if to say, "You'd be a traitor too for an extralarge pepperoni with cheese," before pivoting and heading for her water bowl.

"Want some?" Gio held up a slice.

"I'd rather have a cupcake." I started for the kitchen, but he stopped me.

"I, um, sort of ate them all."

I arched an eyebrow. "My Twinkies?"

"Gone."

"Snickers bars?"

"History."

I eyed him, noting the circles under his eyes and the tired expression on his face. "Why don't you call her?"

"I tried. She won't talk to me. She said to take a flying leap."

"And instead you headed for the kitchen?"

He shrugged. "What was I supposed to do? I'm desperate."

I knew the feeling.

Cutter was MIA, and while I was trying to stay superpissed because he'd up and disappeared without so much as a text, I actually *missed* him. My hunger stirred and my optimism took a nosedive.

An entire evening without sugar?

To heck with that. I snatched up my car keys and motioned to Gio. "Walmart, here we come."

21

"I still don't understand why you want us both to go to the bridal expo."

"Because we work with brides."

"In Houston," Burke pointed out. "Why are you sending us all the way to Boston?"

Because it was the only wedding extravaganza taking place this weekend, with the exception of the Beaverville Bridal Bash in Beaverville, Alaska. Um, yeah. Not that I had anything against Alaska. But the bash was a Saturday-only event and I needed my faithful assistants out of my hair and far, *far* away from the demonic wedding about to take place this weekend. The Boston expo ran Thursday through Sunday, which made it the perfect distraction.

"Boston?" Burke prodded again. "Really?"

"Boston is the new New York when it comes to designer bridal couture." My mind raced for a convincing argument. "*Modern Bride* did a big write-up about how Boston is a virtual hotbed of wedding trends."

"Which issue?" Andrew cut a glance at me. "I've read every issue cover to cover and I don't remember any such article."

"I think it was an online exclusive." I waved a hand, dismissing the subject, before he could ask any more questions. "Come on, we're rising stars in the wedding biz. We need to be front and center. Since I can't go, I need the next best thing. You guys. My right hand and my left hand. The geniuses behind Happily Ever After Events." Andrew blushed and Burke flexed. "I need you guys," I added, heaping on a steaming side of guilt. "Happily Ever After needs you."

"We are good at what we do," Andrew added before lapsing into a pout. "But why do we have to leave today?"

Because it was already Tuesday and things were getting stranger by the second. Case in point, the wedding gifts that had started to arrive earlier that morning.

My gaze shifted to the far corner, where several gifts were already piled high. My attention snagged on one in particular, wrapped in shiny white paper with a huge silver bow. The package rattled ever so slightly. A low moan vibrated from inside and I made a big pretense of clearing my throat to mask the sound.

Where was a yapping Snooki when you really needed her?

"You're both such wonderful assistants that I want you to have some time to relax and sightsee while you're there. Do some shopping. Have a spa day. Kick your feet up." I beamed. "You both deserve it."

"We have been working hard," Andrew pointed out. "I've been so busy I can't even remember my last pedicure."

I nodded frantically. "Pedicures are *so* important."

"What about Momzilla?" Burke persisted. "Who's going to help you pull off her wedding? We've only got four days."

"The details are all taken care of and I've got the entire staff at the Bell Tower for everything on-site the day of. Why, I won't even be working. I'll just be overseeing things."

"But I really wanted to see how proud Momzilla is going to be when you give her a superspectacular wedding—" Andrew's words stalled as he glanced around. "What's that noise?"

"Me," I blurted, clearing my throat again as I fumbled for my iPod dock. I hit the on button and Rihanna wailed through the speakers, drowning out the otherworldly wailing coming from the gift corner. "Don't worry about missing anything. I'll get you a copy of the wedding DVD. Now, here's your itinerary and hotel info. Your flight leaves in three hours from Hobby Airport."

* * *

Once Andrew and Burke had left to go pack, I pulled out my cell, gathered my courage, and called my mother.

After three hours, twenty-eight minutes, and four seconds spent with my family at the baby shower last Thursday, I was desperate to avoid the bridesmaids' luncheon—the next detail on my Momzilla list—at all costs.

"I know you're busy," I told my mother when she finally picked up, "especially now that you're trying to fit all of this wedding stuff into your schedule. So I was thinking, why clutter up your schedule with one of those stuffy bridesmaids' luncheons? Besides, a bridesmaids' luncheon is all about you fussing over the wedding party. A time to say thank you. To pamper *them*, so I thought we could just lose that and keep things focused on you."

"I see your point. We *should* keep things focused on me."

"Exactly. We can easily hand out thank-you gifts at the rehearsal dinner. Speaking of which, do you have something in mind or would you like me to help pick something?"

"Samael and I took an engagement picture. I had Cheryl order extra prints for my sisters. That way they will have a constant reminder that I married first."

"I was thinking jewelry or perfume, but that could work too."

As a dartboard, at the very least, if my aunties weren't feeling the whole memento vibe.

"About the rehearsal dinner," my mother went on. "I need details so I can text them to your grandfather. Not that he's going to make it. He's finishing up a tournament on Friday and I doubt he'll be done in time. But I still want him aware of every step of the process."

"I've booked a restaurant near the Galleria area."

"Houston's? They're my favorite."

"Jimmy J's. They were the only steak house that would let me bring in a private chef," I added when a tense silence filled my ear.

"I guess it'll do," she finally said. "It's not like it really matters anyway. It's the ceremony that's most important."

I tamped down a wave of *oh, no* and summoned my most optimistic voice. "I booked Chef Lorenzo DeMarco." I played my only good hand. "You love his tonsil tartare."

She grunted what sounded like *whatever* and a wave of anxiety went through me. If I couldn't amp up her excitement with Chef Lorenzo (to whom I'd had to promise an arm and a leg—not my own, but those of some poor schmuck Lorenzo had chosen to be the star of Friday night's menu), no way would she be wowed by the other wedding details. Especially since they weren't nearly as dark and creepy as she'd requested.

"You know, it's not just about the ceremony. It's about all the little steps leading up to the main event," I said, trying to pump up her lack of enthusiasm. "You're actually getting *married*."

"True," she said after a long moment. "I *am* getting married. Even more, I'm this close to ruling the world."

"That too."

"I should be counting down the minutes."

"I was thinking you should slow down and enjoy the moment."

"Are you insane? I've been waiting for this my entire existence and it can't come a second too soon. Just make sure everything is in place for a really good show."

That's all this was to her. A show. A chance to one-up everyone and thumb her nose at her sisters.

The notion went against everything I believed in. My mother was making a mockery of the sacred institution of marriage, and I was smack-dab in the middle of it.

And there wasn't anything I could do except see it through.

Or quit.

The possibility played in my head all of five seconds before I dismissed it. However much I wanted to bail—and not because of the blood warnings and the invisible nooses and the spidery chocolate chips, though those made for a good argument—I couldn't. Despite our differences—despite her indifference—I didn't want to let my mother down. Not just because I was afraid of her. For the first time, she'd asked me to step up, to do something for her, and I was determined not to fail.

"It's going to be a great wedding," I promised her. "The biggest and the baddest ever."

Now all I had to do was follow through and I'd be home free.

At least for a little while.

Until she saw the magazine and sent me spiraling back down to Hell.

I ignored the depressing thought, held tight to my fast-waning optimism, and focused on the next item on my list.

The bachelorette party.

Aka the bridal party (my aunties) and the bride (my ma) all in one room at the same time.

I pictured several possible scenarios even worse than the burned-out bridal salon and the singed dressmaker, and the optimism vanished.

On second thought, maybe quitting wasn't such a bad idea.

22

"Tell me again why I have to be here?" Blythe demanded on Thursday night as we stood in the doorway of the Ab Factory, Houston's version of Chippendales.

While I was killing myself trying to plan a wedding befitting the princess of darkness herself (complete with a bat release when the happy couple officially said *I do*), the bachelorette party was a different story. Sure, I was terrified of having the aunties together after the fiasco picking out the bridesmaids' dresses, but the actual party details were a no-brainer.

My mother was no different from any other bride in that she wanted a chance to cut loose, lust after a few hot male bodies, and store up enough memories to last her entire married existence. Hence the male strippers and overpriced drinks.

"You're here because you're my BFF and I desperately need moral support right now," I told Blythe.

She glanced at the clipboard I handed her. "I can do moral support without a pen and paper."

"All right, so I desperately need an extra set of hands. And eyes. And ears. Mother had me invite every female relative in our family." Including a few third cousins and my cousin Renee, who had four arms. "I need an extra sober person to help keep track of everyone on the list and prevent any disasters."

"Like your aunt Bella and your aunt Levita fighting over who gets to eat the Candy Man?"

"No one gets to eat the Candy Man. No one gets to eat anything tonight except the appetizers."

"Tell that to Aunt Bella." Blythe's gaze slid past me and I turned in time to see Bella with a dagger in her hand while a really hot Latino dressed in a red-and-white peppermint-striped thong gyrated in front of her.

"Stop!" I shrieked, darting across the room in time to catch the blade before it turned Raoul from a he to a she. "No slicing and dicing the dancers."

Despite my diabolical-looking Aunt Bella and a near-death experience, the Candy Man kept time to LMFAO's "Sexy and I Know It" without missing a beat. All hail my quick-thinking glam powers.

Aunt Bella shifted her full attention to me and I instantly felt the heat on my face. She frowned and fire swept from my head to my toes. The first wafts of smoke curled in the air and panic bolted through me.

My hair.

I knew it even before I smelled the sickeningly sweet aroma of burned shampoo. This was no warning. This was the real thing—my complete annihilation—and it was happening right here in front of everyone.

"Aunt Bella," I croaked despite my suddenly dry lips. "Please—"

"Bella," Aunt Lucy declared, sliding an arm around her oldest sister's shoulder and drawing her attention. The heat subsided and I managed to catch my breath. "I was just looking for you. We're doing Bloody Mary shots." Lucy winked at me as she steered Bella around toward the bar. "Nobody sucks down a Bloody Mary like you, old girl."

"I do have superior sucking powers," Bella growled. "But I'd much rather have the real thing."

"And the rest of us would rather not be party to a felony. At least not in public."

"Pshaw," Aunt Bella scoffed. "Back in my day, we didn't worry about silly felonies…"

They disappeared toward the bar and I managed to draw a much-needed breath. After a quick glance to make sure I wasn't still sizzling—yes, my hair was slightly singed on the ends, but nothing a quick trim wouldn't fix—I gave in to a surge of relief. I sent up a silent thank-you (do *not* tell my mother) for my aunt Lucy.

"Are you okay?" Blythe was beside me in that next instant. "You're smoking."

"Still?"

She eyed me, doing a quick look around. "A little, but there's no fire. Your aunt is totally psychotic."

"Tell me about it." My mind flashed back to the bloody threat on my bathroom mirror, the invisible noose, the spiders. Yep, Bella was psychotic, all right.

But in a bold, in-your-face way.

I'd just seen that for myself. She hadn't waited for me to slip off to the ladies' room so that she could exact her revenge. Rather, she had set me on fire in front of everyone, or at least she'd tried.

No, Bella wasn't behind the cryptic message on my bathroom mirror. Or any of the other threats. Subtlety wasn't her style.

Was it Aunt Levita who'd been terrorizing me? Or one of the cousins? Maybe they'd just been blowing off steam over the nuptials.

I shivered, still really, *really* wanting to believe. My family gave new meaning to the word *crazy*, but better the devil you know.

"I think I need a drink," I croaked, my lips suddenly dry.

"You and me both. Do you know I caught your cousins trying on thongs in the back dressing room with the dancers?"

"Let's hope that's the worst we have to deal with. Last time I had the aunts together, the building caught fire."

And this time *I'd* caught fire.

"I'd invest in an extinguisher if I were you. It's probably going to get worse. Agarth said there's far too much demon activity going on for one city. Something is bound to happen."

"Way to lighten my mood."

She shrugged. "I just want you to be careful. I worry about you."

And I was starting to worry about Cutter.

I admitted that to myself over the next few hours as I sucked down not one, but three margaritas and thought about the situation.

Cutter had been forced off the grid because of all the demon activity. I knew that much. But why? Because he was in danger?

That had to be it.

He was in danger, so he'd bailed and assigned Smith to keep an eye on me.

Because *I* was in danger?

Duh. I'd been neck-deep in it from the get-go.

If only I wasn't starting to think that I had more to worry about than a few crazy relatives. Much more.

I tried to drown the notion in another margarita while I watched Blythe stand guard near the restroom, her clipboard in one hand and her cell phone in the other. She read an incoming text and her face brightened.

What were the odds Agarth was at the other end?

I smiled and then I frowned, because while I was superhappy that Blythe had found someone (even if she wouldn't admit it), I was super*un*happy that I had found zip.

Just a demon slayer who didn't know how to call or text or drop by.

And the problem was?

The last thing I needed was to start something that could only end in disaster. Cutter would find out the truth and lop off my head, or I would take a nosedive south thanks to some unseen force out to get me. Either way, we're talking bad with a capital B.

All the more reason to try to relax and enjoy the time I had left. And the hot guys. Everywhere.

I summoned my inner slut puppy and focused on a nearby waiter with broad shoulders and muscular biceps and six-pack abs that would make any woman's mouth water.

I waited for the appropriate reaction. I was a succubus, for Pete's sake. There should be an instant rush of *give it to me, baby.*

Instead, the only thing I felt was a churning in my stomach courtesy of my stress level.

Seriously. I felt more excitement for the chocolate-truffle gift boxes stacked on the main table than I did for Mr. Six-Pack.

Uh-oh.

I reached for another drink. And then another. And then another.

I was drowning my troubles with a sixth margarita and trying not to cringe as eight of my cousins sang a really bad karaoke version of "We Are Family" when Aunt Lucy finally slid into the seat next to me.

"I never thought I'd say this"—she took a long swig of her own appletini—"but I'm actually having a good time. And so is your mother."

My attention shifted to Lillith, sitting at a nearby table. She wore a white veil dotted with condom packages and a T-shirt that said *The Bride Wants a Ride!*—all courtesy of Aunt Lucy, of course.

"Can you believe she actually put on that getup?" Lucy finished off the appletini and grinned.

"Only because she likes being the center of attention." My gaze shifted to the hunk strutting his stuff across the stage in front of her. His name was Count Wonderful and he wore a black cape, black leather pants, and enough body oil to grease a fifty-foot Slip'N Slide.

"He's so hot," cried Aunt Levita, who sat next to my mom. She nudged Lillith before hopping up on her chair and waving a dollar bill. "Come and get it, Mr. McHunky."

In typical one-up fashion, my mother pulled out a twenty. "Over here, man slave."

Aunt Bella, who sat on my mother's left, was the only one who didn't look the least bit engaged, but then I'd confiscated her dagger, so I couldn't really blame her. She'd given up sex years ago in favor of blood and destruction.

"I think Bella needs another drink." Lucy signaled the bartender. A minute later, she sashayed over to her oldest sister, a Screaming Orgasm in hand. She nudged the oldest Damon and handed over the drink. A few gulps and, surprisingly, the stern set of Bella's features seemed to ease. She looked almost human. Harmless. *Family.*

The hunch that I was sinking deep and fast into something I didn't understand hit me again and I blinked against the burning at the backs of my eyes.

I shifted my attention to Cheryl and George, who stood near one of the adjacent stages. Cheryl, whose face looked ready to explode, peeled off several dollar bills from a huge roll and waved them at a tall, buff construction worker who went by the name of the Drill Bit. He shook his moneymaker in front of an embarrassed Cheryl before plucking the dollar bill from her hand. He whirled, shimmied, and backed it up right in George's shrouded face.

The hellish messenger waved a hand and the pants slid up into a very painful-looking wedgie. The construction worker squealed. I cringed.

Ouch.

If I hadn't known better, I would have sworn I saw a crack of white in the black shadow that was George's face. But then the construction worker did a quick rip and yank, and the pants went flying. The demons cheered. George growled. And I reached for another drink.

* * *

"So?" I asked my mother when we climbed into a waiting limo just after three a.m. Everyone else had called it a night and it was just the two of us. "Did you have a good time?"

She shrugged. "I s'pose."

It wasn't the gushing *yessss!* I'd been hoping for, but it was still the nicest thing my mother had said to me in a long, long time.

Maybe ever.

Warmth stole through me, a feeling that had nothing to do with the ridiculous amount of alcohol I'd consumed and everything to do with the fact that deep down, I still longed for my mother's approval. What daughter didn't? "I'm glad it didn't suck."

"Not at all. But it is a great deal later than I intended. I told Samael I'd be home early." I thought I saw a glimpse of regret. But then it faded and I realized I was just punchy from lack of sleep and too much tequila.

Regret?

This was Satan we were talking about.

"Oh, well. He'll get over it." She rested her head back against the seat and closed her eyes.

A comfortable silence descended, and for the first time I didn't feel so on edge. Gone was the obsessive worry that I wasn't good enough. Likewise, she didn't seem the least bit anxious to criticize me.

Because I wasn't a total screwup?

She was my *mother*, for Pete's sake. Genetically wired to care about me regardless of how much I disappointed her. Which meant she would totally want to know that someone wanted me dead, right?

"Mom, I need to talk to you."

She grunted what sounded like a "Hmmm?"

"Someone is after me." I launched into a five-minute explanation about everything from the bloody warning to tonight's near-death experience. "At first I thought it was Aunt Bella or Aunt Levita, or even one of the cousins. But now I'm not so sure. If one of them wanted to get rid of me, they could have done it easily enough. They've been popping in and out of my apartment regularly over the past two weeks. Which makes me think that it's someone else who wants me dead."

There. I'd said it.

Relief rolled through me. Short-lived when I heard the low, guttural, unearthly growl coming from my ma.

"Now don't go getting all worked up. Please. I just don't know where else to turn—" The words died as I slid a sideways glance to find Lillith's head lolled back, her mouth wide open. Another growl slid past her lips.

Okay, make that a snore.

Grrrrrrrrrrrrrrr...

The sound vibrated through the car and my relief vanished quicker than the last truffle in my gift box. Alarm rushed in, reminding me that I had a full forty-eight hours to go until the wedding was over and there was no longer any reason to kill me.

Hopefully.

Which explained why I dropped off my mother and gave the limo driver directions to Blythe's place. After I swung by my extremely dark, extremely intimidating apartment to get Snooki, that is.

Agarth had picked up Blythe at the club just after midnight under the pretense that her car was messed up and he was just giving her a lift home. One that obviously involved an overnight sleepover, since he answered the door when I knocked.

"What ye be needing at this hour of the bloody night?" His eyes flashed murderous intent at the barking Snooki in my arms.

Talk about rotten timing. I should have shown a little decorum, pretended not to notice that he was wearing only a pair of boxers and an irritated expression, and walked away.

"Can we sleep on your couch?" I blurted instead. "Please."

If survival meant being an unwanted third wheel, then bring on the lug nuts and call me Goodyear.

2 3

"Mmmm...lick me again," I murmured to the tall, dark hunk of demon slayer who loomed over me.

A smile played at Cutter's lips and his green eyes sparkled. He dipped his head. A quick, leisurely sensation lapped at the side of my neck, and my nipples pebbled. Another lap and my toes curled.

"More," I begged as the tip of his tongue touched the outer shell of my ear. Desire swept my nerve endings.

He had the most sinful mouth and I'd been waiting so long and—

"Ruuuufffff!"

My eyes snapped open a split second before Snooki's tongue caught me right on the lips.

"Stop," I sputtered and pushed her away. She yapped, determined to get in a few more licks before retreating.

"This is just between you and me," I said firmly to the tiny Yorkie. I scrambled to a sitting position just as Blythe walked out of the bathroom.

"What are you doing?" She didn't miss my blazing-hot cheeks and rumpled hair.

"Wrestling with Snooki." Yeah. That's it. "We were, um, just playing."

"And here I thought you were having a lewd, lascivious dream about that demon slayer."

"He's not my type."

"Sexy. Good-looking. Single. Yeah, I can see how he's not your type."

"He's a slayer."

"Who has the hots for you."

"He does not have the hots for me."

"Fine." She shrugged. "*You* have the hots for *him*."

"I'm a succubus. I have the hots for every man. And speaking of men, was that Agarth who answered your door last night? And don't tell me he was sleeping over because he was too tired to go home after fixing your car. Your car wasn't broken."

"It might be broken. If Agarth weren't doing the upkeep. He gave me an oil change."

"Among other things."

She shrugged. "Okay, so we're friends with benefits."

"Just friends?"

"Of course. He's *so* not my type."

"And yet he spent the entire night." I sniffed. "And made coffee."

"Maybe I made the coffee."

"You hate coffee."

"It's not so bad." I gave her a pointed look, which she avoided. "You're welcome to a cup. And there's Excedrin," she added when I closed my eyes against the blinding sunlight that spilled through the window when she pushed the curtains aside.

"What about a gun?"

Laughter vibrated, making my head pound that much harder. "You'll live. Dump a few tablets into a Red Bull and you'll be up and around in no time."

Unfortunately, *no time* amounted to five hours and thirty-eight minutes of excruciating headache.

Still, I dragged myself into the office and spent every moment nailing down last-minute arrangements for tomorrow and making accommodations for out-of-town guests.

The Hyatt for those in this realm. The morgue for those spirits coming from Down Under who needed a body more than a minibar. While demons usually went for live bodies, there wasn't time to scope out walking, talking humans with spirits weak enough to make possession a possibility. The basement at Methodist Hospital afforded a quick alternative.

Once five o'clock rolled around, I headed over to the restaurant to check on the details for the rehearsal dinner.

Chef Lorenzo (a second-tier demon who'd cooked for my grandfather for eons back in the day) was hard at work finishing up the prep for a scrumptious feast starring my mother's all-time favorite tonsil tartare and complete with chocolate-dipped baby rodents and roasted kidneys.

Needless to say, I spent as little time in the kitchen as possible before making a pass through the dining room to check that all the flowers had been delivered, and appropriately shriveled, and the place settings laid out—black chargers with black china edged in silver.

I also did a double check that the chocolate fountain worked properly. What? Someone had to do it.

After that, I rushed home to change clothes, check on Snooki, and mentally prep for tonight's event. My definition of prep? Sucking down two Red Bulls and six Excedrin and dashing off a quick last will and testament naming Blythe as Snooki's guardian should I bite the bullet.

Hey, it never hurt to be prepared. Particularly since I couldn't shake the unease that sat in the pit of my stomach. A sensation that exploded the moment I returned to the restaurant to find my mother in a fierce argument with Chef Lorenzo.

"What's going on?" I asked her when the demon of devilish chow threw up his hands and disappeared in a puff of smoke. "Where'd he go?"

"Don't worry." She waved a hand. "He'll be back. He's just blowing off steam because he's mad."

"And he's mad because?" I prompted.

"I may have made a tiny little menu change."

"But I worked hard with the chef to come up with that menu. It's nasty, and it could turn a cast-iron stomach. It's perfect for tonight."

"Maybe." She motioned to the platters of tonsils being dumped into the trash. "But I thought we'd go with more normal wedding fare. A pecan-crusted salmon and some julienne carrots."

"Isn't everyone in our family allergic to normal?"

"Exactly." My mother smiled and my blood ran cold. "Lucy will refuse to eat. Levita will pout. And Bella will be climbing the walls. Literally. The last time she was faced with a plate of human food, she scaled the Sheetrock in search of spiders to tide her over. But I've already checked the dining room and there isn't a stray bug in sight." She beamed. "If only your grandfather could be here to see it. But, of course, he's got an awards banquet to attend—he placed second in his tournament today. He promised he'd be here tomorrow. In the meantime, it's going to be a glorious evening."

Um, yeah. If by *glorious* she meant an enraged demonic bridal party desperate for sustenance.

Trepidation rolled through me. If my instincts were right and my aunties truly weren't the ones out for my blood, the next few hours were sure to change that. I was the wedding planner, after all, and ultimately the one responsible for tonight's menu.

I was *so* dead.

* * *

I didn't die.

No, it was Lorenzo who bit the bullet when he refused to serve the salmon and my mother nailed him with a butter knife right between the eyes. His body dropped and his spirit took a flying leap back to Hell, smack-dab to the end of that long, *long* line.

A vivid reminder of the fate that awaited me should I screw up Lillith's big event.

"The food sucks," Aunt Lucy murmured halfway through the appetizer—Santa Fe chicken wraps with sweet-and-sour sauce. She ignored the wrap and went straight for the cup of sauce, which she downed in one quick gulp. "This is the worst rehearsal dinner I've ever been to. Then again, this is the only rehearsal dinner I've ever been to." When my eyes started to burn, she quickly added, "Not that any of this is your fault, sweetie. It's obvious my dear sister wants us as miserable as possible." My gaze shifted to my mother, who looked as fierce and as beautiful as ever in a bloodred suit, diamond earrings, and a chilling smile. She sat next to a very stoic-looking man with a receding hairline, watery blue eyes, and an extra chin.

I'd expected the chief demon of war to look more like Vin Diesel, but Samael appeared to be working the Napoleon angle. Smart man. Being underestimated because of his size and appearance probably gave him a huge advantage on the battlefield, and I had no doubt that Samael played to win. Just like my mother.

I watched as she touched Samael's arm and whispered something in his ear. He leaned toward her, and his features softened. If I hadn't known better, I would have sworn my mother actually laughed.

But then she pulled away. Samael stiffened. And I was left to wonder if all that Red Bull was making me hallucinate.

"It's not enough that she's taking control," Lucy went on. "She wants to rub everyone's nose in it. Even the judge looks pissed."

I turned my attention to the man sitting on my mother's right. Judge Landon Parks, aka chief demon of slavery and oppression. He had salt-and-pepper hair, regal features, and a grim expression that said he'd like to slap a pair of handcuffs on whoever was responsible for the plate in front of him.

I swallowed. Hard.

"Maybe Ma changed the menu because she really likes salmon," I heard myself say.

"And maybe Bella will make a heartfelt toast to the happy couple." Lucy motioned to her sister, who sat across the table looking as gloomy as ever in her usual old-lady black dress. Her eyes blazed with fury.

Eyes that were trained solely on me.

Uh-oh.

"I'll be right back. I need to check on the dessert." I retreated into the kitchen, only to run smack-dab into the young Legion rookie who'd become my shadow over the past few days.

Could my night get *any* worse?

"Are you crazy?" I gripped Smith's arm and tried to steer him toward the back door, but he wouldn't budge. "There are two dozen hungry demons in the next room who would love to rip off your head and have it as the main entrée."

"So?" He shrugged away and puffed out his chest. "I'm not scared."

"Yeah, right."

"I'm not. Really." He glanced nervously around at the prep cooks, who seemed oblivious to us as they rushed to plate the entrée. "I need to talk to you."

"It'll have to wait. I'm in the middle of a rehearsal dinner."

"I know. Satan's getting married and you're in charge. This is important." His mouth tightened as he seemed to gather his courage. "I've got a message from Cutter."

I glanced over my shoulder to make sure the statement hadn't snagged anyone's attention, and then I grabbed Smith by the arm and steered him into a nearby walk-in refrigerator.

My teeth started to chatter as soon as I pushed the door shut behind us. Hey, it's a demon thing. Any cold is too cold, which meant the fridge was the safest place for this conversation.

I hugged my arms and nodded. "You've got five minutes."

"It's about the plan for tomorrow."

"What does he want me to do?" I managed, my teeth knocking as I tried to get the words out.

"When the target shows up at the wedding, your job is to steer him outside into a waiting car."

"I'm supposed to send him away when the whole point is for him to be at the wedding in the first place?"

He nodded. "Tell him he was only invited to the reception, not the actual ceremony. Brides do that all the time, right?"

"I suppose."

"Tell him you're sending him for cocktails or something at a different location until it's time for the reception. Tell him you've got limos shuttling everyone over. We'll have one there to pick him up and drive him to a takedown location."

"Where?"

"Someplace dark and empty."

"What if Azazel realizes that something is up?"

"He won't. Not until he's in the car, and then it'll be too late. I'll be following just in case." When I arched an eyebrow, he added, "I can handle myself."

"Will there be other backup?"

He shifted uncomfortably. "The thing is, this isn't technically a Legion-sanctioned kill. Not that they don't want Azazel dead. It's just that Cutter can't risk bringing anyone else in. He can't risk another Legion officer making the actual kill."

Because in order to gain his soul, Cutter had to be the one to deal the final blow to Azazel.

"You're involved," I pointed out.

"True, but I'm not an official slayer." He actually looked sheepish. "Cutter's been training me for tryouts when I turn twenty-one, but I'm still a civilian. Which is why I'm the one watching you. There are some bad forces out there and Cutter didn't want to draw any more unwanted attention to you. Putting a bona fide demon hunter on your tail would have been a red flag, and it would have meant alerting other Legion members."

Any more unwanted attention? My brain snagged on the words and my chest tightened. Had I already drawn someone's attention? That would explain the threats and confirm the nagging feeling that my family wasn't really out to kill me.

It was someone else. Another demon? Or a Legion member?

I opened my mouth to beg for more info, but Smith reached for the door. "I have to get out of here. I've already said way too much—"

"Wait." I grabbed his arm. "I need to talk to Cutter."

"Do you have questions about the plan?"

I shook my head. I didn't have questions so much as comments. *Be safe. Watch your back. I miss you.* "Where is he?"

"Still off the grid, and he'll stay that way until tomorrow night."

"I need help with these plates!" The headwaiter's voice boomed nearby.

As much as I wanted to keep Smith there and grill him for more information, I knew it wasn't safe. "You should go before the entrées get sent out." I ducked my head outside the fridge to make sure the coast was clear. "I have a feeling the natives are going to riot." I walked out first, blocking the way so he could scoot by and slip out the back door.

I spent the next two hours scarfing down ladyfingers—soaked sponge cake, thankfully, since my mother had ditched the real thing—and praying for divine intervention.

I know, right? But let's face it, the forces of evil, all of whom were less than ten feet away, cared little about my success. I needed something bigger on my side, so I sent up a prayer to the Big Guy that I made it through tonight and tomorrow in one piece, and that Cutter stayed safe and sound and managed to reclaim his soul. *And that my ma never found out I'd gone over her head on this one.*

Ask and ye shall receive.

At least when it came to tonight. Other than a small fire at the head table (Aunt Bella) and a sword fight between Samael and the best man (his brother Mordrad), the rest of the evening was pretty uneventful.

Even Cheryl, who'd been the only human in attendance, looked pleased as she steered my mother and Samael toward a waiting car. "I wasn't too sure about tonight, but you pulled it off without a hitch," she told me after the door had shut and she was just about to climb in next to the driver.

"Don't kid yourself. We were in a roomful of bloodthirsty demons. The salmon was a definite hitch."

"Maybe, but it went well, all things considered. Let's hope tomorrow is the same." She drew a deep breath as if saying her own silent prayer. *Attagirl, Cheryl.* "Speaking of which, I've got to have your mother at the salon by two. All the bridesmaids are meeting there to get ready as well." A shudder ripped through her and I knew she was envisioning what three hours smack-dab in the middle of the crown princesses of Hell would be like. Forget the paraffin wax. Tomorrow's special would surely be a bloodbath.

She seemed to shake away the thought. "Your grandfather flies in at two thirty. That was the earliest flight he could manage since he refuses to miss the celebratory breakfast after today's tournament win."

The win was a given. I wanted to point out that Gramps could also pop in and out anytime he wanted, but I had a feeling Cheryl had already thought of that.

"He insisted on flying in with his golf buddies." She waved a hand. "You know how he is about golf. Anyhow, I'll have my hands full, so can you pick him up and drop him at the Hyatt? I would send a car, but your mother wants the VIP treatment."

"I'm on it."

That is, if whoever was after me didn't kill me in my sleep tonight. A definite possibility, too, since I was still flying solo sans my coveted demon-busting powder. I seriously doubted my newly acquired collection of Vera Bradley was going to ward off any evil spirits.

Cheryl must have noted my sudden worry because she tried for a smile despite her own obvious misgivings. "Keep your chin up," she said as she climbed in next to the driver. At least you get to see your sweetie tomorrow night. Maybe he'll even bring his pooch."

Azazel.

The name echoed in my head as I watched the car pull away.

I glanced at the Datsun parked across the street. Smith sat behind the wheel, a slice of pizza in one hand, binoculars hanging around his neck. I gave him a small wave and he waved back.

A sliver of comfort stole through me. Cutter was out there somewhere, still keeping an eye on me even if it was through the Legion's most inexperienced man.

I marched back inside, back to the kitchen where the dishes were being washed and put away, and pulled out my phone. I spent the next few minutes on the phone with Blythe going over the plan to detour Azazel. If I had to pick up Gramps from the airport, I'd need someone else to catch Azazel when he arrived at the Bell Tower.

"Sounds so James Bond-ey," Blythe murmured, her voice unusually breathless.

I heard a muffled giggle, followed by a deep, guttural, "I've got a big surprise for ye."

Ugh. Too much info.

"Blythe? Is someone there with you?"

"Of course not." Another giggle. "I mean, um, yeah. But it's just Agarth. We're messing around. It's nothing serious. So, um, why not just have Cutter intercept Azazel at the Bell Tower? Wouldn't that be easier?"

"If I wanted a knock-down, drag-out in the middle of my mom's wedding, which I don't. Can you do this for me? *Please...*"

"Okay, but when this is over you're going to owe me big-time for all the favors."

And I knew just how I was going to pay her back—with free planning and a discount on all wedding services.

That is, if she ever admitted that Agarth was more than just an FWB.

I spent the next thirty minutes boxing up the rented linens and dinnerware. I was making one last pass through the restaurant when I noticed that Landon Parks was still sitting in the small bar area near the front entrance, a glass of whiskey in his hand.

"Big day tomorrow," I said, and he nodded. "Shouldn't you call it a night?"

"Not just yet." He eyed the bartender at the far end. "After that atrocious dinner, I need some sort of sustenance."

"But he's a demon," I quickly pointed out.

"Perhaps." His gaze shifted to the wall of windows just beyond the bartender. "But he isn't." The beat-up Datsun sat across the street. I watched Smith reach for another slice of pizza.

A growl vibrated in my ear and my attention shifted back to Landon. "He looks so innocent, doesn't he?" His eyes gleamed as he licked his lips, and my stomach did a somersault because I knew what he had in mind.

He was the chief demon of slavery and oppression. Which meant he would more than likely tie Smith up and force him into a lifetime of servitude. That is, if he didn't eat him first.

He downed the whiskey with one large gulp and slid off the bar stool. "Time to have some real fun."

I had a gruesome vision of poor Smith wearing a leather bondage suit. "You can't leave yet." I dogged the judge toward the door. "We need to go over the vows for tomorrow."

"Already done."

"What about the reception?" I grabbed his arm and held tight.

He tried to shrug me loose. "What are you doing?"

"You don't know where you're supposed to sit."

"I don't care."

"But I do. Let's go back to the kitchen where I've got my iPad. You can take a look at the seating chart and I'll show you—"

"*Let go.*" The deep, guttural voice seemed to come from nowhere and everywhere at the same time.

Cold horror washed through me and the air lodged in my chest. My gaze shot to Landon, but he looked as surprised as I felt.

Because the voice hadn't come from him.

My mind raced. Aunt Bella?

Maybe. Hopefully.

My head snapped around. My gaze traveled through the dimly lit room. Other than the bartender, who seemed oblivious to what was happening, there was no one else there.

My grip on Landon tightened, and he tried to pull free. "Release me," he growled.

"I can't."

"Nonsense. Just loosen your hand."

"No, really. I can't." My fingers contracted of their own will, desperate to cling to something, to fight for survival against the panic punching through me.

Coldness slithered over my feet. I glanced down to see dozens of deadly reptiles circling my ankles. My calves. My knees.

Snakes. Honest-to-goodness *snakes*.

"What the hell?" Landon's voice echoed and my head swiveled sideways in time to see he had his own troubles. The serpents surrounded him too, moving higher, winding tighter.

My ribs seemed to cave under the viselike pressure, and I fought for a breath. Then it felt as if someone yanked the floor out from under me and I started to fall.

My head slammed against the hardwood and bright specks of light exploded behind my eyes. I felt a quick nanosecond of hope. Smith was right outside. He would see what was happening and call Cutter and—

The speeding train of thought shattered as pain slashed through me. And then everything went black.

Aunt Bella had the hairiest feet I'd ever seen.

That was my first thought when I finally blinked away the fog and managed to focus my bleary eyes on a pair of long, wide feet sprinkled with coarse black hair. My gaze snagged on the stubby toes tipped with jagged nails, and I knew what I was getting her for her birthday.

A gift certificate for a pedicure.

I held tight to the hope. Aunt Bella I could deal with. Or Aunt Levita. Or even Portia or Monique or Hester, or any of my other cousins. They were evil, but they were *my* evil. My family.

If only.

This was something infinitely worse. I could feel it in the churning deep in my stomach. I summoned what little strength I had and tried to lift my head, but it throbbed relentlessly. I blinked a few more times against the grittiness in my eyes. "Where am I?" I rasped, my tongue thick.

"A basement in the Bayou City," came the deep, guttural voice from last night.

The words sank in and I became acutely aware of the stiff chair where I sat, my arms behind me, my feet attached to the wooden legs. An icy slickness bound my hands and ankles. The sensation moved and a wave of *ickkkkk* rushed through me, along with a replay of those few frantic seconds before I'd passed out at the restaurant.

I was tied up with several very lethal-looking snakes.

Fear squeezed the air out of my lungs. My head snapped up, and I drank in the scenery along the way—hairier calves, thick knees, khaki shorts, and a powder-blue sports shirt—

"Grandfather?" I croaked.

"You're awake." Gramps had gray hair, tanned skin, and a relieved expression. "Thankfully."

Panic receded enough for me to drag air into my lungs. Like, I know my gramps was the ultimate Evil One, but he really wasn't all that bad a guy. Maybe to the millions of poor souls who'd faced off with him and lost, but to his grandkids he was just Pop-Pop, who'd never missed a birthday—a card and a crisp one-hundred-dollar bill—or a special occasion. He'd even taken me to Disneyland once. Sure, I'd been fully grown at the time, since he'd done it right before retiring for the PGA, but still. It had been the thought that had meant the most—plus I was a sucker for a good roller coaster.

Bottom line, as the proverbial Devil he'd been hell on wheels in his day, but as Pop-Pop? Not so much.

Or so I'd thought.

The past two weeks rushed at me—the bloody mirror, the invisible noose, the spiders—and the panic washed back in, drenching me in a wave of disbelief. "You're the one who's been threatening me?"

"Threatening you?" He looked at me as if I'd grown another head. "Why, I haven't done any such thing. Though I did technically kidnap you last night." Guilt seeped into his voice. "But that wasn't on purpose, mind you. I had no intention of nabbing you. I wanted Judge Parks. You just happened to be holding on to him. I told you to let go," Gramps accused, reminding me of the unearthly command I'd heard last night.

He walked over to a putting green that had been set up in the middle of a concrete room with bleak gray walls. There were several old-fashioned torture devices as well, including a boiling cauldron of oil in the far corner and a dark-robed figure who stood, somber and frightening, a paddle in his hand as he stirred the menacing pot.

"I don't understand. Why would you want to kidnap Landon Parks?"

"To stop the wedding, of course." He pointed away from the torture devices to a far section of the room that looked more like a man cave than a dungeon. A monstrous flat-screen TV filled one wall and a bar area occupied the corner. Judge Parks sat on a black leather sofa, his gaze hooked on a football game. "Landon there has to perform the ceremony for it to be legitimate both Down Under and here. No Landon, no wedding. It's so simple, but brilliant. I'd been avoiding all the wedding preparations, thinking that if I didn't show, Lillith would cease all this nonsense. But then she proceeded with the rehearsal dinner last night, and I realized it wasn't enough that I boycott the damned thing. That's when I thought of Landon and how she wouldn't be able to get married without him. So I snatched him, and here we are."

"Let me get this straight." I blinked, desperately trying to clear away the remaining cobwebs and focus. "You're *against* the wedding?"

"Of course. Why would I want my daughter to marry a weasel like Samael?" He pulled a driver from a nearby bag of golf clubs and lined up his shot on the putting green. "He's an idiot."

"But it was your idea in the first place. You specifically said you would hand over control of Hell if one of your daughters married a chief."

"Yeah, well, I didn't think your mother would choose the most contrary, defiant, backstabbing one of them all."

Okay, so, like, hadn't he just described every demon in existence?

"She was supposed to pick Argeniou or Syrialish or any of the top-tier leaders," he went on. "But Samael?" He snorted and grabbed a golf ball. "He's short. And he's got beady eyes. And he looks like a rodent."

"Maybe he can find a better-looking body for the ceremony?"

"*And* he completely defied me back in Egypt when he enslaved all of those Israelites. I told him it wasn't the right time. I told him to let the people go and show 'em he wasn't such a bad pharaoh, but *noooo*. He refused to concede. Instead, Moses played the hero and gained their trust, and bam, good wins again." He pointed the driver at me. "Samael is a control freak. He never considers another perspective, even when it's a direct order." He practiced his swing. Once. Twice. "I punished him for a thousand years, but it did nothing to curb his control issues. He's not reasonable enough to rule Hell, and he certainly isn't good enough for your mother." He swung a third time. The ball went spiraling toward the hole with practiced control. *Plop.* "This wedding can't happen."

I remembered my mother leaning into Samael and that fleeting moment when I'd felt the intimacy between them. "What if she loves him?"

Gramps's head snapped up. His eyes fired a bright red. His lips pulled back and his teeth sharpened.

Whoops. "What I mean is, what if she *lusts* after him?" I know I said my gramps isn't a bad guy, but I'd never really seen him upset. Like now. "Speaking from personal experience, lust is a mysterious thing. When it's really powerful, there's simply no accounting for tastes. It's chemical. Maybe they have great chemistry."

His eyes cooled and his features softened. He shrugged. "She can spend as much time with him as she desires. She just can't marry him." He smacked another ball. "I never should have advocated this matrimonial business in the first place. From this moment on, weddings are forbidden among demons."

Oh, no, he didn't.

The past two years of searching and hoping rose up inside me and the words poured out before I could think better of them. "But you can't do that!" I was on my way to finding my One and Only, and when I did, I wanted a traditional *I do*, complete with big centerpieces and a monster cake. I *deserved* it. "Is it really fair to ban all weddings when it's just this particular one that you're dead set against?"

"I don't care about being fair." He waved his golf club at me. "I don't want your mother to marry Samael. That's why Landon will stay right here until this bunch of nonsense is over with."

"What about me?"

"You're free to go." I stared pointedly at the snakes binding my legs to the chair and he waved a hand. The snakes loosened and slithered away.

I rubbed my sore wrists and my gramps actually looked embarrassed. "You kept slumping over." He shrugged. "Bob here had to do something to keep you from sliding to the floor." He motioned to the robed figure with the paddle. Bob nodded and kept stirring.

"So he's not going to torture me?"

"He's not here for torture. He's here for nostalgia. I adore golfing, but living out of a suitcase is hard. I bring Bob and the toys along because they remind me of home. They also come in handy when I don't get good room service, but that's another story."

"Replay!" Landon shouted from his corner before settling back, a beer in one hand and a bowl of popcorn in the other.

Reality slammed into me and I realized that two weeks of careful planning was about to go to Hell in a handbasket, and I was going down with it.

"So that's it?" I pushed to my feet and caught the edge of the chair when the floor seemed to tilt. "You're just going to hang out here and hold Landon hostage?"

"That's the plan." Gramps bypassed the torture devices and headed for the man cave.

I followed on his heels. "Why not just tell Ma that you hate Samael?"

"And admit I made a mistake?" Popping the top on a beer, he took a long sip. "I was the one who advised her to marry in the first place. I just didn't think she'd pick such a loser." He shook his head. "No, from this moment on, I decree that weddings are completely forbidden. Anyone caught engaging in one will be sentenced to servitude Down Under."

Which meant I was damned if I did and damned if I didn't.

I thought of Cutter and the way he'd looked at me those few seconds before he'd kissed me. As if he'd wanted more than just a kiss from me. More than just a touch. *More.*

I blinked against the sudden burning in my eyes, but the tears came anyway, spilling over onto my cheeks, coursing down my face. A sob burst past my lips and my grandfather's gaze swiveled toward me.

"W-what are you doing?" He looked horrified.

"It's called crying," I said between sobs.

"I know that." He waved a nervous hand. "Why are you doing it?"

"Because," sniffle, "I'm upset," sniffle, sniffle. "My life sucks." The emotional wall that I'd bricked around my deepest, darkest fears cracked, and suddenly the words spilled out before I could stop them. "*Everything* sucks. My mom doesn't really like me. And my family is crazy. And I spent last Valentine's Day all by myself. And now the only thing I'm actually good at—my business—is about to be ripped away because you hate Samael and—"

"Stop," he cut in. "Just stop all the crying."

"Okay." But the tears kept coming.

"I mean it." He went from mortified to angry in a heartbeat. "I order you to stop right now." His eyes fired a bright, vicious red and his teeth sharpened again. "Otherwise I'm going to banish you from this realm."

And there it was. My worst fear. Forget failing my mother. I was being banished. Right here. Right now.

No more weddings.

No happily-ever-afters.

No Cutter.

The truth crystallized and the tears came harder. Faster. "Fine," I cried. I was going down anyway. What was the point of fighting it? I was through being worried and terrified. *Through.* "Just do it. Get it over with."

"I will."

"Go ahead."

"I will. I really will. That, or I'll let Bob take over and torture you until you stop all that blubbering."

As if on cue, Bob held up the paddle. A few drops of oil sizzled and popped on the floor.

"So do it." I stiffened. "Boil me in oil. Ban me from this realm. None of it matters because when I don't show up, my mother will go ahead and do it herself. Don't you see? It's hopeless. I'm doomed regardless. And I never even got to find out if he's The One." The last word caught on a wail and the sobs came, racking my body and stirring a look of pure terror on my grandfather's face.

"Stop," he begged, his voice more desperate than depraved.

"I—I can't. It's just that it's been so stressful trying to do everything and now it's all ruined and my life is pretty much over and—"

"Don't worry about Bob," he cut me off. "I was just trying to scare you. I won't let him boil you in oil. And I won't banish you."

"But my mother will still hate me and I'll never find true love and—"

"I'll go to the wedding. Just stop. *Stop.*"

His plea finally registered through all the doom and gloom and I sniffled. "Really?" He nodded and I wiped frantically at my cheeks. "What about Judge Parks?"

His mouth drew into a tight line. "Don't push it."

Where I would have backed off before because, hey, we're talking *timeless* evil, I now had an entirely different perspective on things. I'd faced the absolute *worst* a few moments ago and won. Which meant I wasn't backing down.

I walked over to the sofa and sank down next to Landon, much to the surprise of both men.

Gramps narrowed his gaze. "What do you think you're doing?"

"Making myself comfortable." I propped my feet on the coffee table and snatched the bowl of popcorn out of the judge's hand. "I might as well spend my last few moments right here with the two of you, because Mom is sure to banish me when I show up without the judge." I reached for the remote control and switched the channel to TLC. The latest episode of *Say Yes to the Dress* blazed across the screen. "I just love this show. They're running a marathon right now. The entire first season back-to-back, which means we get to watch fourteen whole episodes—"

"He'll go," Gramps cut in. "We'll both go."

I grinned. "Smart man."

"Where in Hades have you been?" Blythe demanded the minute I finally walked into the foyer of the Bell Tower, my grandfather and Judge Parks in tow. Unfortunately, I'd been unconscious for most of the day. When I'd finally opened my eyes and stood up to Gramps, the sun had already set. "The wedding was supposed to start five minutes ago. Your mother is about to pop an artery."

"I got tied up." I thought of the slimy snakes slithering around my hands and feet thanks to Gramps.

And the mirror? The noose? The spiders?

Someone else had been responsible.

But who?

"Where's Azazel?" I blurted.

"We have to get started," Blythe rushed on, obviously scared and flustered and ready to bail.

I *so* knew the feeling.

"Your mom already zapped the beverage manager for not bringing in enough preceremony cocktails and she started a fire in the bridal suite and—"

"*Where is he?*" The screech flew out of my mouth, surprising both of us.

"I told him he was only invited for the reception and sent him out to the car waiting at the curb just like you said."

"How long ago?"

"About ten minutes, I think."

"You think or you know?"

"I know. That is, I think I know." She shook her head. "Give me a break. It's been crazy around here. George got bit by Cerberus and was late picking up a bunch of guests." She motioned to a robed George, who stood in the corner, a white bandage covering half his arm. "Luckily we have a few doctors in the house."

Possessed doctors, but who was I to argue semantics?

"That idiot dog," my grandfather growled. "He should have saved it for the groom."

"Zip it." I glared at Gramps. "Or I'm telling everyone that you freak at the first sign of tears."

He opened his mouth, but then snapped it shut again. His eyes flashed red before cooling to a deep, fathomless black that scared me almost as much as the bright crimson.

I snatched a boutonniere from a nearby table and pinned it on Judge Parks before grabbing another and turning to my sour-faced grandfather. He started to protest and I poked him. Just to keep the current balance of power intact.

I had a feeling it wouldn't last for long.

"I don't know what's going on here"—Blythe glanced at my gramps and the judge before shifting her attention back to me— "but we *really* have to get started."

Ten minutes. My gaze zigzagged to the street out front and I did a quick search for the Datsun. Smith was nowhere to be seen.

Because he's helping Cutter.

The plan was already in motion. Azazel had climbed into the waiting car, and Cutter was reclaiming his soul at that very moment in some dark and quiet place where no one would interfere. I had delivered on my end, and it was time to forget everything else and shift into David Tutera mode.

I celebrated all of two seconds before Blythe handed me my purse. My cell phone bleeped from inside. "The restaurant sent this over, along with your iPad and a box of your stuff. You must have forgotten it last night."

"Yeah." I gave Gramps an accusing look. "I must have."

I fished out the bleeping phone and glanced at the display. Forty-eight voice messages in the past two hours. Thirty-three texts, too. All from the same phone number. All with the same message.

Cutter never picked up the limo. I can't reach him. Something's wrong. Call me!!!!

My heart thumped. I hit *Return* and waited for Smith to pick up. The call went straight to voice mail, and my anxiety morphed into full-blown terror.

"What kind of car did Azazel get into?"

"I don't know." Blythe shrugged. "Maybe a BMW or a Lincoln. I just know it was short and black. Some sort of compact, I think."

My stomach bottomed out. "It was supposed to be a limo."

"Maybe there were car problems and they had to switch at the last minute."

If only. But if that had been the case, Cutter would have communicated the change to Smith. The young rookie was his only backup.

"What difference does it make?" Blythe shrugged. "Azazel wasn't the least bit put out that it wasn't a limo. In fact, he looked really pleased when he climbed into the car."

Pleased because he didn't have to attend a long, boring wedding ceremony?

Or because he'd managed to turn the tables on Cutter and strike first?

"Forget Azazel. We've got bigger problems." Blythe snagged my phone and tried to shoo me toward the bridal suite. "I've got a change of clothes waiting for you." George moaned and she gave him a look that said *Suck it up, big boy.* "We'll all be begging for a rabies shot if we don't get this show on the road. Your mom will sic that dog on every one of us. If she doesn't zap us first."

A very likely possibility, given the yelling and smoke coming from the room down the hall.

"Tell Mother that we're here and everything is fine." I stuffed my phone back into my purse. "Get the judge into position. Then get Gramps seated and stall."

"But—"

"Which way was the car headed?"

"East. But—"

"I'll be back." Or so I hoped.

I left a stunned Blythe staring after me as I darted out of the Bell Tower, snagged the first cab I could find, and hightailed it down the street to save Cutter's ass. I knew Azazel wouldn't go far. Regardless of what he had in store for Cutter, he still had to put in an appearance at the reception or risk my mother's wrath.

He had to be close by. I knew that much.

It was just a matter of pinpointing exactly where before he stole more than Cutter's soul.

* * *

It was the only abandoned building in the vicinity.

I stared up at the monstrous structure as I fished some money out of my purse and paid the cab driver. The place had once housed several offices before the economy took a nosedive and the housing market bottomed out. Several real-estate agents and a mortgage company had closed down, leaving the building vacant. A FOR LEASE sign sat out front, but I could tell by the broken windows on the second floor that it had been vacant for quite a while.

It was just the sort of place where a demon might take a kidnapped demon slayer. Or vice versa.

I tuned my senses, searching for some sign of life inside the building, but it was quiet. Dark.

Perfect.

The notion struck and I bolted forward. My gut instinct was to race through the double glass doors at the front, but a strange sensation crawled through me as I reached for the handle. I stalled. A heartbeat later, I did an about-face and started around the building, searching for a back door or a window or something—*there.*

I eyed the half-rusted metal door barely hanging onto its hinges. A soft push and metal groaned. I ducked my head inside, peering into the blackness for a few breathless moments, then I slipped inside and started down the pitch-black hallway.

Luckily I was a fierce and foreboding demon, otherwise I would have been terrified of the dark.

Okay, so I was a little terrified of *this* dark, particularly since zero moonlight pushed through the sparse windows, but desperation kicked a candy-ass any day. Cutter might be inside, possibly hurt and bleeding, and I had to *do* something.

And if he's already opened up a can of whup-ass on Azazel and is now sucking down lattes at a nearby Starbucks?

He wasn't. I wasn't sure how I knew, I just knew. First off, he didn't strike me as a latte drinker. Second, I'd been around enough evil in the past one thousand years to know what it felt like.

It felt like *this.*

A tension in the air and a dark sense of foreboding. Of danger. Of death.

I eased down the length of the hall, ducking my head into every doorway, searching every available space before hitting the stairwell at the very end. On the second floor, I started over.

Move forward.

Duck in.

Quick visual.

I was just about to hit door number three when I saw the shimmering shadow at the far end of the hall. It whispered through the open doorway and disappeared into the wall.

I knew that I would find Cutter inside.

I knew, but I wasn't prepared for the reality.

My heart lunged into my throat when I saw his limp body sprawled on the scarred linoleum. It had been six days since I'd seen him, and while I could still picture him alive and sexy, this was so totally opposite that I wasn't prepared for the ice that rushed through my veins.

His face was battered and bruised. One eye was swollen nearly shut, the other closed. He wore a pair of jeans and a black T-shirt that had been ripped halfway down his chest. Blood oozed from an open wound. He was still, so still, and quiet.

I was beside him in that next instant, my hand going to his neck. His pulse thudded against my fingers and my heart started beating again.

"Cutter?" I murmured. "It's me."

"Jess?" His lips were thick around the breath of the word.

He forced his eyelids open a fraction. Pain clouded the familiar green. I had to get him out of here. Now. Quick.

Before Azazel returned.

I wasn't fool enough to think he'd left Cutter alive by accident. No demon would walk away from a still-breathing slayer.

Azazel was still here somewhere.

"Can you walk?" I whispered, trying to pull him into a sitting position.

After a few pained seconds, he was upright. I pulled and was just about to hoist him up with my shoulder when I heard the voice.

"I'm afraid that's mine." The words rushed across the room like an arctic wind and froze me on the spot.

My head snapped up and I stared at the man standing in the doorway.

Azazel was tall, with long, dark, flowing hair and black eyes that drilled through me.

"Nice body choice," I said, desperately trying to keep the tremble out of my voice.

"A grunge band had a massive pileup on the interstate and this was all that was left at the morgue when I came up last week." He glanced down at the battered T-shirt and ripped jeans. "It's not my personal preference, but it'll do."

"You've been in this realm for an entire week?"

"A week and five days if you want to get technical. Who did you think was playing those little tricks on you?" He must have read the shock on my face, because he smirked. "Ah, but you didn't know, did you? Who did you think it was? Bella? Levita? They're all talk and no action. Lillith is the only one with any real balls. She has no problem killing to get her way. Or lying. I bet you think she was the one who tempted Eve, don't you? Everyone does. But it wasn't her. It was me."

I snorted, pretending a calmness I didn't feel. "Yeah, and I'm going to believe that because you're such a stickler for honesty, right?"

"Believe what you want, but it *was* me. Just like it's been me tormenting you these past few weeks." He shook his head. "You poor thing. Tsk, tsk. You couldn't back off, could you? You just had to help the slayer, and so you're here. Both of you." A vicious gleam lit his eyes. "And you're mine."

The truth crystallized as I looked in horror at the ancient demon. Instead of running, Azazel had been keeping tabs on his biggest nemesis. That's why he'd been able to elude Cutter for so long. He'd been one step ahead of the slayer. Watching his every move. Waiting for the chance to eliminate the threat. I'd played right into Azazel's hands by inviting him to the wedding.

And now he was going to kill Cutter.

He was going to kill *me*. I knew it even before he opened his mouth.

"I wonder what Lillith would say if she knew you were getting friendly with the enemy?" Azazel sneered. "Surely she would banish you. Not that she'll need to. I intend to destroy that pretty little body of yours and send you Down Under myself."

"She likes to do her own dirty work. You'll only piss her off."

"Then bravo for me." His expression hardened into sharp lines and angles. "Lillith's a bitch, and it's high time I one-upped her after the garden incident."

Horror gripped me, and I knew that for all my bravado, Azazel would rip out my heart and eat it right in front of me.

He was old. Ancient. And while I was related to Satan herself, that meant little to a backstabbing, two-faced, zillion-year-old, soul-stealing demon. Azazel was supremely powerful thanks to all the souls he'd hoarded. Like all ancients, he was also selfish and all about *me, me, me*.

And he'd obviously decided his allegiance to Gramps was over.

He reached me in the blink of an eye.

I sidestepped the hands that grabbed for me, and whirled. But he kept coming, backing me into a corner so fast that I barely had time to catch a breath.

He reached out and I ducked, but I wasn't fast enough. He caught my throat and squeezed. The pressure cut off my blood flow, and everything went hazy as he slung me around and threw me toward the opposite wall. I slammed into the Sheetrock, pieces shattering against my back. Before I could open my eyes, he reached for me again, tossing me like a rag doll as walls crumbled and ceiling tiles rained down. I ended up flat on my back, the linoleum buckled beneath me, as he moved in for the kill.

I felt the icy fingers at my chest, the slash of pain as his nails tore at my shirt. Desperation welled inside me. I bent my knee and delivered a fierce kick to his groin. He wailed and stumbled backward, and I saw my chance. I went after him, landing another vicious kick to his shin, then his other shin. He reached out, fingernails slicing across my arm. A burning jag of pain hit me hard and fast, but it was nothing compared to my protective instincts kicking into high gear.

He wasn't getting past me. He wasn't getting to Cutter. Not again.

My scream echoed in my head as I threw myself at the ferocious demon, jumping on his back and jamming my thumbs into his eyes as he stumbled around, trying to fling me loose. He finally grabbed a wrist and jerked it toward his mouth. He bit down, his razor-like teeth piercing my skin. My grip faltered and I let go. He flung me off like a bothersome fly and I landed in a heap near Cutter.

The wind rushed from my lungs and my vision clouded. I grasped at the dusty floor, hands searching for something. Anything to protect myself. A few heartbeats later, my hand closed around the sharp edge of a sword. Cutter's sword.

The antique handle flashed in the darkness and a strange shiver went up my arm. I could feel the power radiating from the weapon, and I sent up a silent prayer that I wouldn't die trying to hold on to all that energy.

I was a demon, after all, and this was a demon-killing sword.

I grappled for a good grip, and then Azazel was there. Looming over me. His face a mask of vicious intent.

I saw then what Cutter must have seen in those brief moments before Azazel had reached in and stolen his soul. And I felt the maelstrom of emotion.

The fierce loneliness. The raw pain. The unmistakable torment.

That was the trade. One he'd made unwillingly.

But I didn't have to face the same consequences. I was a demon without a soul to steal, and I was feeling mightily pissed off on behalf of a certain slayer.

"You low-down, dirty snake," I hissed. I hefted the sword and swung. The blade sliced through his shoulder.

He stumbled backward, howling, and I struggled to my feet, the weapon in my hands. I went after him, following him across the room until his back was to the wall. I swung the sword again. Steel flashed in the dim light and—

"No!" Cutter's desperation pushed past the thundering of my heart. "You can't kill him, Jess. Please. Not yet."

Before I could turn, Cutter was next to me, looking as if he might topple over at any moment. His hand closed around my wrist and suddenly he was the one wielding the magical steel.

He lunged, shoving the sword straight into Azazel's heart.

The demon shrieked, his features twisting and morphing from those of a man into something unholy. His chest spilled open and a rush of fluttering wings flew from inside, followed by a shimmer of light. One after the other. Souls. Every soul that Azazel had claimed over the centuries. They filled the room for a brief, blinding moment and then the sky seemed to open above. The ceiling cracked wide and a ray of light beamed down. A roar filled my ears as the building started to shake. The brightness drew the souls into one collective body, gathering them for the journey home.

All except for one.

The flutter of light pivoted, firing straight into Cutter's chest, sending him sailing backward. He slammed into the opposite wall before sliding into a heap on the floor.

The light disappeared and the room went black and grim again.

At the same time, it didn't feel so cold and menacing, and I knew exactly why.

Cutter all but pulsed with life, despite his wounds.

I reached him in that next instant and felt the warmth that radiated from his skin. The fire. The life.

He'd reclaimed his soul and now he was healed.

I held tight to his hand until his eyes finally opened. Sure enough, there was a twinkling light that had been missing from the dark-green depths. A vibrancy that made my heart skip a few beats. "Shouldn't you be throwing a wedding right about now?" he croaked.

His skin pulsed against my fingertips and a smile played at the corner of my mouth. "Yeah, well, I couldn't let you have all the fun."

A grin curved his sexy lips just as a dozen Legion agents barreled through the doorway, swords drawn. All except for Smith. He led the way, worry carving his young face. The expression eased the moment his gaze fixed on Cutter.

"This was a solo project," Cutter said, touching a tentative hand to the wound on his chest. "You were supposed to keep quiet about all of this."

Smith shook his head. "I had to call them when you went missing. I didn't know what else to do."

"How did you find us?"

A tall, muscular man with long blond hair and bright-blue eyes stepped forward. He wore black jeans and a fitted black T-shirt that outlined his brawny shoulders. An intricate slave-band tattoo just like Cutter's encircled a bicep that rippled as he holstered the gleaming silver sword in his hand. "We saw the light show outside." His voice was authoritative, and I knew he was a powerful demon slayer in his own right. He tilted his head at me, his eyes hooded and expressionless. "Who's she?"

"Nobody, Jacob."

Jacob gave me another long, hard look, but I knew he wasn't about to challenge the man who'd just slain one of the oldest demons in existence. He nodded and stepped back while Cutter took my hand.

"You should go," he murmured. His green eyes sparkled with life and my heart stuttered. "You're late."

Mission accomplished. He'd gotten the one thing he'd set out to reclaim, and while I had no idea what that would mean to his future with the Legion—to slay or not to slay—I knew what it meant to me. I'd kept my end of the bargain, so he meant to keep his. My mom was safe and the wedding was still on.

If she hadn't torched the Bell Tower by now.

"But what about you? I could help—"

"Go, Jess. This place will be crawling with even more Legion members in a matter of minutes, including Gabriel. I don't want you caught in the middle of it."

I nodded. "Take care of him," I told Smith.

"Yes, ma'am." He gave me a wink as I turned for the door.

Outside, I ignored the fast-growing collection of black SUVs swarming the front of the building and sprinted the three blocks to the Bell Tower.

Correction—I *tried* to sprint. But the knock-down, drag-out with Azazel had exhausted me. The result? A slow, gasping jog and a silent promise that if I made it through the rest of this night in one piece, I would give up all the sugar and invest my energy in a cardio workout. While I had an ultrahot body, my endurance was for shit.

Faster, I told myself. Just move *faster*.

Finally I reached the venue, my chest heaving and my lungs burning and…I gasped for air and tried to swallow against my dry throat. I needed a drink of water in the worst way.

But there was no time. I was already a full forty-five minutes late and I knew even before I saw the storm clouds gathered overhead that my mother was upset.

A crack of thunder sizzled in the air and the hair on the back of my neck stood on end.

Forget upset. She was downright pissed.

The foyer of the Bell Tower looked as picture-perfect as when I'd left a half hour ago. The giant arrangements of bloodred roses and hand-painted skull accents looked perfect and untouched. No blood. No gore. No fire damage.

The realization scared me even more than a few bodies strewn here and there would have.

What if she'd given up on me and called off the wedding? What if she was, at that very moment, signing a decree that would send me spiraling back to Hell?

I ignored a wave of panic and tuned my senses. I could hear muffled voices coming from the ceremony area as I strode down the hallway toward the bridal suite. At least the guests were still here. I pushed through the double doors leading to a plush sitting room, where I found Cheryl.

She stood near a granite-topped bar off to the left. Her makeup was streaked and her hair was frizzed and full, as if she'd stuck her finger in a light socket.

"Cheryl?"

She was rummaging through the array of bottles sitting on the granite. "Have to find it," she muttered, doing a crackerjack imitation of Rain Man. "Have to find it. Have to find it. Have to find it."

"Cheryl?" I tried again, my voice louder, my anxiety mounting. "Where is it? Where is it? Where is it?"

"Cheryl?"

Her head snapped up and I knew she'd finally heard me. "Jess?"

I nodded. "Yes, it's me, Jess."

Her gaze focused. "You're here," she breathed. "You're really *here*."

"And everything is going to be fine," I added. "Where's my mother?"

She pointed to a closed door that led to an adjoining bathroom. "The ladies' room?"

"She drank all of these when Blythe told her you were running late." She indicated the empty rows of liquor bottles. "She's not good at waiting. Speaking of waiting"—she snatched up a bottle and upended it—"she wants another margarita and we're out of tequila."

"She drank margaritas *and* wine?"

"And a few Bloody Marys, some Cosmos, a couple martinis and half a bottle of Windex." When I arched an eyebrow, she shrugged. "She thought it was a Blue Hawaiian."

"How many drinks total?"

Her gaze collided with mine. "Before or after she zapped me?"

Which totally explained the hot new hair trend.

I watched as wisps of smoke curled above her head before I shifted into Super Wedding Planner. "No more alcohol. Give me the bottle."

"But—"

"Hand it over." I waited until the glass met my hand and then I sent her off to the lobby restroom to regroup. Meanwhile, I grabbed my emergency bag and retrieved my usual black pencil skirt and white silk blouse that Blythe had brought for me.

I shed the bloodstained tee and jeans and pulled on the clean clothes. Then I combed back my hair, tied it up into a ponytail, grabbed my headset and clipboard, and inhaled.

Easy. Calm. Breathe.

I braced myself, pushed open the adjoining door, and smiled at my mother, who was just coming out of the bathroom stall. Her gaze narrowed and electricity crackled in the air. She looked more than ready to throw a few lightning bolts my way.

I squashed the urge to turn and run the other way and instead pasted on my most excited smile. "There's my happy bride. Let's get married!"

* * *

"It's about time," Blythe said as I slid into a seat next to her. The bridal march had already started. Every head swiveled toward the entryway, eager for Lillith's appearance.

Behind me sat my three sisters, who wore black couture dresses and bored expressions. The cousins filled the next twenty rows. Monique frowned, obviously distressed that I'd thumbed my nose at proper etiquette with my hasty arrival. Portia and Hester and the rest of Aunt Bella's brood stared daggers at me.

I ignored a tap on my shoulder from Camille, who whispered that I was late while she'd been on time. And from Tracey, who wanted to tell me how great she looked in her dress. And from Jill, who wanted to tell me that all Tracey could talk about was how good she looked.

As if I didn't already know that.

Blythe sniffed me. "You smell like smoke."

"Trust me, it could be worse. My mother was so liquored up that her aim was a little off." Still, I was going to have to add a nice chunk to the Bell Tower fee to pay for a brick statue of Venus that was now history. "Three lightning bolts and they all went right over my head."

I drew a deep breath, ignored the symphony of whispers behind me (a scandalous wedding + a roomful of female guests = a *lot* of gossip) and watched as my mother reached the front of the aisle, where Judge Parks waited. He wore the same suit as last night, but with Lillith demanding every eye, no one seemed to notice.

Being the attention hog that she was, my mother had decided to give herself away, and so she mounted the steps solo and stopped next to Samael.

"I can't believe you actually pulled it off," Blythe murmured. Her gaze touched on the sprays of withered red roses that lined the front of the ceremony space. The water wall served as a backdrop. I'd swapped the blue up-lighting for red, which made the water look like a sheet of shimmering blood. Totally icky for the typical bride, but this was Satan, so it simply set the mood for the sinister event about to take place.

"Me either." My aunties stood to the bride's right, wearing the hated white bridesmaids' dresses, while the groomsmen looked dark and debonair in black tuxedos and bloodred cummerbunds. My gaze caught Aunt Lucy's and I gave her a grateful smile.

I wasn't sure what she'd had to do or say to get the other aunties into the dresses, but she'd pulled it off and I couldn't have been more thankful.

So far, so good.

Lillith herself wore a black fitted mermaid dress with lots of lace and beadwork. While it wasn't the typical wedding gown, it fit her like a glove and, more importantly, she actually liked it. Not that she'd said as much. But she didn't have to. She'd put on the dress and was now wearing it in front of everyone, and for the most important event of her existence. That alone spoke volumes.

Of course, it wasn't the pat on the back I'd hoped for, but beggars couldn't be choosers.

I let loose a deep sigh and the tension eased just a little. I'd made it. I was here and this was really happening, despite my grandfather going off the deep end and kidnapping the judge and Azazel almost ripping off my head.

"We are gathered here together in the sight of the Evil One"— Judge Parks nodded toward Gramps, who sat to my right, a sour look on his face—"to join this woman and this man in unholy matrimony…"

The judge went on about two people clinging together and ruling the world and I found my thoughts drifting to Cutter and our uncertain future.

I should be happy, right? Cutter had reclaimed his soul and I'd helped. Talk about major brownie points for me. The thing was, I knew deep inside that no matter how I'd helped, it wouldn't make up for the fact that I'd lied to him about my identity.

He would hate me when he found out, which was exactly why I had to keep my mouth shut. While Azazel had known who I was, he'd never said it out loud in front of Cutter. Cutter didn't know, and I didn't want him to ever know. Better to back off and keep my distance from him. No more touching. No more kissing. *No.*

Cutter was the last man on earth for me.

If only he wasn't the one man I really, *really* wanted.

The notion brought a wave of tears to my eyes and I blinked frantically. Not for fear of standing out. There wasn't a dry eye in the place, particularly when it came to my aunties.

Aunt Bella wept openly, obviously mourning the hellish dictatorship about to be born. Aunt Levita moaned. Even Aunt Lucy shed a few tears, though I had the distinct feeling those were more because of the dress she'd been forced to wear than the impending change in leadership.

No, I wept because it wasn't just the kissing and the touching that I would miss with Cutter. It was the camaraderie I'd felt when he'd been in my kitchen and we'd been talking. Or the comfort of knowing he was close by, watching me, protecting me. I'd never felt things like that with any man. I'd never felt anything other than lust. I felt that with Cutter too, but even that was amped up. What I felt for him was different. Special.

I dabbed at my eyes with the tissue Blythe handed me.

"...anyone can show good reason why these two demons should not be joined, let them speak now or forever hold their peace."

Gramps cleared his throat, my stomach dropped to my knees, and I had the sneaking suspicion that things were about to get really ugly.

Don't do it, I begged silently. *Don't open your mouth.*

"I have something that needs to be said."

Yep, ugly was barreling toward me at the speed of light.

Come on. Don't be such a pessimist. Maybe he just wants to wish them a long and happy eternity together. Maybe he learned his lesson earlier about trying to manipulate women. Maybe you're about to stroke out for nothing.

"You can't marry Samael," Gramps declared, rising to his feet as my mother whirled around. "This union is an abomination. And while I have nothing against a good abomination, this is completely unacceptable. It's a travesty and I won't allow it to happen."

Then again, maybe it was time to stop, drop, and roll.

27

"Dad?" My mother zeroed in on my grandfather. "What do you think you're doing?"

"Preventing you from making a huge mistake. You can't marry this sorry excuse for a demon."

"But I thought you wanted me to get married."

"Not to him." He waved a hand. "*Never* to him."

"Why? Because he isn't afraid to speak his mind and disagree with you?"

"Precisely because of that."

"Egypt was ages ago. Just get over it."

"No more loopholes." My grandfather's eyes narrowed and I could feel the anger pulsing around him. "I rescind the decree stating that whoever marries first assumes control. You and your sisters will continue to share. Forever."

My aunt Bella let out a whoop followed by a crack of thunder. Aunt Levita launched into a happy dance. And Aunt Lucy ripped off the monstrous bow adorning her shoulder.

My mother stiffened and her features seemed to stand out in stark contrast. "Let me get this straight," she said, her lips tight, so frighteningly tight. "You let me go to all this trouble"—she waved an arm around her—"and now you're saying you won't *allow* me to follow through?"

Okay, so technically, *I* was the one who'd gone to all this trouble, but I wasn't going to point out that tidbit. Especially with the tension mounting and the temperature in the room climbing several dangerous degrees.

"That's right," Gramps went on. "I forbid you to marry Samael."

"You *forbid* it?" My mother said the words slowly. Carefully.

Uh-oh.

Breaking news alert—Lillith Damon didn't like being ordered around, even if it was my grandfather doing the ordering.

Especially when it was him.

Sure, he was the ultimate evil, but he was her father. A parent. And my mom had a rebellious streak that had caused more than one of the gray hairs on his head.

"No way are you doing this," he said, wagging a talon-tipped finger. "It's not happening. This wedding is officially off."

"But it's not your wedding to call off. It's *my* wedding." Her gaze caught and held his. Her eyes sparked and the air seemed to shimmer around her. "And I say it's on."

It wasn't just Gramps's eyes that flared bloodred in that next instant. His face elongated, his chin jutted down into a point, his cheekbones sharpened. His skin glowed a deep, vivid crimson. "Maybe I didn't make myself clear the first time." His voice had taken on an unearthly quality. "I'm not giving you sole control of Hell. I'm never giving you sole control of Hell. No matter who you marry."

Aunt Levita and Aunt Bella high-fived each other, and Aunt Lucy went for another bow.

He shook his head as if she'd brought home a hated brand of beer right before a Super Bowl party. "I should have known you'd pick the wrong one. Samael, of all demons." Another disgusted shake. "Why, I couldn't rest if I knew he was in charge. Of all the chiefs in my service, you go for this idiot?"

"He's not an idiot," my mother growled, confirming my guess that there was more to the wedding than simply a power maneuver. "Continue," she barked, turning back to face Judge Parks. "Say the words. Now."

"*Lillith*," my grandfather demanded. "Do not defy me."

But my mother had been defying my grandfather for as long as she'd been in existence. All of my aunties had, which was why he'd finally given up the fight in favor of the PGA.

"Say them." My mother touched the judge's arm, her fingers digging into his flesh and overriding his resistance. He was a chief and one of her peers, but she was royalty.

His eyes glazed over. His mouth opened and a steady monotone blared over the microphone. "Do you, Lillith, take this demon, Samael, to be your lawfully wedded husband? To have and to hold? From this day forward—"

"I will," my mother cut in. "I do."

"You'll regret this, Lillith." Smoke steamed out of my grandfather's ears. His eyes spit fire and an excited gasp echoed among the crowd.

What can I say? My relatives love a good fight.

"You've defied me for the last time!" He shimmered and vibrated and more sparks flew. "The last time!" And then he disappeared in a swirling cloud of smoke that choked the oxygen in the room for a long, frantic moment.

When the bitter fog cleared, I caught sight of my mother.

She stared at the empty spot where my gramps had been as if debating his words. For the space of a heartbeat, I thought I saw regret in her eyes, but then the expression hardened into pure, pigheaded determination. She turned back to Samael.

"Looks like this torture is over," Aunt Levita began, but my mother silenced her with a look that said *I may not be the head honcho, but I can still kick your ass*. My auntie shrugged. "Then again, we're already here. Might as well finish what we started."

The entire room went silent, and in a matter of seconds the *I do*s were over and the attention shifted to the reception.

The first few minutes were as tense as the ceremony, but as the guests began sucking down drinks and appetizers, the mood lightened. An hour in and Beelzebub was chasing Ashtoreth with his sword. All was back to normal in the Damon clan.

Or so I thought until my mother cornered me near the sculpture that I'd had Agarth create as my special gift to her.

"I can't believe this." She stared up at the monstrous sculpture that sat center stage, surrounded by platters of braised eyeballs and brain tartare.

Lillith Damon liked herself above all else, so I'd had Agarth sculpt a life-size replica of her in rich, dark chocolate.

"Doesn't it look just like you?" I was desperate to tip the scales in my favor and point out just how thoughtful I truly was. Especially since she was no longer going to be superbusy ruling the Underworld. She would have plenty of time to focus on me and the fact that I'd turned my back on my birthright, which meant I needed to kiss up in a major way.

"Why, it hardly resembles me. I'm much more stern and frightening. There's nothing stern and frightening about chocolate."

"Maybe not, but it's the finest available. It's imported."

She eyed me before reaching out to pop off a finger. "I've had better," she murmured after a quick nibble. "Bella," she growled, her gaze streaking past me to her sister, who raised her sword and sliced the head off a nearby male demon. She tossed it up into the air and my mother went nuts. "I'm the only one allowed to play fetch with Cerberus! He's *my* dog." She popped the rest of the finger into her mouth and went to intercept her three-headed pet before he leaped after the severed head.

I breathed a sigh of relief. I was off the hook.

For the time being.

But the moment of truth was still out there, barreling toward me like an out-of-control freight train. If I didn't want to find myself splattered all over the pavement, I needed to come clean and tell her about the magazine article before she saw it for herself. Just as I had to tell Cutter that I was one of Satan's own before he made the connection himself.

Just do it.

That's what I told myself later that night after the festivities wrapped up and I arrived home to find a Land Rover parked in front of my duplex.

My porch light was off—testimony to the fact that Gio had gone to pour his heart out to Syra and do everything in his power to get her to change her mind about marrying another man.

He wanted her and he didn't intend to give her up without a fight.

Go, Gio.

Meanwhile, my house was dark and quiet. Moonlight spilled onto the front yard, illuminating the man waiting for me.

Cutter still looked as sexy as ever despite the bruises on his face. He leaned one hip against the front bumper of his Rover, his ankles hooked, arms folded. He'd changed into a fresh pair of faded jeans, a black fitted T-shirt—and a determined expression.

Here's your chance. Tell him now.

I gathered my courage and climbed out of the car.

He met me just as I was pulling a box from the front seat.

I could do this. I *would* do this.

Satan's my mom.

Satan is my mother.

Mi madre es el Diablo.

"You've got your soul back," I blurted instead.

"Yes." His gaze locked with mine. "Thanks to you." I didn't miss the gratitude as he said the words. But there was something extra in the brilliant green depths. The vibrancy that I'd seen in those few seconds after he'd slain Azazel.

I couldn't help but smile. A reaction that had nothing to do with the chemistry that sizzled between us and everything to do with the knowledge that he appreciated me.

Of course, the chemistry was still as potent as ever.

Awareness swept over my skin, and my nerves started to hum. "I guess that means you'll hang up the demon-slayer hat and find a real job," I heard myself say.

A girl could dream, couldn't she?

He gave me an odd look before shaking his head. "I wasn't sure what I was going to do at first. I couldn't see past the kill. But now..." He shrugged. "I'm an integral part of the Legion. I take the jobs that no one else wants and, trust me, there are a lot of them. I can't just bail now. Plus, Smith is trying out next month and I know he'll make it. I can't let him do it alone. He needs somebody to keep an eye on him. He's the only relative I've got left."

I remembered the night of the spider incident and Cutter telling me about his last remaining family member. "Smith is your cousin?"

He nodded. "His dad was a big gun enthusiast. He named him after Smith and Wesson."

"And here I thought that was a made-up name to protect his real identity."

Cutter chuckled. "Hardly. He doesn't think that fast on his feet. That's why he needs me. That, and his aim is for shit. He'll have to get a lot better if he wants to run with the big dogs. But it's his dream and I'm going to help him realize it. He's my only family. Him, and the other slayers. We're like family."

"But I thought the only reason you joined the Legion was because you were desperate for revenge. You had a vendetta against demons that was totally understandable since you lost your soul to one. But now you've regained your soul *because* of one. Surely you've come to realize we're not all so bad."

"I realized that a long time ago. But it still doesn't change the fact that I took an oath." He shrugged. "The Legion is what I do, Jess. It's who I am."

"I guess I thought you'd take some time off, maybe go camping and hiking again. Fire up the old grill."

Melancholy played across his expression. "I just might, but it'll have to be on my day off."

"Oh."

He eyed the box in my hands that overflowed with leftover programs and the coffin-shaped chocolates that I'd given away as favors. "I'm guessing you made it to the wedding in time. How'd it go?"

"No earthquakes or tsunamis, though we did have a couple small fires and a minor tornado." A grin played at his lips and my disappointment faded in a swell of warmth. "Thanks for backing off and letting me do my thing."

"We had a deal. I promised not to interfere if you delivered Azazel." He shrugged. "You did, so I didn't." His gaze caught and held mine. "I always keep my promises." His words dripped with implication.

I swallowed against my suddenly dry throat. "Always?"

Hunger carved his features and anticipation shot from my head to my toes. "Always." And then he took the box from my hands and kissed me.

My lips parted and Cutter's tongue met mine and it was the best kiss of my life.

Hotter than I remembered.

More potent.

Yum.

I wasn't sure what happened next. I was so wrapped up in the kiss that one minute I was standing in my driveway, the overflowing box at my feet, and the next I was standing in my bedroom, a frantic Snooki barking in the background.

Cutter broke the kiss and stepped back. He glanced toward the bathroom, a questioning look on his face.

"She doesn't like company," I told him.

"And what about you?"

"Me?" I shrugged. "I'm a lot friendlier."

He grinned.

Buttons slid open. Material slithered and fell away. In a matter of seconds, I stood before him wearing nothing but my high heels, flushed with passion and a growing sense of impatience because, as fast as he was, he wasn't fast enough. I'd been waiting for this far too long.

"You're next," I told him, reaching for the hem of his T-shirt. I pulled the soft cotton up and over his head. My fingers brushed his crotch, popped the top button on his jeans, and gripped the zipper. The metal teeth gave and he sprang hard and hot into my hands.

I stroked his long, pulsing length, my fingertips tracing the head before sweeping back up and brushing the silky dark hair that surrounded the base of his shaft. He groaned.

The sound rumbled in my ears and stirred the lust I'd fought so hard to bury over the past two years. It was out now, unearthed in a matter of seconds, and suddenly I couldn't wait to get him inside of me.

I finished undressing him, kicked off my shoes, and pushed him down onto the bed. I straddled him and was this close to sliding down onto his erection when his hands closed around my waist and he stopped me.

"Wait," he breathed.

I stalled, my body poised over the head of his penis. "For what?"

"More of this." He leaned up and caught my lips with his own. His mouth plundered mine, his tongue plunging deep.

The kiss was the wildest, most intimate thing I'd ever experienced. Crazy, right? I was the queen of intimacy, with a long list of conquests to prove it. But this was different. There was something more intense about this. It had power. Depth. Meaning.

The One.

Tell him.

The thought blared through my head and I pulled back. Guilt rushed through me and I opened my mouth.

But then he flipped me onto my back, parted my legs, and thrust into me.

Okay, so maybe now wasn't the best time.

I lifted my hips, welcoming him in. I wanted to feel him deeper...harder...there.

Right. *There.*

His groan echoed in my head and I forced my eyes open to see him braced above me, his breaths coming hard and fast. His gaze drilled into mine and I had the unnerving thought that he could see right through me, to all of my deep, dark secrets.

I clamped my eyes shut, breaking the spell, and concentrated on enjoying myself.

That's all this was. Sex. Phenomenal. Overwhelming. But still, it was just sex. Purely physical with zero emotions involved.

Because Cutter Owens was *not* The One I'd been hoping for the past two years.

No matter how much I wished otherwise. His loyalty was to the Legion, which meant he could never pledge himself to a demon.

And that's what I wanted.

A pledge.

A future.

I slid my arms around his shoulders, surrendered to the delicious sensation swamping my senses, and focused on having the hottest, wildest, most memorable night of my life.

If only I didn't have the sinking suspicion that I'd been waiting for Cutter a lot longer than just a measly few years.

I'd been waiting for him my entire existence.

Waiting and hoping and praying. All for this.

For him.

EPILOGUE

I was through waiting on Cutter Owens.

Done. Over. *Fini.*

It had been three weeks since my mother's wedding and the most incredible after-wedding sex of my existence. And not once in twenty-one days had he called. Or sent an e-mail. Or even a text.

Because he was busy helping Smith on his first assignment.

I knew that because he'd said as much in a voice mail just before disappearing off the face of the earth.

Still, I couldn't shake the bone-deep feeling that somehow, someway, he'd discovered that I was Satan's daughter and he now hated my guts.

I chewed on my lower lip as I stood in the bridal suite of Galveston's infamous Moody Gardens (think a man-made Jamaica in Texas—no, really) and watched Delaney fidget with her hair in front of the mirror. She was breathtaking in a floor-length A-line with a sequined bodice and Swarovski crystals lining the train. Bouquets of tropical flowers filled the interior of the room, along with a huge box overflowing with three dozen long-stemmed roses. A recent token of the groom's affection.

Delaney abandoned her hair to read the card on the flowers. She blinked back tears.

Not the happy kind, either. She looked as if she were about to face a firing squad.

My chest hitched. *Don't do it,* I told myself. *Remember the three years of hell she put you through, with all the indecisiveness and stalling.*

My pain was about to end. She would waltz down the aisle and I would collect my final check and there would be another group of successful pics to load onto the digital frame in my office.

"You don't want to marry him, do you?" I heard myself ask.

Was I a glutton for punishment or what?

"Of course I do." She blinked frantically. "I'm just rethinking this dress." She glanced down. "It's a little too fitted. I feel like I can't breathe."

"That's not the dress. It's the anxiety."

"What are you trying to say?"

Yeah, what *are* you trying to say?

I was supposed to be encouraging this wedding. I was supposed to tell her everything would be fine and the wedding would be beautiful. I was supposed to tell her she was the most stunning bride I'd ever seen and that the groom was one lucky guy and that they would live happily ever after.

I knew the routine.

I lived it week after week.

But as much as I wanted to say those things, I just couldn't. Not when I saw the apprehension in her eyes. It was an emotion I knew all too well. The dread of facing the future, of admitting the truth.

To my mother.

To Cutter.

"You don't want to marry him," I told her.

"How do you know that?"

"Because I've seen my share of excited brides, and you aren't one of them. You've changed your mind about a million times."

"That's just because I want every detail to be perfect."

"Maybe. Or maybe you're more worried about the groom than the details." I caught and held her gaze. "Seriously, Delaney. Do you *really* love him?"

"I should." She turned back toward the mirror and stared at her reflection for a long moment. "But I don't." Her eyes met mine. "What's wrong with me, Jess?"

"The only thing wrong is that you're living a lie. You'll never be happy as long as you're doing that."

"Which means I should tell the truth?"

"The truth shall set you free."

I knew as I recited the words to Delaney that I had to follow my own advice. I would never find my own happily-ever-after as long as I was living a lie.

And if you come clean?

I wouldn't find it then, either.

Surprisingly, my mother had been so preoccupied over the past weeks with trying to convince my grandfather to accept Samael that she hadn't noticed the magazine on her own.

Likewise, my family was so fixated on the will-he–won't-he? drama between Satan and his eldest daughter that they seemed oblivious to yours truly as well.

Even Hester wasn't paying any attention to me, despite the fact that she was still pissed because I hadn't brought enough brownies to her shower.

Still, I had no doubt my mother would doom me the moment she found out. That was, if Cutter didn't beat her to the punch, chop off my head with his magic sword, and end my miserable existence for good.

Miserable. That's what I was. Miserable and riddled with guilt and fear. Dreading the worst was just as bad as living it.

No more. I was done living a lie. I had to come clean and save my conscience if nothing else.

It had worked for Gio. While Syra hadn't called off the wedding, she'd at least postponed it for a while. Gio now had a chance to make his case and prove his love. And all because he'd put himself out there and confessed the truth.

"You want me to buy a copy of what magazine?" Cheryl asked when I called her after loading Delaney into a cab and announcing to everyone, including the groom, that the merger—er, the wedding—was off.

"*Texas Brides.* Just buy a copy of this month's issue and give it to my mother. It's urgent." Before she could ask any more questions (and before my courage ran out), I killed the connection and texted Cutter to please, please, *please* meet me ASAP. If that wasn't tempting enough, I added a line about having a lead on a very ancient, very evil demon.

"Who is it? Where is he? What's going on?" he demanded when I pulled up to my duplex a half hour later to find him sitting in the driveway. He wore a rumpled white T-shirt, worn jeans, and dusty black biker boots. A shadow of a beard covered his jaw and there was a weariness in his eyes that said he hadn't slept in a long, long time.

"You look tired."

"I've been working." Regret gleamed in his gaze. "Listen, I've been meaning to call you—"

"It's fine, really." *Not.* At the same time, at least I knew he hadn't stayed away because he hated my guts. He *had* been working. Day and night, from the look of him. "Thanks for coming."

"What's up?"

Easy. Calm. Breathe.

I gathered my courage. I was through being scared and lonely. I was going to do this. For better or for worse.

"I've got something I need to tell you."

And then I did just that.

KEEP READING FOR A SNEAK PEEK AT *THE DEVIL MADE ME DO IT.*

1

"We want an outdoor theme," said the woman sitting across from me. "Something at night beneath a star-studded sky."

"Outdoors." I entered the information into my iPad. "I can do that." Because I was Jess Damon, Houston's hottest up-and-coming wedding planner—at least according to the last issue of *Texas Brides* magazine. My sole mission in life was to make matrimonial dreams come true.

"With lots of candles."

"Candles." My fingers flew across the touch screen. "Check."

"Black candles."

"Black. Check."

Okay, so I wasn't just any ordinary wedding planner. Jess is short for Jezebel. *The* Jezebel.

Yep, that's right. I'm a 1,026-year-old demon slut puppy (the not-so-PC term for succubus) with a weakness for all things sugar, a rockin' bod (a demon can only exist in this realm by occupying a human body), and a crazy extended family. We're talking a control-freak mom (aka Satan, one of the four crown princesses of Hell), three aunts (the Big H's other three), thirty-six cousins, and a zillion second cousins. All female.

Um, yeah.

Anyhow, I'd been carrying on my birthright by plowing through men faster than I went through my favorite Krispy

Kreme doughnuts up until two years ago, when I'd watched an old hookup marry the love of his life. A lightbulb had gone off then and I'd realized how empty and meaningless my existence had truly been.

Forget mindless lust.

I wanted the real deal. Forever and ever. Till death do us part.

And I wanted it in a big, massive ceremony with those cute little bubbles, a five-tiered wedding cake, and tons of flowers.

What? A demon can't be a hopeless romantic?

Anyway, since true love wasn't hanging around every street corner, I'd had to settle for planning happily-ever-afters for everyone else while eagerly awaiting my own. I'd started out with a strictly human clientele, but a recent wedding uniting Mommie Dearest with a demon general named Samael had opened up my employment options.

Enter Henry Martin—that's human speak for Heneraminzanen, aka chief demon of foul-smelling gases (and I don't mean the fuel kind)—and his one and only Eloise Macallister—Elimaneezercalis, i.e., the chief demon of bad timing. They'd been front and center at Mom's big event and properly awed by my planning skills. While they'd obviously teamed up a long, long time ago, now they wanted to make it official with a big ceremony and an ever-growing guest list.

"And we need lots and lots of shrunken heads," Eloise went on. "Henry has a thing for shrunken heads." She beamed at the fortyish-looking man sitting next to her. "And we'd like to do a mini bonfire at the center of every table and ceremonial knives at each place setting and we definitely want to spit roast a few virgins."

"Four," Henry chimed in. "We need at least four."

"A wedding is a happy occasion," I reminded them. "Why don't we save the human sacrifice for the first anniversary?" That, and since we demons existed in this realm and weren't too anxious to find ourselves sucked back Down Under, we tried to play it as safe as possible. That meant looking both ways before crossing the street, turning off the oven before bedtime, and refraining from any major felonies that might lead to the death penalty.

"I think I've got enough information to get started," I said after making a few more notes. "I'll call as soon as I've lined up some location prospects."

"Great." Eloise smiled and motioned to Henry. "Pay the woman."

Henry pulled out a Visa Gold card and my heartbeat kicked up a notch. While I was scheduled to make a nice profit off my mom's wedding, I had no idea when, or if, I would see the money. I'd sent her an invoice two weeks ago, right along with a copy of *Texas Brides* featuring yours truly. No big deal, except that my mom had been under the impression that my new career was nothing more than a front to boff hunky groomsmen and spoil Big Days. The magazine was proof that I'd gone legit.

I'd expected a few lightning bolts and maybe a plague when she'd discovered the truth.

But complete and utter silence? Talk about scaring the bejesus out of me.

In more ways than one.

My chest tightened as my thoughts shifted to a certain hunky demon slayer. While Cutter Owens and I had gotten superclose (we're talking phenomenal sex and the fact that I'd helped him hunt down an ancient demon and reclaim his soul), I'd failed to reveal my true identity. Instead, I'd led him to believe I was just a lower-level demon. Insignificant in the hierarchy of Hell. And, therefore, hardly worth a Legion member's time, much less his sword.

But in my flurry of guilt, I'd not only sent my mother a copy of the magazine, I'd gone for a full confession with Cutter.

"My mother is the Devil," I'd blurted just as he'd gotten an urgent text from his higher-ups. He'd stared at me for a nanosecond, muttered a gruff, "We'll talk later," and then he'd hauled ass in the opposite direction.

I hadn't seen or heard from him since.

A good thing, I told myself for the umpteenth time. If he'd been *really* pissed, he would have come back to slice and dice me by now.

No, he was probably just taking his time to process the info.

That, or he'd gone straight to the Legion with the news, because he couldn't do the deed himself since I'd rocked his world and he was madly in love with me. They'd no doubt issued a bounty on my head and every demon slayer within a thousand-mile radius was now stalking me, waiting for the perfect moment to—

"...much up front?" Henry's voice pushed past the humming in my ears and yanked me from my morbid thoughts.

"What? When? What?"

"The down payment." He motioned to the credit card in my hand. "How much are you putting on the card?"

I forced Cutter from my thoughts, tamped down the gut feeling that something bad was about to happen, and focused on the couple sitting across from me.

"For the size of your wedding and all the extras"—I did a quick mental calculation and added twenty percent—"a fifty-thousand-dollar retainer should do the trick."

Henry didn't flinch. Thankfully. While I wasn't exactly living off ramen noodles, I still had bills to pay, not to mention I was desperate to move my growing business from the first floor of my duplex into an actual storefront.

I was just about to run the credit card when the intercom buzzed.

"Jess?" Burke Carmichael's voice floated over the line.

Burke and his twin brother, Andrew, were my devoted assistants. With blond hair, brown eyes, and ripped bods, they were two of the hottest guys I'd ever seen. They were also extremely gay, a big plus for me because, as a succubus, I oozed massive sex appeal, which proved far too distracting to the average heterosexual male. The twins fixated on flowers and centerpieces rather than boinking yours truly, so we tended to get massive amounts of work done.

"I know you're with a bride and groom right now," he went on, "but I think there's something out here you should see."

"I'll be right there just as soon as I finish up." I slid the card through the reader and keyed in the amount.

"It's really important."

"Ditto in here." I grabbed a twenty-off referral coupon while I waited for the receipt to print.

"I bet this is more important."

"I bet it's not." I handed Henry the credit card slip and a pen. "If you'll just sign right here—"

"Get your ass out here now!" His frantic voice shattered my train of thought. I punched the off button and pushed to my feet. "If you'll excuse me for just a minute. What's the big emergency?" I demanded when I waltzed into the outer office to find an ashen-faced Burke.

"I opened the closet and there it was." He clutched his hands. "So then I slammed the door shut and tried to tell myself that I shouldn't have had two mimosas this morning, but the thing is, I always have two mimosas after a morning facial because they relax me, you know, but maybe I should have had just one because two might be getting to be a bit much and so now I'm seeing things, really bad things and—"

"Burke!" I grabbed him by the shoulders. "Get a grip." I stared past him at the closed door. "It's just a closet."

"Says you." He shook his head. "It's in there, I tell you."

"What is? A rat? A raccoon? A dead body?"

What? I'm a demon, for Pete's sake. It's not like I haven't seen it all. Then again, Burke wasn't privy to my demon status, so I definitely should have kept my mouth shut.

He didn't so much as bat a wide, terrified eye. "I think it's a vortex," he managed a split second before the door seemed to swell. A roar started. Hinges creaked. Wood cracked.

Okay, so maybe I haven't seen it all.

The roar grew louder, deafening. I grabbed a fistful of Burke's shirt and dived for the floor just as the door blew.

And all Hell rained down on us.

Don't miss these other great reads from
***USA Today* bestselling author Kimberly Raye!**

ACKNOWLEDGMENTS

Writing is the hardest job in the world and the most solitary, but luckily I have a few key people who help make the job easier and a little less lonely: my wonderful agent, Natasha Kern, for her continuing faith in me and my work; my loving husband, Curt, who keeps me going through every trial and tribulation and slaps the remote out of my hand when I'm on a reality TV binge; and my best bud, Debbie, for always listening when I need to talk, or cry, or gossip about people we used to know.

My heartfelt thanks to all of you!

And many, *many* thanks to my readers who send notes and e-mails and visit me on Facebook. Your encouragement means the world to me!

ABOUT THE AUTHOR

Photo by Curt Groff, 2008

Kimberly Raye penned her first novel in high school and hasn't stopped writing since. Today she is the bestselling author of more than fifty-five novels, two of them prestigious RITA Award finalists. The first title in her romantic vampire mystery series, *Dead End Dating*, has been optioned by Disney for television. A diehard romantic who loves weddings, she lives with her husband and their children deep in the heart of the Texas hill country. To learn more about Kim, visit www.kimberlyraye.com or friend her on Facebook.